"I wouldn't want anything to happen to you."

Hart's gaze moved to the wharves, as if he saw a gang of marauding pirates rather than busy longshoremen.

Beth stared at him.

"I'd hate to have to explain to your brothers," he added.

Well! She was about to tell him exactly what she thought of the idea when she noticed a light in his eyes. Was that a twinkle in the gray?

Beth tossed her head. "Oh, they'll take your side. They always say I have more enthusiasm than sense."

He shrugged. "I know a few women who match that description."

Beth grinned. "But none as pretty as me."

"That's the truth." His gaze warmed, and she caught her breath. Hart, flirting with her? It couldn't be!

Silly! Why did she keep reacting that way? He wasn't interested in her. He'd told her so himself. And she wasn't about to allow herself to take a chance on love again, especially not with Hart McCormick.

Regina Scott has always wanted to be a writer. Since her first book was published in 1998, her stories have traveled the globe, with translations in many languages. Fascinated by history, she learned to fence and sail a tall ship. She and her husband reside in Washington State with an overactive Irish terrier. You can find her online, blogging at nineteenteen.com. Learn more about her at reginascott.com or connect with her on Facebook at Facebook.com/authorreginascott.

Books by Regina Scott

Love Inspired Historical

Frontier Bachelors

Lone Star Cowboy League: Multiple Blessings

Lone Star Cowboy League: The Founding Years

The Master Matchmakers

Visit the Author Profile page at Harlequin.com.

REGINA SCOTT

Frontier Matchmaker Bride

HHARLEQUIN® LOVE INSPIRED® HISTORICAL

Recycling programs
for this product may
not exist in your area.

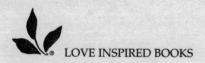 LOVE INSPIRED BOOKS

ISBN-13: 978-1-335-36958-1

Frontier Matchmaker Bride

www.Harlequin.com

Printed in U.S.A.

And we have known and believed the love that God hath to us. God is love; and he that dwelleth in love dwelleth in God, and God in him.
—*1 John* 4:16

To Tina James, for making my books the best they can be across nineteen stories, and to the Lord, without whom there would be no stories.

Chapter One

Seattle, Washington Territory
March 1875

It simply wasn't easy to save a man's life.

Beth Wallin blew out a breath as she stood in front of the Kellogg Brothers' mercantile, a cold breeze tugging at her feathered hat. Hart McCormick always rode down Second Avenue between ten and noon on Tuesdays. She'd studied his movements every time she came to town, and the pattern hadn't changed in the ten years she'd known him. Here it was nearly noon, and she hadn't so much as caught a glimpse of the lawman.

Her booted foot was tapping against the boardwalk under her pink-and-white-striped skirts. She forced it to stop. The muddy street was thronged with riders on horseback and farmers with wagons. She loved the bustle, the purposefulness. Men in warm wool coats and ladies with swaying skirts passed her for the shops on either side. She smiled and nodded in turn. After all, it wouldn't do her reputation or Hart's any good if the truth about their past was known.

But really, was it too much to ask that the man be punctual?

She shook her head. She shouldn't be so annoyed with him. Hart had no idea she was waiting. He might be off chasing bandits, lying in wait for vandals, rescuing children from raging rapids. That's what he did: safeguard the citizens of King County, standing between them and the forces of evil.

"He's just a man," she muttered aloud. "Opinionated, stubborn, bullheaded..."

"May I help you, Miss Wallin?"

Beth put on her sunniest smile and turned to the clerk who had come out of the store. Mr. Weinclef couldn't help that he resembled a rat with his lank brown hair, long nose and close-set brown eyes.

"How very kind of you," Beth told him. "But I'm simply trying to decide where to go next."

He waved a hand back to the store, the movement tugging at the green apron looped around his neck and tied at his slender waist. "Why go anywhere else but Kelloggs'? We can meet all your shopping needs." He leaned closer, his flowery cologne washing over her. "And I just marked down that pink crepe you've been eying to half price."

"Oh!" Beth started toward the store. "Thank you! I might have just enough egg money to..." She drew herself up short of the door. "That is, I really should wait." She bit her lip, then met his gaze. "I don't suppose you could set aside two yards?"

He straightened, adjusting his spruce-colored neck cloth. "First come, first served. That is the Kellogg rule."

Beth sagged. "Of course. I wouldn't want you to

break the rules. Perhaps you could just keep Mary Ann Denny from buying it all."

"I'll see what I can do," he murmured, glancing either way as if to make sure no one overheard his concession. "Just don't delay too long." He whisked back into the store.

Beth turned her gaze to the street, eyes narrowing. Hart McCormick would be in even more trouble if he cost her that material. A deep pink, it would make the perfect overskirt. She could see the creation now, the material swept back over her hips with pleated trim all along the hem and tiny white bows dotting the pleats, just like the latest fashion plates in *Godey's Lady's Book*. Pink always complemented her fair coloring and blond hair. If she could convince her sisters-in-law, Nora, Catherine, Dottie and Callie, to help her, she could finish the dress in time for Easter.

But not if she had to stand here woolgathering all day!

Another noise caught her attention, and she glanced to the right. A group of men lounged outside the Pastry Emporium on the next block. The roughly dressed fellows ought to be working at the sawmill at the foot of Mill Street, but perhaps it was their meal break. Either way, they elbowed each other and grinned at her, and she knew it was only a matter of time before one of them worked up the courage to come speak to her.

She was one of the only unmarried females over the age of eighteen within a fifty-mile radius, so that sort of thing happened a lot. Normally, she didn't mind. Their approach allowed her to put her matchmaking skills to the test, suggesting other ladies who might better appreciate their attentions. She loved playing matchmaker, helping couples reach their wonderful happy-ever-after. Her success with her brothers had brought her to the attention of the Literary Society, an august group of women she had dreamed of joining. All were established, respected, admired for their civic contributions and taste. She'd felt nearly giddy taking tea with them, eager to volunteer for any of the worthy causes they supported—women's suffrage, literacy, medical treatment for the poor.

Unfortunately, the opportunity they suggested she volunteer to champion was the most difficult she could have imagined, taking her back to a day nearly two years ago, a day she'd tried in vain to forget.

Beth put her back to the men now, straightened her shoulders in her gray wool cape, but still the memory intruded. She'd just turned one-and-twenty and had filed for her claim. That was what was expected of her, choosing one hundred and sixty acres that would augment the town her family was building at the northern end of Lake Union. She was proud to do it.

She was too proud.

She saw that now. A young lady on the frontier might accomplish much at such an important age—file for her own claim, pursue a career.

Select a groom.

She didn't have to look far. She'd admired Deputy Sheriff Hart McCormick since she was fourteen and he'd ridden out to Wallin Landing the first time. Tall, handsome, worldly even at the age of four-and-twenty then, he'd been the embodiment of the heroes in the romantic adventure novels their father had left her and her brothers. He was the knight Ivanhoe, fighting to save England; the dashing John Alden petitioning the fair Priscilla Mullins to wed. She'd smiled and primped and giggled at him every time he came near. He never seemed to notice.

But when she turned one-and-twenty, she became determined to make him notice. She was certain God had a plan for her life, and it included Hart McCormick. She just needed to give God a little help in moving things along.

She'd dressed in her best gown, a vivid blue with white piping, styled her pale blond curls to spill down behind her. She'd borrowed her brother James's famous steel dusts and driven the horses in to Seattle to tell Hart how she felt. It hadn't been hard to locate him. Then as now, Seattle consisted of a few business streets hugging the shoreline with residences and churches on the hillside above, backed by the forest from which they'd been carved. She could scarcely breathe when he'd agreed to walk with her. They'd passed the Brown Church when she'd stopped him, gazing up into his dark eyes.

"I admire you far more than any lady should," she'd said, voice ringing in her ears. "I don't suppose you might feel the same."

He'd gazed down at her a moment, and she'd thought she would slide into the mud of the street, her bones had turned so liquid. She waited for his gaze to warm, his arms to go about her, his lips to profess his undying devotion. That was what happened in her father's novels. That was the way she'd always dreamed it would be for her.

He'd tipped his black hat to her instead. "That's mighty kind of you to say, Miss Wallin. But I have no interest in courting you. Best you go on home now."

She had. She'd run all the way back to the livery,

startling the owner, and urged her brother's horses Lance and Percy into a frenzy to get them back to Wallin Landing. She very much doubted she'd be willing to risk her heart again, for him or any other fellow. It seemed her role in life was to encourage others to marry. Perhaps it was easier to see from a distance how two people might become a couple. She'd certainly misjudged her own circumstances. Even now, she avoided spending time with Hart.

Yet how could she allow him to be pushed beyond his endurance? For that was what would happen if the ladies of the Literary Society thought she had failed in her commission.

Farther up the street, a movement caught her eye. A black horse, sides glossy, head high and proud, trotted toward her. The man riding him was no less impressive—carriage firm and controlled, gaze sweeping the street. She knew those eyes could be as dark and unyielding as a rifle barrel. Her heart slammed against the bodice of her dress.

She made herself step to the edge of the boardwalk and raised a hand. "Deputy McCormick! A word, if you please."

His gaze swung her way, and the world seemed to narrow until she could see nothing but him. Shoulders broad in his worn black leather duster, the flash of metal that was the badge on his chest. Long legs in denim and black boots. Her breath was hard to find as he guided his horse across the street and reined in in front of her.

Gloved fingers brushed the brim of his black hat. "Miss Wallin. What can I do for you?"

Beth swallowed. Where was the speech she'd so carefully rehearsed? Why did one look at those chiseled features still serve to make her tremble?

She refused to be a ninny in front of him again. He wasn't the man for her. Her experience and his determination had confirmed that.

"Hitch Arno a moment," she directed him. "We need to talk."

He leaned back in the saddle. "I thought you and I were done talking."

Heat rushed up her. He had to remind her of the most ignoble moment of her nearly twenty-three years, as if she wasn't reminded of it every time she saw him.

"This is different," she told him, catching a stray hair the wind had freed from her bun and tucking it behind her ear. "There's a plot afoot, and you must be wary."

He stiffened, but then there was nothing soft about him. She wasn't sure why she hadn't noticed before confessing her feelings. Hart was all planes and angles, his brows a slash, his lips an uncompromising line. Some in Seattle were afraid of him. She wasn't. She wouldn't allow it.

He slung his leg over the saddle and dropped to the ground. Tying his horse Arno to the hitching post in front of Kelloggs', he followed Beth around the corner onto a quiet side street.

"What's this about a plot?"

His gravelly voice stroked her skin. Beth stood taller, even though that brought the top of her feathered hat just under his chin.

"The Literary Society has designs on you," she informed him.

His brows shot up. "The Literary Society? Mrs.

Howard, Mrs. Yesler, Mrs. Wyckoff, the Denny ladies and Mrs. Maynard?"

Beth nodded. "The most influential women in Seattle. They are determined that every upstanding citizen do his or her part to grow the territory."

He relaxed, arms hanging loose at his sides. "As deputy sheriff, I'm available to help as needed."

Beth licked her lips. "Not in this particular area, I fear."

He shrugged. "If they need a lawman, they have only to ask. They didn't need to enlist your aid to turn me up sweet."

"As if that would work," Beth muttered.

His eyes narrowed. "See? I told you we were done talking."

And she hadn't noticed how stubborn he could be, either. Beth stamped her foot. "Oh! Will you listen for once? I'm trying to save your life!"

Once more tension slid over him. "What do you mean?"

Finally! Beth met his gaze. "The ladies of the Literary Society have decided it's time for you to wed. They've even compiled a list of candidates. And they've asked me to play matchmaker."

Hart stared at her. For a moment, when she'd mentioned saving his life, he'd thought she'd stumbled into something dangerous. She couldn't know how the suggestion chilled him. He'd have cheerfully walked barefoot through a raging forest fire before he saw her harmed. But marriage?

He barked a laugh. "Well, you can try, but we both know it won't work."

The pink was rising in her cheeks again. Better that than the pallor she'd worn the day he'd refused her overtures. He'd been shocked when she'd confessed she admired him. He'd known her since she was a girl, had thought her sweet, had nothing but respect for her older brothers and their wives. That day he'd looked closer and recoiled as if he'd run into a brick wall.

Little Beth Wallin had grown into a fine woman.

That didn't mean she was the right woman for him. She had always been everything pure and bright, her enthusiasm as shiny as a new penny. She didn't need his shadow covering her. He'd been curt, almost rude in refusing her. It was for the best, or so he'd told himself every time he'd seen her since.

"You don't understand," she said now. "If I had declined the request, they would have asked someone else."

Perhaps they would. He knew each of the ladies. They were used to getting their own way. They had been the vision and the drive to transform the tiny frontier town into the second biggest city in the territory. There was nothing more dangerous than a woman with a vision.

"I'll speak to Mrs. Wyckoff," he told her. "There's no need to look for a bride for me. I'm not marrying."

She sighed. "That's what my brothers said, and look at them now."

Her five older brothers were happily married, and she'd had a hand in it.

"I'm not your brothers," he replied. "I'm not pining for a wife."

Her head came up. How did such a little chin look so hard? Everything about her was feminine, from the silvery-gold curls tumbling down behind her head to the curves hinted at when her cape swung about her. But Beth Wallin was another lady who wasn't used to being told no.

"And why don't you want a wife?" she demanded. "You have a position of authority. You're well respected in the region. You're not getting any younger, you know."

Despite himself, he winced. Two-and-thirty wasn't so old, for all he sometimes felt twice that. Chasing after criminals could sap the joy from life at times.

Watching the woman you love die in your arms, knowing she'd sacrificed herself for you, did worse.

"Some men aren't meant to wed," he said. "Thank you for the warning, but I'll be fine."

She shook her head. "You really think it's that easy? They'll be throwing women at you. You won't be able to turn around without stepping on one."

He chuckled. "I'll take my chances."

"I give it a month. Maybe two."

Hart turned for Second Avenue. "Good day, Miss Wallin. Give my regards to your family."

"Oh! It would serve you right if I followed through with the agreement to match you up."

A chill ran through him again, and he turned up his collar, even though he knew the feeling had nothing to do with the brisk March weather. "You do what you have to do. So will I. No one can make me walk down the aisle, say my vows before a preacher. Not even you, Beth."

"I know."

The words held such pain, such sorrow, he nearly turned back. But if he did, he'd only give in to the need to gather her close, be the man she wanted him to be, promise to protect her.

And he could only protect her if he kept his distance.

"You don't have to encourage them," he murmured, gaze on the busier street beyond. "Tell them you have better things to do. It's only the truth."

He heard her sigh, the rustle of cloth as she must have shifted on her feet. "But Hart, if I decline, the next person they ask might not have your best interests in mind."

And she did. Whatever their differences, he knew that. Beth Wallin only ever acted from love and compassion. He had refused to accept her as his bride, but she would willingly find him another, if that pleased him.

How did anyone grow up so selfless? He'd been practicing for more than ten years, and he still failed some days.

And was he doing any better today? As much as the high-handed machinations of the Literary Society annoyed him, the ladies were right. Settling the frontier took men and women of courage and tenacity, and partnerships like marriage only made sense. You needed someone you could count on at your side, in good times and bad, a helpmate, a comforter and encourager.

Only Sheriff Wyckoff knew that Hart had already found all that, and lost it. He couldn't go through that pain again. The best he could do was work to make sure no one else lost a love to an outlaw's bullet.

And he could try to see this from Beth's perspective. She'd once confessed herself in love with him—nothing more than a schoolgirl infatuation, he was sure. However much it had hurt at the moment to be denied, she'd be better off in the future with another man less burdened by his past. Yet how mortifying now to be asked to play matchmaker to the man she'd hoped to wed, and by the mighty Literary Society, no less. Every lady in Seattle wanted to join the elite group. Beth likely wasn't immune. Besides, if any lady had a right to be admired, respected, it was her.

"Follow through as you promised," he said. "Just know I won't agree. It won't matter which lady you parade in front of me. The answer will always be no."

She scurried around him to block his way forward. That pink hat with its silk bows and white feathers was far too frivolous for the concerned look in her deep blue eyes. "Are you sure, Hart? You have a lot to offer a lady."

"And a great deal no lady should have to bear."

Her eyes lit, as if he'd given her the key to unlock his heart. He tugged on the brim of his hat, started around her, intent on escaping before he betrayed himself further.

"You wait, Hart McCormick," she called after him. "I'll find you the perfect bride, one you can't refuse."

He didn't respond. He'd already had the perfect sweetheart. Her loss had left a gaping hole, sharper than a knife and deeper than a bullet. And he doubted even the pretty, sweet-natured Beth Wallin could heal it.

Chapter Two

Stubborn, obstinate, annoying man! Beth picked up her skirts and climbed onto the boardwalk, fully aware that Hart was standing beside Arno, watching her. Couldn't he see he was only making matters worse for them both by fighting this edict? The Literary Society would think she had no gumption, no perseverance. And they would certainly begin to question his character. Why refuse matchmaking when it could result in a happy future? Truly, at times like this she'd had her fill of males. And was it any wonder?

Her oldest brother Drew had played father far longer than necessary after he'd taken over the family on Pa's death. He still had trouble accepting any fellow who came courting her, claiming this one wasn't well enough established, that one hadn't sufficiently developed his faith. Why, he'd once warned her away from a suitor because he thought the fellow had shifty eyes! Not that she'd been heartbroken to see any of them sent packing, but still.

Then there was Simon. Even after marrying her favorite sister-in-law, Nora, her second oldest brother was far too logical. He persisted in pointing out all the reasons she would benefit from a marriage, including potentially adding another one hundred and sixty acres of land from her husband to contribute to the town. Hadn't he noticed she scarcely had time to improve her own claim, much less work a second?

Her next two brothers were more understanding. James was always up for a lark. He'd helped her scare off two particularly persistent suitors. John completely endorsed her decision to marry only for love. But both seemed a little mystified that she hadn't found someone she admired enough to accept. And her youngest brother, the recently married Levi, was so besotted with his dear Callie and the family he had adopted that he hadn't even remarked upon her single state. No doubt he'd start harping on the matter shortly. Those in love always wanted everyone else to be as happy.

And she couldn't forget about Scout. Her brother Levi's best friend growing up, Scout Rankin had recently returned from the gold fields a wealthy man. He was as reticent as she was about romance. But even he encouraged her to find a beau.

She knew her brothers and Scout only wanted the best for her. She'd thought she'd found the best. The best hadn't wanted her. And she couldn't tell any of them that her heart hadn't healed from Hart's rejection.

For one, the whole situation was entirely too embarrassing. She was a noted matchmaker. What confidence would anyone have in her abilities if she couldn't even catch the eye of the gentleman she fancied? For another, she couldn't count on her brothers not to pick a fight with the lawman over his refusal. And that would make everything so much worse.

The main reason she'd accepted the Literary Society's request to find him a match was the chance to be of service to Hart. It seemed she wasn't the woman for him, but it didn't follow that there wasn't some paragon out there who would make him happy. If he was safely married to another, perhaps she could finally remove him from her thoughts. She could impress the ladies of the Literary Society at the same time.

And she did love a challenge.

So, she turned her back on him and swept into Kelloggs'.

He followed her.

Beth scowled at him. "What? Not only do you doubt my ability to find you a bride but I can't even complete my own shopping?"

He grabbed her hand and pulled her behind a display of tinned goods in the crowded mercantile. "Keep the bride business to yourself."

Oh, but those cool eyes could look fiery. "How exactly can I do that when I must talk to the various women involved?" she demanded. "Springing it on them as a surprise won't work. Trust me on that."

"I meant you don't need to discuss it in front of every Tom, Dick and Harry," he gritted out.

Beth fluttered her lashes at him. "But Deputy McCormick, I left Tom, Dickie and Harry at Wallin Landing."

He blinked, and she held back a giggle. Not for the first time she found herself pleased that the names of her brother's logging crew made for such interesting commentary. Still, she couldn't help noticing how Hart glanced around the store, as if expecting a desperado to leap out from behind the salt casks or sprigged muslin.

"I won't breathe a word to anyone unless absolutely necessary," Beth promised him. "Now, may I go, Deputy? Or do you intend to charge me? If I stand here much longer, you'd have every right to arrest me for loitering."

He stepped back and inclined his head. "Just doing my duty to protect the citizenry, ma'am. In case you hadn't noticed, Seattle can be a rough place. I aim to make sure you head for home safely."

He didn't trust her. Her! She'd kept secrets about birthday presents, Christmas presents and wedding presents and never said a word to others. She'd listened to stories about lost horses, lost funding and lost loves and never whispered about it. She was the keeper of all family knowledge. Nora liked to say there was nothing that wasn't wound onto Beth's spool.

And Hart thought she'd blab to anyone who came along!

"Suit yourself," she said, detouring around a pile of furs brought in from the winter trapping season. "But I've never met a man who had the stamina to match mine for shopping."

Head high, she swept up to the counter, where Mr. Weinclef stood waiting.

With a decidedly pinched look on his narrow face.

She thought perhaps it was because of Hart looming behind her, but the clerk immediately disabused her of that notion.

"I'm sorry, Miss Wallin," he said, Adam's apple bobbing as he swallowed. "Another customer asked for all the pink crepe."

Oh! Beth spared Hart a glare. He wisely went to look at rifle cartridges.

Beth turned to the clerk. "Are you sure? You wouldn't have a yard or two tucked away?"

Weinclef positively squirmed. "I'm very sorry, miss."

Beth sagged. "It's all right. I'm sure you did your best. If any more comes in, you'll send word?"

He bowed. "Of course."

Beth turned, started for the door, and Hart fell into step beside her.

"You heading home now?"

She sighed. "I suppose I must."

He held the door open for her. "Don't think I've ever seen you so discouraged. That pink whatever-it-was mean so much to you?"

How could she explain? She loved fabric—how it looked, how it felt, how it made her feel, the many things she could imagine creating with it. Some of the men of her acquaintance turned positively glassy-eyed when she started talking about fabric and fashion. Of course, there were those who consistently complimented her on her sense of style.

And there was Hart, who never seemed to notice what she was wearing.

"I'm just disappointed," she told him. "I had plans for that crepe."

He pulled up. "Wait here."

Before she could ask why, he strode back into the store. Someone yelped, and something fell with a thud. Beth peered through the open door, but saw nothing amiss.

Hart returned to her side. "The lady who bought the fabric is named Jamison. She's the new seamstress down on Commercial."

The day brightened. "New seamstress?"

He started in that direction. "I figured we could ask if she'd be willing to part with it." He led her to the corner and down the block to turn onto the busy street. As much as she wanted that crepe, she knew what he was doing. He was trying to take her mind off her purpose—finding him a bride. He ought to know she wasn't deterred so easily.

Even by fabric.

"By the way," she said, stepping up onto the boardwalk, "some of the candidates on the list I was given are simply unsuitable for your wife. You have too much experience to favor a dewy-eyed debutante, even if Seattle had boasted more than two of them."

His boots thudded against the rough wood, as if he'd put excessive energy into his walk. "Too much experience or too many years?"

Was he touchy about his age? She wouldn't have guessed him to be so vain. But then again, he had proven that he wasn't the man she'd originally thought him.

"Either," she answered breezily. "And I've ruled out the widow with seven children."

She thought she heard a chuckle. "Kind of you."

Beth waved her hand, causing a gentleman in a top hat to veer around them. "Most men would have to ease into the role of father. Even Drew nearly buckled when our family was thrust upon him."

"He was only eighteen, if I recall the story."

"Eighteen and unsure," Beth agreed, glancing up at the placards over each storefront. Ah, there was the shop, sandwiched between the bootmaker's and the haberdashery. "You are neither."

She reached for the handle and pushed open the door.

A bell tinkled. The scent of roses drifted over her as her foot sank into the carpet. Hart, her commission, her family faded away as she stepped inside and turned in a circle. Her gaze flew from the bolts of bright satin and rich velvet to the soft wool and crisp cambric. And the ribbons—wide and narrow, in every possible color. Spools of thread to match. Lace in white, cream, black and, oh! Pink. Dressmaker forms with half-finished gowns she would be proud to wear when completed. She nearly swooned.

A curtain at the back parted, and a tall woman glided into the room. Her raven hair was piled up behind her head to spill artfully around her shoulders. Her creamy complexion set off liberally lashed eyes of a delicate shade of violet, Beth saw as the woman approached. Every inch of her black gown was tucked and pleated, draped with lace and dotted with bows, the very height of elegance.

"Good afternoon," she said in a cultured voice. "How may I help you?"

A dozen ideas presented themselves, but Beth set them all aside. Very likely she hadn't enough money in her pocketbook to afford one of this lady's creations. "I understand you purchased the last of the pink crepe from Kelloggs', and I was hoping you'd part with some."

The woman wandered to the nearest wall, trailed a long-fingered hand along the bolts of wool. "An inferior material to be sure, but it was perfect for a day dress I am constructing for Mrs. Yesler."

Beth brightened. "I know Mrs. Yesler. I'm sure she wouldn't mind. Tell her Beth Wallin asked."

The proprietress turned and held out a hand. "Mrs.

Wallin, Mr. Wallin, a pleasure. I'm Mrs. Evangeline Jamison."

Too late she remembered Hart. Turning, she found him just behind her, a dark shadow among all the pink and white.

Beth turned to accept the seamstress's hand. "It's Miss Wallin, and this is Deputy McCormick."

Mrs. Jamison fluttered sable lashes as she dropped her gaze. "Deputy, an honor."

"Ma'am," Hart said.

He gave no explanation for his presence, didn't so much as attempt to look at material or notions. A slight frown marred the perfection of Mrs. Jamison's countenance.

"I'm delighted to make your acquaintance," Beth said, moving the lady's attention back to her. "Your shop is lovely. You obviously have excellent taste."

She inclined her head as she pulled back her hand. "As do you. I'm certain I saw that gown in *Godey's*."

Beth touched the striped fabric. "Oh, do you take *Godey's*?"

"Of course. One must remain *au courant* with what other designers are attempting. I'm sure they study my designs depicted there."

Beth head jerked up. "Your designs were in *Godey's*?"

She thought she heard a choked sound. It might have been Hart.

It might have been her.

"Most recently the January issue." She said it as if the tremendous honor was commonplace. "And I'm working on one now for June."

"May I...may I see it?" Despite her best efforts, her voice came out breathless.

Mrs. Jamison's smile was tight. "Now, why would I show my best work to the competition before it was complete?"

Beth blinked. "Competition?"

Mrs. Jamison spread her hands. "Come now, dear. Someone made that fetching gown."

Beth glanced down at the pink skirts again. "Not me. My sister-in-law Nora sewed it for me."

"Nora Wallin." Mrs. Jamison cocked her head, sending curls cascading across her shoulder. "Customers have mentioned her, but I haven't seen a shop with her name on it."

"She takes commissions out of Kelloggs'," Beth explained. "Or she did until you came to town. I very much doubt Nora will be a competitor. Every lady will be flocking to your door. You and Mr. Jamison must be very proud."

The seamstress lowered her gaze. "Alas, Mr. Jamison has gone to his just reward. It's only me and my younger brother here in Seattle, but I must say everyone has been so welcoming." She raised her head and made sure to include Hart in her smile.

Beth glanced between the two of them. An accomplished widow of grace and beauty, a lonely lawman established in his career. What better match could she envision?

And why did everything in her rebel at the very idea?

Hart had thought his work difficult. He'd grown thirsty or hungry as he chased a culprit across the county for days. He'd been bruised and battered by men fighting to remain at large. Nothing was as painful as waiting for Beth to finish her transactions in the frilly, overly perfumed shop. And he didn't much like the looks the proprietress was directing his way. For all her sweet smiles and fluttering fingers, he sensed calculation. He could only hope Beth didn't suggest her as a likely bride.

Finally, she left, fabric folded under one arm. Pink, like much of her wardrobe. The fresh, youthful color suited her. Not that he paid much attention.

"What next?" he asked, pacing her as she started down Commercial.

She cast him a glance. "Tiring already?"

Hart stretched his arms over his head. "I can last as long as you can."

She shook her head. "Perhaps you can. But I refuse to monopolize Seattle's only deputy. Think what dire crimes are being committed even as we speak!"

Hart chuckled. "It's Tuesday. Most of the dire crimes happen over the weekend."

"Really?"

Those blue eyes were so trusting. She believed anything he said. While he had tried to walk the narrow path since that dark day in Ohio ten years ago, he still found her belief gratifying.

She probably hadn't noticed that Seattle had too many troublemakers these days. Some of the men coming to work in the coal mines across the lake were harder types than the original pioneers. The steamship route from San Francisco that had started this week added dozens more strangers to the city. Worse, there had been reports of newcomers being enticed from the docks so a gang of ruffians could relieve them of any valuables. Mortified, the immigrants hadn't been willing to come to the sheriff for help, according to the locals who had found the victims. So far, he hadn't been able to convince the immigrants to talk, and he hadn't located the criminals, but he wasn't about to stop trying.

Seattle had one duly appointed constable, but he mostly served as a watchman, raising the hue and cry when something happened. If criminals were to be stopped, it was up to Hart, Sheriff Wyckoff, and any other man he might deputize. Which meant Beth was right, and he had work to do.

Something of what he was feeling must have shown on his face, for she sighed. "I'm finished for today, Hart. You can see me back to the livery."

She sounded so defeated he moved closer. "Didn't you get what you wanted?"

"Oh, yes." Her grin reappeared, forming a dimple at the side of her mouth. "At least, purchase-wise. But don't think you can get rid of me so easily. I'll come back to town and meet with you tomorrow. I'll have better candidates in mind then."

Not if he could help it.

As soon as he saw Beth on the road north toward Wallin Landing, driving a wagon with her brother's famous steel dusts in the traces, Hart went straight to his superior's home on the outskirts of Seattle to speak to Mrs. Wyckoff.

Ursula Wyckoff was a pillar of the town. A handsome woman in her late forties, she worked on most civic and church committees, donated flowers for every funeral and supported any number of charitable causes. Her stern demeanor reminded Hart of the woman who had run the orphanage where he'd been raised. Still, Mrs. Wyckoff invited him in and offered him a glass of lemonade, which he declined, before sitting across from him in the parlor.

"Is something wrong, Mr. McCormick?" she asked, blue eyes bright.

Had she noticed the way he shifted on the horsehair-covered sofa? The Wyckoffs had one of the finer homes in Seattle, the walls covered with floral paper, the wood floors by thick carpets. The furnishings were dark and heavy, while crystal draped the lamps. He always felt like an interloper.

Now he balanced his hat on his knee. "Not wrong, ma'am, just of concern. I understand you and the other ladies of the Literary Society persuaded Miss Wallin to find me a bride."

She didn't look the least embarrassed to be caught in her machinations. "Ah. I had hoped Miss Wallin would be more circumspect."

Hart raised a brow. "So you wanted her to lie, too?"

She waved a hand, the sleeve of her gown dripping lace. "You make it sound so sordid. We were only trying to help."

"I don't need help," Hart told her. "I'm perfectly capable of finding myself a wife if I wanted one. And I don't."

She leaned forward, frown gathering. "And why not?"

Her husband knew the full story of his past, his upbringing in the crowded orphanage, his short time as an outlaw, the deadly consequences of his decision to testify against the gang. Would Wyckoff be strong enough to deny this woman if she asked him about it? Would the story have any chance of remaining hidden if the sheriff or Hart told her?

Would he escape this room without giving her something?

He squared his shoulders. "I was in love once. She died. I don't much care to try again."

Mrs. Wyckoff made a commiserating noise. Then she rose and went to the sideboard. "I don't believe you met my daughter, Ursula." She returned to hand him a daguerreotype. "I thought my first husband silly for insisting that we name her after me and even sillier for going to the expense of having this made."

Hart gazed down at the little girl with a riot of pale curls and a grin that likely tugged at her father's heart. "Is that why you call her Miss Eugenie now?"

Mrs. Wyckoff retrieved the image. "This isn't Eugenie, Mr. McCormick. It's her older sister. My Ursula died when she was seven. She wandered too close to the hearth, and her dress caught on fire."

His stomach clenched. "I'm sorry, ma'am."

She stroked the picture as if she would have liked to stroke her daughter's curls. "So am I. I still miss her." She dropped her hand. "But my point is this: Where would Eugenie and my son John be now if I had been afraid to try again? Where would any of them be if I had refused to marry after my first husband died?"

He sat straighter. "It's different for a woman. You don't have much choice but to wed."

She set down the picture. "I had choices, Mr. McCormick. I could have kept all my suitors dangling and raised my children in peace. I chose to marry and continue with life. So must you."

"Begging your pardon, ma'am," Hart said with a shake of his head, "but there's no *must* about it. Besides, my job keeps me too busy to take a wife."

She nodded. "I'll speak to Lewis about changing your schedule."

That was not what he'd had in mind. He enjoyed his work, knew he made a difference. "I live in a small cabin on the Howards' land. It doesn't have room for another."

"I'm certain your wife wouldn't mind staying in a hotel while you build her a house. Or perhaps Clay Howard can be persuaded to sell you one of his properties in town."

He wasn't about to ask the successful businessman for another favor besides allowing Hart to live in the cabin. "Mrs. Wyckoff, I won't go along with this."

She eyed him. "Is it Beth Wallin?"

She could not have guessed his feelings. He kept his face impassive from long practice. "No."

She sighed. "I thought she might be too young to join the Literary Society and accept this assignment, but Mrs. Howard assured us she was a woman of character despite her years and had had much success with her own family. Perhaps I should take on the task instead. After all, you would have a difficult time refusing your superior's wife."

He would indeed. Except for a short stint last year when Henry Adkins had been elected, Lewis Wyckoff had been sheriff since Hart had arrived in 1865. He'd listened to Hart's story, his dreams, and taken a chance that a onetime outlaw would make a good deputy. Hart had never given him reason to regret his decision. He wasn't about to start now.

"Why are you doing this, Mrs. Wyckoff?" he asked. "You and your husband have been nothing but kindness. Why force me to wed?"

For the first time, her face softened. "Oh, Hart. I'm not trying to harm you. Seattle needs men like you—strong, certain, forthright. But keeping everyone at arm's length is no way to live. If Miss Wallin cannot find you a woman you'd be proud to call wife, I'll simply have to delay her entrance into the Society and undertake the commission myself."

He couldn't do that to Beth. Hart rose and slipped on his hat. "Don't trouble yourself, Mrs. Wyckoff. The Literary Society would be fortunate to have Beth Wallin as a member. I promise you, if there's any woman on this earth who could make me consider matrimony, it's her."

Chapter Three

As Beth went about her chores that afternoon and the next morning, she gave considerable thought as to who might be the right match for Hart. She didn't believe his protests. Her brothers had all reacted that way to courting, only to fall in love when they found the right brides. Hart might bluster all he liked, but the ladies of the Literary Society were right—he'd make some woman a fine husband.

She decided as she cleaned out the main cabin, which served as a rooming house for her brother's logging crew, that he needed a woman of substance, maturity. As she helped John's wife, Dottie, bring in the wash hanging on the line before a squall came in, she determined that an impoverished lady might touch on his sense of chivalry and convince him to help. And she kept her promise. She said nothing to any of her family about her plan.

She had a few women in mind when she went to fetch the mail on Wednesday. Wallin Landing had its own post office, sanctioned by the Postmaster General of the United States, no less, but someone had to carry the letters and parcels from Seattle to her brother James's store and back. When she stopped at the mercantile on Front Street, however, Seattle's postmaster was apologetic.

"A big storm ran down the Strait," Mr. Pumphrey told her, rubbing at the counter with his thick fingers. "I heard it even toppled houses in Victoria. All ships have been delayed, alas."

"We'll send someone back later in the week," Beth promised. "Have you seen Deputy McCormick today?"

"He rode past not a quarter hour ago, heading toward the docks." He leaned across the counter, heavy features lifting. "If you see him, will you tell him his books arrived?"

Beth glanced to the far wall, where leather spines promised adventure and romance. Mr. Pumphrey had stocked the largest collection of books and magazines of any mercantile in Seattle. Her brother John usually had to be dragged from the store before he spent all his money.

"What did he order?" she asked.

His smile brightened his green eyes. "Dime novels— cowboys, train robberies, kidnapped maidens. Perhaps he learns something about being a deputy by reading them."

She promised to let Hart know. Leaving her brother's horses tied in front of the store, she started for the docks. Dime novels. Who would have thought? They were thrilling, sensationalist, romantic. A shame he hadn't learned more from them than the importance of enforcing the law.

The docks were busy as she approached. When she was a girl, Seattle had boasted only one wharf. Now six others stretched across the shores of Elliott Bay.

Three ships had made it to port before the big storm. Sailors and teamsters were still working to unload the cargo. The steamer from San Francisco had also docked, longboats heading out to ferry the passengers and luggage ashore.

Even in all the movement, she easily spotted Hart's black hat, his tall figure. Because it was useless to call over the whine and whir of the nearby sawmill, she stepped out onto the dock. Her rosy skirts were a sharp contrast to the weathered wood, the clumps of lichen and moss, the dark clouds hanging heavy. But it wasn't the threat of rain that made work screech to a halt as she passed. Men lowered their end of boxes to tip their caps. Others offered smiles and nods. One enterprising fellow with dark hair darted in front of her.

"Can I help you, miss?"

A blond elbowed him aside, one thumb hooked in the suspenders that covered his flannel shirt. "I'm the man for the job, miss. Anything you need."

His colleague shoved him. "Back off, you lout. I saw her first."

The other man raised a fist.

"Gents." Both the men froze at Hart's raspy drawl as the lawman moved up behind them. "I believe the lady is looking for me."

"Yes, please," Beth said with a smile to the would-be brawlers. "But thank you for your eagerness to help."

The first swept her a bow. "Anything for you, mi-lady."

His colleague pushed on his shoulders, nearly oversetting him, then ran off with a laugh, the first in hot pursuit.

"They're so cute at that age," Beth said.

Hart shook his head. "You're not much older."

"But so much wiser." She linked her arm with his. "So, tell me. When shall we meet to discuss the next steps in finding you a match?"

He glanced around, likely concerned the men might overhear as work resumed. "Not here." He tugged on her arm, and she allowed him to lead her back up to the shore and pointed him toward Pumphrey and Company, where Lance and Percy waited in their traces.

"Mr. Pumphrey wanted you to know the new dime novels are in," she told Hart. "I understand you're fond of them."

He cast her a glance. "Against the advice of the Literary Society, no doubt. Probably not up to their standards."

Beth raised her chin. "I would never disparage another person's taste in literature. Besides, I've always enjoyed them. Have you read *The Adventures of Black Bess*?"

His smile brightened, and something inside her wanted to dance in its light. "Now, there's a lady. Nothing stopped her—kidnapping, tornado, bandits."

Beth grinned. "Of course you remember the bandits."

He shrugged. "Part of the job."

"I'd have thought you'd want something different from the job to read," she said as they approached the team.

"I started reading them before I was a lawman."

"And they made you dream of becoming one," Beth guessed.

He seemed to be studying the horses. Over the years, many men had responded that way to her brother's horses. They were steel dusts, the first in the area, their shorter necks and powerful hindquarters making them uniquely suited to run far and fast.

About as far and as fast as Hart likely wanted to run from her idea of matching him up.

"Would you be willing to meet me at the Pastry Emporium at two?" she asked. "I'd like to introduce you to someone."

His eyes narrowed, but he nodded. "All right. Until then, stay away from the docks. There are some rough sorts down there."

The two workers hadn't seemed all that rough to her. "You forget. I have five brothers."

"Your brothers are gentlemen. Some of those workers aren't."

She really shouldn't take his statements as anything more than his duty as a lawman. "Very well. I'll be careful."

His gaze moved to the wharves, as if he saw a gang of marauding pirates rather than busy longshoremen. "Good. I wouldn't want anything to happen to you."

Beth stared at him.

"I'd hate to have to explain to your brothers," he added.

Well! She was about to tell him exactly what she thought of the idea when she noticed a light in his eyes. Was that a twinkle in the gray?

Beth tossed her head. "Oh, they'll take your side. You know they will. They always say I have more enthusiasm than sense."

He shrugged. "I know a few women who match that description."

Beth grinned. "But none as pretty as me."

"That's the truth." His gaze warmed, and she caught

her breath. Hart McCormick, flirting with her? It couldn't be!

Fingers fumbling, she untied the horses and hurried for the bench. "I should go. Lots to do before two. See you at the Emporium."

He followed her around. Before she knew what he was about, he'd placed his hands on her waist. For one moment, she stood in his embrace. Her stomach fluttered. She traced the lines around his mouth with her eyes, tried not to think about how those lips might feel against her own.

He lifted her easily onto the bench and stepped back, face impassive as if he hadn't been affected in the slightest. "Until two, Miss Wallin."

Her heart didn't slow until she'd rounded the corner.

Silly! Why did she keep reacting that way? He wasn't interested in her. He'd told her so himself. She was not about to offer him her heart. There was no reason to behave like a giddy schoolgirl on her first infatuation.

Even if he had been her schoolgirl infatuation.

She was a woman now, with opportunities, plans, dreams for a future. If those dreams sometimes seemed nebulous, it was only because she hadn't firmed them up yet. She needed time, more information. She'd figure it out eventually. And she wasn't about to allow herself to take a chance on love again, especially not with Hart McCormick.

For now, the important thing was to find the perfect woman for him, and she knew just where to look. She drove the wagon up Mill Street for the houses that lined the ridge.

Mrs. Dunbar was happy to entertain her, until Beth eased into her reason for visiting. The tall blonde widow leaned back in her leather-upholstered chair with up-raised brow at the idea of working with a matchmaker. When Beth confessed she'd come about Hart McCormick specifically, the woman held up a hand.

"Oh, not him. I appreciate you thinking of me, Miss Wallin, but I have no interest in having Deputy McCormick court me."

Beth couldn't help frowning. "May I ask why? He seems to me to be everything a gentleman should be."

The pretty widow went so far as to shudder. "You were raised in the wilderness, I hear. Some ladies have more exacting standards. Deputy McCormick is far too gruff, far too uncompromising. And those eyes." She shuddered again. "I'd not like to see those looking at me across the dining table every day."

Beth stood, shaking out her skirts. "I understand. You'd prefer a gentleman you can bend to your will, preferably with pale eyes and a wan constitution. If I find one in Seattle, I'll be sure to send him your way. I'll just see myself out."

She was still steaming as she climbed up onto the bench. Uncompromising, Mrs. Dunbar had said. Who wanted a man who compromised his values? What was wrong with having a strong moral compass? And to judge a fellow by the color of his eyes? Mrs. Dunbar was no better than Drew, coming up with reasons to refuse a man without having any idea of his character! Hart could do better.

Unfortunately, the next two ladies she visited were equally uninterested. One thought him too opinionated, the other too quiet. He certainly held strong opinions, but she generally agreed with them, except for a certain decision on whether to wed. And he wasn't garrulous.

When he spoke, he spoke with substance, imparting information, concern. Why did they see those traits as weaknesses rather than strengths?

The final lady agreed to come with her to meet Hart, but so timidly that Beth could only wonder. Perhaps he wasn't showing himself to best effect. If these women had encountered him in the middle of some investigation, Beth could see why they might find him uncompromising. He would have been focused on doing his job. Perhaps they needed to see another side of him, a man who could show to advantage in society.

Not that she'd ever seen that side of him, come to think of it. But it had to be there. She merely had to bring it out.

As in the tale of the ugly duckling she'd read as a child, she was certain Hart McCormick had a swan inside. He just didn't know it yet. But, with her at his side, Seattle would soon see what a fine man held the position of deputy sheriff. And then the ladies would come running.

Hart dragged his feet going to the Pastry Emporium that afternoon. He told himself he had work to do. That was why he'd been out on the docks, after all. Weinclef at Kelloggs' had confessed to finding another newcomer beaten in the alley beside the store. Hart wasn't about to let the gang claim another victim. Whoever recruited the poor fellows must have a pleasing disguise, because the immigrants went willingly and didn't want to implicate their benefactor in their troubles.

So, after seeing Beth off, he returned to the top of the docks, watching as the passengers from the San Francisco run climbed up onto the planks. The first

pair were grizzled sourdoughs, looking for better pick-
ings, it seemed. Likely they'd be too savvy to run afoul
of Seattle's newest gang. Next up the ladder from the
longboat was a dapper gentleman with a lady and two
lads in tow. They were probably safe as well. Single
fellows were easier to peel away.

The next fellow was the perfect candidate. Tailored
coat and plaid trousers, big grin on his face, as if even
the frontier town delighted him. Carpetbag in hand, he
strutted up the pier.

A lad materialized from behind a crate, startling
the fellow. Hart frowned as the pair exchanged words.
Then the youth fell into step beside the newcomer, as
if guiding him along the dock.

Hart met them at the top of the wharf, feet planted
and stance wide. The youth blanched. He could have
been as old as fourteen, though his slender build and
short stature made it equally likely he was younger. He
quickly tugged down on his tweed cap and lowered his
gaze, but not before Hart made out thick black hair.

"Afternoon," Hart drawled. "I'm Deputy McCormick. Where might you be going?"

The man beamed at him. "My new friend here was
about to show me a suitable place for a gentleman to
lodge in your fair city."

"Wasn't that neighborly of him?" Hart eyed the
youth. "Where are you headed, son?"

He bolted.

While the newcomer called out in protest, Hart gave
chase. The adolescent darted among the wagons waiting
to be loaded. Horses shifted, wagons swayed, drivers
shouted a complaint. Nothing stopped the youth. Nothing stopped Hart either.

His quarry wove in and out among the traffic on Commercial Street, then paused before a shop. Was he daring Hart to follow him? Hart didn't look at the name of the proprietor before diving after him.

Three women cried out, and he managed to stop himself before plowing into them. He recognized the two Denny ladies. He couldn't mistake the woman with them.

Mrs. Jamison drew herself up. "Really, Deputy! What is the meaning of this?"

Hart nodded to her, gaze sweeping the shop. It ought to have been easy to spot a lad among all the fripperies, yet everything looked much as it had yesterday. "Forgive the interruption, Mrs. Jamison. I followed a possible felon into this shop. Did you see where he went?"

The Denny ladies clutched their chests as if fearing for their lives.

Mrs. Jamison narrowed her eyes. "Felon? What nonsense. The only person of the male persuasion to come through those doors in the last hour was my brother."

Mrs. Arthur Denny, wife of the railroad president, collected herself and stepped forward, blue skirts swinging. "There must be some mistake, Deputy. Mrs. Jamison and her brother are new to our shores."

"And she is a terribly talented seamstress," her sister, who had married the wealthy land developer David Denny, brother of Arthur, added. "She and her brother are a credit to our town."

Hart nodded. "Good to know. I'd like to meet the fellow."

The Denny ladies looked to their hostess. Mrs. Jamison's bow of a mouth was pressed tight together. Then it widened to a smile. "Why, certainly, Deputy.

I'll just fetch him for you." She passed through the curtain at the back of the shop.

The two dark-haired sisters busied themselves with the sketches they must have been perusing before he'd burst in on them. He could imagine Beth poring over the things as avidly.

He cleared his throat even though he hadn't spoken his thoughts aloud. Both of the ladies were members of the Literary Society. No sense giving them more ideas.

Mrs. Jamison floated back in with a young man at her side. He wore no coat over his cambric shirt and wool trousers, and his black hair was parted to fall neatly on either side of his face. He acted more diffident, but Hart was certain the lad was the same one he'd chased from the wharf.

Mrs. Jamison's long-fingered hand rested on her brother's shoulder. "Bobby, this is Deputy McCormick. He wanted to meet you. Deputy, this is my brother, Robert Donovan."

Hart inclined his head. The adolescent gazed back, mute.

"Donovan," he acknowledged. "I'm glad to meet you. Tell me what you were doing down by the dock."

Mrs. Jamison's fingers must have tightened on his shoulder, for the cambric stretched under her hand. "You must be mistaken, Deputy. My brother knows better than to visit such a dangerous place."

Still the lad said nothing. Hart cocked his head. "We know otherwise, don't we?"

Donovan swallowed.

His sister's hand slipped around his shoulders. "Oh, Bobby, you didn't. I told you it was no good meeting the ship. None of your friends are coming north. And we don't have the money to send you back to San Francisco."

Donovan hung his head.

Mrs. Jamison met Hart's gaze, tears shimmering in her violet eyes. "I'm sorry, Deputy. Bobby didn't want to come north, but there was nothing for us in San Francisco after my husband died. Please forgive him if he caused any trouble. He just wanted to find a friend."

As if fighting tears himself, Donovan gave a brave sniff.

Hart straightened. "No harm done. But do as your sister says, lad, and stay away from the docks. If you want to make friends, you'd do better to attend school."

Mrs. Jamison beamed at her brother. "Of course. We'll be enrolling him at the North School at the start of next term." She turned her look on Hart. "Thank you, Deputy, for your kind concern. May I send something home to your sweetheart to show my appreciation? Perhaps a length of ribbon?"

"Mr. McCormick doesn't have a sweetheart," the elder Mrs. Denny put in with a sly look to Hart.

"Though many of his dear friends would like to see that remedied," her sister added with a giggle.

Mrs. Jamison turned the same shade of pink as her wallpaper. "Then you must send her to see me when you propose. I specialize in wedding dresses."

Hart tipped his hat. "Very kind of you, ma'am, but I'm afraid that time might be a long while coming."

The seamstress fluttered her dark lashes. "Perhaps not as long as you fear. A lawman like you would make a devoted husband and father. See how well you did with Bobby?"

The boy glanced up at him, eyes narrowed. "I hope you'll come by often, Deputy."

His sister's smile tightened. "Now, now, Bobby. Deputy McCormick must be very busy. We'll be fine. Haven't I always taken care of you?"

Her brother didn't answer, dropping his gaze and shuffling his feet.

He didn't fool Hart. There was something going on with Bobby Donovan and his lovely older sister. Hart made up his mind to keep an eye on them both. Right after he made sure Beth hadn't settled on a bride.

Chapter Four

"Are you certain this is advisable, Miss Wallin?"

Beth smiled encouragement to the woman sitting beside her in the Pastry Emporium. Honoria Jenkins was a gentle lady who had been hired to teach at the newly opened North School, starting after Easter. Her light brown hair, cornflower-blue eyes and rosy cheeks made her resemble one of the glass-eyed dolls on display at Kelloggs'.

"We are in a public place," Beth assured her, waving at the neat little wrought-iron tables and glass display case the bakery boasted. "And I'm here as a chaperone."

Miss Jenkins adjusted the brown velvet hat on her sleek hair. "But won't Deputy McCormick suspect this is more than a casual meeting?"

Beth certainly hoped so. "As I mentioned, Mr. McCormick is seeking a wife. I'm merely facilitating introductions as his good friend."

The schoolteacher eyed the door as if expecting Father Christmas to arrive with a bag of presents. "He sounds like quite a catch."

"Oh, he is." Beth picked up the cup of chamomile she

had ordered. "Upstanding, loyal, a hard worker. He's the law in this area."

Miss Jenkins sighed. "How heroic." She turned her blue gaze back to Beth. "Why aren't you pursuing him yourself?"

Beth's face heated. She set down her cup and selected one of the lemon drop cookies, her personal favorite, then took a bite and swallowed before answering.

"He's like a brother to me."

The lemon drop was like dust in Beth's mouth. Maddie Haggerty, longtime friend and owner of the Pastry Emporium, must have had an off day. Beth took another sip of the tea to wash things down. It didn't help.

Suddenly the couple sitting closest to the window gasped, and others began rising. Beth caught a glimpse of a dark-coated rider and a black horse pelting past, heard the shouts accompanying them. Her heart started beating faster.

Miss Jenkins pressed a hand to the ruffles at her throat. "What is it?"

"Deputy McCormick, I believe," Beth answered, rising. "Come on."

She hurried to the window, where the other patrons had collected, voices buzzing as they vied for the best position to watch. Beth squeezed in and pulled Miss Jenkins with her. Down the block, Hart and Arno veered against a team of horses thundering along, reins flapping. As she watched, he leaned over in the saddle, caught the reins, and pulled both Arno and the team to a halt. The elderly driver trembled while his wife buried her face in his shoulder.

"Runaway team," someone said. "Good thing McCormick was on duty."

"As usual," Beth said, drawing a breath.

Miss Jenkins pulled her gaze from the street to stare at Beth as the others returned to their seats. "How can you be so calm? Someone might have been killed."

"Possibly," Beth allowed, taking her arm to lead her back to their table. "But you see how he rescued them. Mr. McCormick is a gentleman who can be counted upon."

Miss Jenkins looked thoughtful.

They had no sooner settled themselves than the door opened to the ring of the shop bell. Hart stepped inside, leather duster settling against his black boots. His hard gaze bypassed the display counter with its dozens of frosted and spiced treats, and narrowed in instead on the patrons gathered at the tables. Some of the other patrons applauded. He gave them a nod.

Beth rose as he approached.

He removed his hat, the sunlight from the window gilding his short-cropped black hair. "Miss Wallin." His look moved to her companion.

As if she was guilty of some crime, Miss Jenkins paled, and she pushed the cookies away from her.

"Good afternoon, Deputy," Beth said determinedly. "May I introduce a new acquaintance of mine, Honoria Jenkins. Miss Jenkins, this is Deputy Hart McCormick."

Hart inclined his head. "Ma'am."

She dropped her gaze. "Deputy. Won't you join us?"

With a look to Beth that held any number of misgivings, he drew up a chair.

"Cookie?" Miss Jenkins asked, offering the plate. "They're quite good."

"No, thanks," he said. "Never was too partial to lemon."

She set down the plate, wrinkling her nose. "Too tart. I quite agree."

Odd. She'd consumed four of the things before Hart had arrived and even agreed with Beth they were one of Maddie's best.

"That was very brave of you just now," the schoolteacher continued, folding her gloved hands demurely on the table. "Miss Wallin told me you're quite the hero, but now I've seen the evidence with my own eyes."

His gaze swung Beth's way, and she had to stop herself from squirming. She raised her chin instead. "Everyone here saw what you did. We all know you stand between the citizens of the county and every sort of danger."

He snorted, leaning back in his chair as if to distance himself from the very notion. "Folks in King County are pretty good about spotting danger and protecting themselves. I'm just here for when things get out of hand."

Miss Jenkins leaned closer to him. "And do they get out of hand often?" she asked.

Hart frowned as if he could not understand her breathless interest.

"Miss Jenkins is new to our shores," Beth explained. "I'm sure she'd appreciate your assessment of the area."

Hart shrugged. "Things are fairly safe. Only had one cougar attack in the last month, and Sheriff Wyckoff and his dogs chased it off. Natives left on this side of the Sound are friendly for the most part. Last time anyone was murdered was a few months ago—family out Columbia way—shot in their beds. We strung up the killers."

Miss Jenkins was turning whiter with each word.

"But everything in Seattle is fine," Beth rushed to assure her. "Kind people, industrious…"

"Few drunken brawls on the weekend, petty theft in the mercantiles…"

"Four churches now," Beth continued, raising her voice.

"A gang along the waterfront, beating and robbing newcomers."

Beth gave up and glared at him. "A vicious gang, in Seattle?"

"Never underestimate man's ability to prey on man, Miss Wallin," he insisted, with a nod to Miss Jenkins. "Or woman."

She rose in a flutter of brown, like a sparrow startled from its nest. "Thank you for inviting me to tea, Miss Wallin. I fear I must be going. I'll be starting work shortly, and I won't have time for more of these…social events. Deputy."

Hart had risen when she did, but she scooted out the door before he could bid her farewell. With a frown, he settled himself back onto his chair. "Curious woman. Doesn't say much."

"Because you wouldn't let her get a word in," Beth accused. "What were you thinking, filling her head with dangers and drama? I'll be surprised if she sets one foot outside her door the next two days."

Hart reached for a cookie. "If she's that timid, she shouldn't have come to Seattle."

Beth stared at him as he popped the morsel whole into his mouth. "I thought you didn't like lemon drops."

"They're tolerable," he allowed, reaching for another.

Heat flushed through her and not from embarrassment this time. "You did that on purpose."

"Did what?" His face and voice were bland, but he didn't fool her.

"You went out of your way to be unpleasant to Miss Jenkins. Surely you guessed I was trying to match you up with her."

"Couldn't think of any other reason she'd be here."

Beth threw up her hands. "You didn't even try to see if she was suitable."

"We won't suit." He'd finished the last of the cookies and pushed the plate away. "No man wants a wife who can't stomach to hear about his work."

There was that. Beth sighed. "Very well. I suppose she might be too timid for a fellow like you."

He nodded, leaning back in his chair as if satisfied. Something inside her itched to remove that smug smile.

"I should have thought to ask," she said sweetly. "What do you prefer in your bride?"

His smile snuffed out. "I'm not looking for a bride."

Stubborn! Like most of his kind. Beth smiled at him. "You're quite right. *I'm* seeking you a bride." She leaned forward. "You don't have all that many choices, you know. There are still far more men than women here. And the other ladies I've approached have been reticent."

He nodded. "Good. I always knew the ladies of Seattle were a smart lot."

"But that doesn't mean there aren't ladies who would be willing to have you court them," Beth insisted. "I'll try to take your ideas into consideration, if you'd care to share."

He crossed his arms over his chest, setting his badge to winking in the light. "Never gave it much thought."

"Really? I know women who have the gown all picked out and are just waiting for the fellow to go on their arm." When he frowned, she pushed on. "Let's start with physique. Slender or ample?"

Was that a touch of color working its way into his firm cheeks? "I am not having this conversation with you."

She smothered a laugh, keeping her tone pleasant. "Whyever not? It's in your best interest. I certainly don't want to waste my time on women you wouldn't look at twice."

"This whole thing is a waste of time," he grumbled, shifting in his seat.

"Blonde, brunette, raven-haired, redhead?" Beth persisted.

He glanced toward the curtain covering the opening to the bakery kitchen, where the redheaded Maddie Haggerty was likely hard at work. "There's something to be said for red hair."

She'd wondered from time to time whether Hart had had a soft spot for the spunky Irish baker before Maddie had married her dashing husband, Michael. She must have been sitting too long, for the little chair seemed suddenly hard.

"Not too easy to find them," she said. "What else?"

She heard his sigh. "Can't you leave well enough alone?"

She almost gave up. His shoulders were tight, his hands braced on the table as if he wanted nothing more than to escape. She reached out, laid her hand atop one of his.

"I'm only trying to help, Hart."

He blew out a breath. "I know. Being a matchmaker is a fine calling, for men who want a wife."

Once more Beth smiled encouragement. "But not any wife. What's the perfect woman for you?"

He straightened. "You want to hear what kind of woman I'd accept as a wife? Tall enough to fit under my chin, sunny hair, warm disposition, backbone to argue her side of the matter, grace to give in when she sees it's important to me. Someone who understands what I do and respects me for it. You find me a woman like that, and I may have to rethink my decision not to wed." He pushed back from the table and headed for the door.

Beth watched him go, too surprised to move. She'd thought it might be difficult finding him someone who met his criteria, but she knew a woman who embodied all those traits.

Her.

Hart strode down the boardwalk, the sound of his boots beating in time with his pulse. Why'd he give her a target to shoot at? Her brothers bragged that Beth was a crack shot. Once she set her sights on a lady, Hart was as good as married, even with so few women in the area.

"Hart! Deputy McCormick!"

Her breathless call pulled him up short. She hurried down the boardwalk after him, one hand clamping her dainty little hat to her head. The gray net veil fluttered behind her as if trying to escape. He knew the feeling.

"I said my piece," he told her, widening his stance. What, was she planning to draw on her? Why did he feel as if he'd been backed into a corner by an outlaw gang bent on destruction?

"And I appreciate your candor," she assured him as she came abreast. "But we haven't determined our next steps."

He started down the street for the sheriff's office, where he'd left Arno with a feed sack. "You tried. No lady will have me. That's the end of it."

Her skirts flapped as she lengthened her stride to keep up with him. "I didn't say no lady would have you, only the ones I've approached so far. I would never give up so easily. We have merely encountered a challenge." She shot him a grin. "And I love challenges."

Truth be told, he liked a challenge as well. But this was something more. "You said it yourself—there are only so many unmarried women in these parts. What can you do about a lack of ladies? The women Mercer brought back were all married within a year."

"Except Lizzie Ordway," she reminded him. "She chose to devote herself to teaching."

"Wise woman." He offered her his arm as they came to the end of the boardwalk, but she used both hands to gather her skirts out of the mud instead.

"I agree."

She said it so firmly. Why did he doubt she believed it?

"If you and the Literary Society are so determined that every gentleman take a wife, why would you allow some ladies to avoid taking a husband?"

There was a prim set to her mouth. "Some people of either gender lack the spirit of compromise and congeniality necessary for a good marriage."

"And what makes you think I'm not one of them?"

"Because I know you."

So she thought, but Hart had gone out of his way to

keep his past quiet, his present private. It was best not to make too many friends you'd only end up having to investigate one day.

"If you know me so well, you ought to understand this isn't going to work," he told her.

"Nonsense. I must insist that any number of fine, upstanding women might meet your criteria and win your heart, but for one thing."

From what he'd seen, there were few enough women who could truly appreciate the life of a lawman on the frontier. But he found himself curious as to what might stop them from agreeing to his suit.

"What's that?" he asked as they rounded the corner.

She met his gaze. "You."

Hart jerked to a stop, then recovered himself. "Well, I could have told you that. And I'm not changing."

"Not in character," she assured him as he set out once more. "Although you might work on some traits. Patience, openness to new ideas…"

His glare only made her giggle. The happy sound could not fail but make him chuckle too.

"Very well," she acknowledged as they neared the sheriff's office. "You don't want to change. Personally, I'm not sure why you would need to do much. I would have thought any lady could see from your exploits reported in the papers that you have high morals, an outstanding work ethic and a chivalrous nature."

He wasn't sure whether to thank her or laugh. What a paragon she thought him. He settled for a *humph* as they reached Arno. The gelding bobbed his head as if agreeing with everything Beth had said.

Traitor.

"If I'd make the perfect husband," Hart said, "why is it a challenge to find me a wife?"

He'd hoped to prick her bubble of optimism, but she merely raised her chin, the breeze tugging at her platinum curls. "A woman wants more in a husband. She seeks a gentleman, a fellow who appreciates music, the arts."

He raised a brow, and Arno snorted as if doubting Hart could ever measure up. "In Seattle?" Hart asked.

"Anywhere," she insisted. "And I cannot believe you insensible to such refinement of spirit. You read literature."

"Dime novels," he reminded her. "Adventures, mysteries."

"And what are the great novels of the past if not adventures. Dickens, Scott, Fenimore Cooper."

He hadn't read anything by those authors, but he'd have to ask Mr. Pumphrey about them. Or perhaps her brother John. It wouldn't be the first time he'd borrowed books from the scholarly logger.

"No," Beth continued, "we merely need to prove to the ladies that you are Seattle's most eligible bachelor."

A weight fell across his shoulders. It was not unlike the feeling that came over him before he moved in to apprehend a felon, as if he was about to meet his destiny. "What do you mean, Beth?"

She gazed up at him, eyes shining with a light that sent a chill through him. "I intend to show you to best advantage—grooming, clothing, domicile, social prominence."

Hart's stomach sank. "Now, wait a minute…"

She gave Arno a pat and stepped back. "No time to waste. I can see this will require all my time, all my energy. I'll have to move into town for a while."

"Town." The whole idea seemed to be spinning out of control. "Your brothers won't like that."

She waved a hand as she was so fond of doing, as if the movement wiped away all his arguments. "They'll survive. They have their wives to assist them now in any event. And I don't expect it will take more than a month or two."

Two months of this? He'd never survive.

"You can't put up in a hotel," he protested. He certainly couldn't protect her there. "Too many men."

"I'll speak to Allegra Howard. I'm sure she'd let me stay with her and Clay."

Very likely she would. The Howards and the Wallins were old friends. But if Beth was staying with the Howards, she'd be just across the paddock from his cabin. He could see her every morning before he left for work, every night when he returned. Likely she'd be at the table when he ate with the Howards as he sometimes did.

She beamed at him as if she had no idea she'd boxed him into a canyon and was standing guard at the entrance. "Just think, I'll be right at hand to help whenever you need."

That was what he feared.

Chapter Five

Hart hadn't been enthused about Beth's idea to move into town from Wallin Landing, but Allegra was as welcoming as Beth had hoped when she called that afternoon to ask a favor. The dark-haired beauty had come with Beth's sisters-in-law and Maddie Haggerty in the second Mercer expedition bringing brides to Seattle, but the widow had become engaged before she ever reached Seattle's shores. Her onetime sweetheart had sailed with the expedition and convinced her to marry him instead.

Now her daughter from her first marriage, Gillian, had been joined by a little brother, Georgie. Beth had watched both children grow. Gillian was thirteen, and Georgie was seven, fair-haired like their fathers but with their mother's refined features. They were equally excited to have Beth come stay with them.

"You can tell me all about the latest styles," Gillian gushed.

Georgie made a face. "Dresses, bah. You can show me how to shoot. Pa says you're better than he is."

"Well, I don't know about that," Beth demurred,

thinking of the stalwart businessman who was the boy's father. Clay Howard had traveled the country, including working on the California gold fields, before settling in Seattle. He knew how to take care of himself.

Her family, however, wasn't so sure about her. The first people she told about her plans when she returned to Wallin Landing that evening were Drew and his wife, Catherine. She generally cooked and kept house for her oldest brother's logging crew, after all. Drew would have to make other arrangements while she was in town.

"Out of the question," he said when she went to his cabin across the big clearing at Wallin Landing. "You have too much to do here."

He seemed so determined, arms crossed over his chest, eyes narrowed. Strangers took one look at his broad shoulders, his muscular build, and concluded the blond giant must be a bear of a man. His family and friends knew the warm heart that beat inside that massive chest, and felt free to ignore his edicts.

Catherine, ever the reasonable one, put a hand on his arm as if to restrain further comments. Raised near Boston and trained to be a nurse, she had an elegant way about her Beth could only admire. She was certain it had something to do with Catherine's pale blond hair and light blue eyes.

"What will you be doing in Seattle, Beth?" she asked politely.

Beth couldn't tell them the whole truth. She'd promised Hart to keep quiet about the matter. And her brothers didn't like to encourage her matchmaking, for all none of them might have married without her help.

"I've promised to assist Allegra and the Literary Society in a matter," she said.

Catherine eyed her husband. "The Literary Society? How nice that the most influential ladies in Seattle would enlist the aid of a Wallin."

If Drew was impressed, he didn't show it. "If they're so important they ought to be able to take care of the matter themselves," he grumbled in his deep voice. "You have work here."

Beth put her hands on her hips. "May I remind you that I took on cooking for the crew, without pay I might add, because you were concerned they couldn't fend for themselves? They are grown men, Drew. Surely they can make their own way without me for a little while."

Drew leaned back. "That wasn't the work I meant, though I am grateful for your help. You have a claim to improve. You're still living in Simon's old cabin. You haven't even built one for yourself yet, and you've had the land for nearly two of the five years allowed. If the territorial land office learns you aren't living on the claim, you could lose it."

Why did talking with her brothers always make her feel like a child again? "I know the law. I must live on the property six months of the year. I'll be back after Easter, and we can decide on plans for the cabin then."

His arms fell. "After Easter? You won't be here for the celebration?"

He sounded so forlorn that her heart went out to him. "Of course I'll come home for Easter. You couldn't keep me away. Rina, Nora, Catherine and I have already been planning. I'm sure they can continue without my input."

Drew looked as if he would keep arguing, but Catherine nodded. "It won't be the same without you being here to direct things with your usual energy, but I'm sure we'll make do. Dottie and Callie can help."

Drew sighed. "Very well, if no one else has any objections."

Of course, there were more objections. Her other brothers were nearly as argumentative when they learned of her plans. Drew must have sent his children around with the news, for the rest of her brothers descended on the main cabin shortly after she'd finished serving the logging crew dinner. Harry, Tom and Dickie wisely beat a retreat at the sight of them crowding into the front room. Beth only wished she could get away so easily.

"You'll be too far from home," Simon pointed out, long legs eating up the plank flooring as he paced before the stone hearth. "We can't reach you if there's trouble."

"I'll be staying at the Howards'," Beth told him. "What sort of trouble do you expect?"

She was sorry she asked, for he stopped to tick off his concerns on his fingers. "Cholera has been reported in the territory. The town is becoming increasingly crowded with men of every sort. That windstorm cut off supplies—another could do so as well, leading to rioting in the streets."

"Worse," James intoned, voice like a church bell, "she might come back engaged to a sawmill worker." He gasped and clutched his chest.

Simon looked daggers at him, but Beth shook her head at his teasing. So did her brother John.

"I'm sure we could deal with that," he told James. "But Beth, Simon has a point. Here you have all of us for support if you need it. Who will you rely on in Seattle?"

Her middle brother, John, was such a dear, always concerned about the family. Before she could protest that she could take care of herself, Levi, her closest brother in age, spoke up.

"I have similar concerns. You need someone you can count on, Beth."

Beth threw up her hands. "And you don't believe Allegra and Clay are reliable? Look at the lives they've built—successful, admired."

Levi had learned something about the tact required in his position of minister, for he made a sad face as if commiserating with her. "Allegra and Clay are good friends, but they aren't family."

"Precisely," Simon said. "Someone should go with her."

That was all she needed. Immediately they set about arguing who could spare time from their families and work. Beth stamped her foot to get their attention.

"No," she said. "I don't need anyone to look out for me. I'm not a child."

"That," James said, "is exactly why we're concerned."

Oh! Brothers!

"I have a solution," Levi put in. "There's someone in town as close as family who'd be glad to help Beth. Scout."

Her brothers all nodded, stances relaxing, mouths smiling. Even Beth thought she could live with that solution. She'd known Scout Rankin all her life. Only three years her senior, he and Levi had been nearly inseparable growing up. Before James's wife, Rina, had come to Wallin Landing as the first official schoolteacher, Beth, Levi and Scout had sat for lessons with Ma in the main cabin. The three of them had fished and hunted together, climbed trees together, chased each other through the woods. Only when Levi and Scout had set off to seek their fortunes on the gold fields of the British territories to the north had the trio been parted.

Scout and Levi had had a falling-out along the way, but since their friend's return to Seattle last month, they had made up. Scout had come back a wealthy man and had purchased a fine house in town. And he had proven himself a good friend.

But while her brothers were certain Scout could keep an eye on Beth, Beth was equally certain she ought to be keeping an eye on Scout. He'd returned to Seattle triumphant, just as he and Levi had always dreamed. But his quiet nature and the wariness learned under his abusive father seemed to be keeping him from accepting the place he'd earned in society.

What he needed was a wife.

She told him as much when they met at the Pastry Emporium two days later, after she'd moved in with the Howards and made arrangements to start the next phase of her plan to find Hart a bride.

She smiled at her old friend sitting across one of the wrought-iron tables from her, looking rather dapper in an olive coat and tan trousers. Scout had never been as tall or muscular as her brothers. His dark hair was longer than currently fashionable, brushing his collar. His narrow face was marred by a crooked nose that had been broken years ago, and his left cheek bore a scar he had received while he'd been away.

"Oh, you needn't worry," he said, soft brown gaze dropping to the tabletop. "I doubt anyone will want to marry me."

Beth nudged his foot with her own, and he glanced up.

"You are a gentleman," she reminded him.

Scout quirked a smile. "I suppose money will do that for a fellow."

"Nonsense," Beth said, applying herself to the cinnamon roll Maddie had placed between them, white sugar icing dripping from the still-warm sides. "You were a gentleman before you left for the gold fields. Money doesn't change who you are."

He rubbed a hand on the olive-colored sleeve of his coat, as if uncomfortable with the elegant cut of the wool fabric. "It sure doesn't."

This time, Beth's nudge was sharper, and he looked up, brows raised in obvious surprise.

"You stop that immediately," she scolded. "You are a fine man, Thomas Rankin. Any lady in Seattle would be blessed to have you."

Whether it was the use of his formal name or the tone of her voice, she wasn't sure, but Scout grinned at her. "Well, there's one lady I'd like to impress, but she's awfully bossy."

Beth stuck out her tongue at him.

Scout laughed. "See? You don't stand for any nonsense from me or your brothers. Never have."

"Never will," Beth promised him.

"And that tells me it isn't anything about me that keeps you from letting me court you. I know which way the wind blows there."

Like her brothers, Scout had witnessed her earlier infatuation with the deputy.

"The wind has changed, Scout," she murmured, keeping her gaze on the cinnamon roll. "I've changed. I don't think I'll ever marry either."

"What?" He leaned closer, and she could feel him searching her face. "But you're the matchmaker!"

"Just because I can match other people doesn't mean I can pick my own husband reliably," she said, voice prim. "That's why people need a matchmaker, you know. They lack the vision to see the right person for them."

"Funny," Scout said, leaning back. "I thought it was lack of skills in society or lack of confidence."

"Those can be overcome," Beth assured him, raising her gaze with certainty. "But I'm beginning to believe none of us can reliably choose a mate on our own."

"The human race is doomed," he teased.

"No," she replied with a grin. "I'll save it."

He laughed. "We're a pair, I guess. I doubt any woman would want me given my family history. You doubt the man you want will return your affections."

"I don't doubt," Beth told him. "I asked him. He doesn't."

She wasn't sure why she told him. He could very well take the tale back to Levi and the rest of her brothers. But there was something about Scout, something sweet, something approachable.

And it was very nice to have someone commiserate with her.

His reaction was everything she might have hoped for. He drew himself up, color rushing back into his lean cheeks. "Then Deputy McCormick is nothing but a low-down skunk, and you're better off without him."

"That's what I keep telling her," Hart said as he stopped by their table.

He watched as Beth washed white. She'd been so intent on her conversation with Scout Rankin she probably hadn't heard the shop bell. Georgie Howard had told him Beth had come to visit. The boy often joined Hart at the paddock to help him rub down Arno. But Beth hadn't approached Hart, and he found himself eager to speak to her. After all, he needed to know how she intended to follow through on her threat to find him a wife. Then he'd spotted her through the window and had decided to ask.

Besides, he still wasn't any too sure about Scout. He'd known the fellow since Scout was seventeen. He'd seemed the sneaky, weak-natured son of a crooked, cruel father. Ben Rankin's homemade liquor and high-stakes card games had been the ruin of many a man in Seattle. His son might be living in a fancy house instead of the shack along Lake Union where his father had raised him. He might be wearing better clothes than the torn trousers and rough wool shirt that had been his habitual outfit, but until Hart knew this apple had fallen farther from the tree, he couldn't feel comfortable with Scout spending time with Beth.

Scout flushed now, but he rose to his feet and met Hart's gaze unflinchingly. "Deputy. I'm glad to hear we're in agreement."

"Stranger things have happened." He turned to Beth, who seemed to have recovered by the way her chin came up. "What brings you to Seattle, Miss Wallin?"

Scout bristled. "Seems to me this is a free country. Beth can go wherever she likes."

"Deputy McCormick isn't questioning my rights, Scout," she said, keeping her dark blue gaze on Hart. "He's concerned what I may be doing. You must know I've deposited my things with the Howards, Deputy. I will stay in Seattle as long as it takes to accomplish my goal."

At least she hadn't mentioned that goal aloud. It was bad enough the Literary Society had been discussing his matrimonial prospects. He didn't need Scout Rankin laughing behind his back.

"Your family will miss you," he told her.

Her look softened. "And I will miss them. All the more reason to settle things quickly. I believe you have this afternoon off?"

How did she know? He took care to vary the days and times so no criminal would guess when the law might be absent. Had Mrs. Wyckoff learned his schedule from her husband?

"I do," he acknowledged.

She nodded. "Good. You have an appointment at Ganzel's at two."

The barber? He certainly hadn't made that appointment. "Do I, now?"

"You do." The twinkle in her eyes was unmistakable. "And I believe Messieurs Black and Powell are expecting you at three."

The tailors as well. She had been busy.

"And if I had other plans for the afternoon?"

The twinkle became a gleam. "Cancel them." She rose suddenly, and Scout stepped to her side as if protecting her, his gaze defiant as he looked toward Hart.

"I must be going," she said. "Scout, it was lovely to see you. Let's keep in touch while I'm in town. I haven't given up on our plans." In her usual impetuous manner, she gave him a hug.

Hart was more interested in her words. Plans? What plans did she have with the fellow? Was Rankin looking for a bride, too?

Releasing Scout, Beth nodded to Hart. "Deputy.

Don't disappoint me." She swept from the shop to the chime of the bell.

Scout sighed like a moonstruck schoolboy.

"Someone should marry her," Hart spat out.

Scout started, then peered more closely at him. "I have it on good authority the only man she ever wanted turned her down."

Had she confessed? He had been under the impression she'd told no one. After all, none of her brothers had come calling demanding an explanation. If Beth trusted Scout so much that she'd share her secret, perhaps Hart had been mistaken about the man.

On the other hand, the gang along the waterfront had risen to prominence in the month since Scout had come back. Maybe he hadn't returned wealthy. Maybe his money was coming from somewhere else. Maybe, like his father, he saw other men as victims rather than friends.

Hart straddled Beth's chair. "Sit down, Rankin. I'd like a word with you."

The sullen look reminded Hart of Scout as a youth. One of Scout's jobs had been to come in to Seattle and entice men out to his father's place to drink and gamble. It struck Hart now that the pattern was a great deal like what the gang was doing.

Still, Scout obeyed his command and sat, gaze hard on Hart's face.

Hart leaned back. "You arrived in town the middle of February, didn't you?"

Scout nodded.

"Any particular reason you wanted to return?"

Scout's smile was more sneer. "It's home."

Hart stuck out his lower lip. "Not much of a home to return to. Your pa's gone. He lost his claim."

"Because you drove him out."

Now, there was some venom. The color was rising in his cheeks again.

"Guilty," Hart said. "But then, so was he, of moonshining, cheating at cards."

"Oh, he was guilty, all right." Scout leaned across the table, gaze drilling into Hart. "But I'm not. I intend to be a fine, upstanding citizen, Deputy. You have no call to hound me."

Hart nodded, and Scout rose. Instead of leaving, however, he came around the table, forcing Hart to his feet. Though Scout was a good six inches shorter, the heat radiating off him made Hart take a step back.

"And you have no need to hound Beth Wallin, either," Scout said, tenor voice surprisingly hard. "She's been through enough on account of you. If I hear you've hurt her further, you'll have to deal with me. And I promise you, Deputy, I can be even less forgiving than my father."

Chapter Six

Hart shook his head as he left the Pastry Emporium. Who'd have thought Scout Rankin had such courage? He seemed to have developed backbone on the gold fields. Of course, it shouldn't surprise him that Scout was determined to protect Beth. Scout had grown up with her and her brothers. And she was the kind of woman to inspire acts of valor. Every man in Seattle would likely be willing to do her a service.

Even, it seemed, the barber.

"Deputy McCormick," he said, welcoming Hart with a warm smile. "What a pleasure."

A neat fellow with a gap-toothed grin and meaty hands, David Ganzel had been shaving faces and cutting hair for Seattle's bachelors for fifteen years. Hart generally trimmed his own hair and shaved himself. He'd never been partial to another man holding a razor to his neck.

Still, he made himself climb into the leather-bound chair. "Let's get this over with."

Ganzel bustled about, whipping up the lather in a porcelain cup, stropping his razor. "I appreciate you leaving a note about when you intended to come," he said, eyeing Hart in the mirror. "Most fellows just wander in. Sometimes there's quite a wait."

So that's how Beth was making the appointments. He'd wondered how she could do so without someone questioning her association with him.

The barber came around and draped a cloth over Hart's chin. The warm moisture sank in. Despite his misgivings, his shoulders relaxed. This wasn't so bad.

"Lots of new people in town," the barber said, pulling the cloth away. Hart willed himself not to flinch as the shiny silver razor approached. "Keeping you busy?"

"Some," he allowed, fingers gripping the ends of the armrests.

Ganzel continued to chatter away, not seeming to expect an answer. Indeed, Hart didn't like the idea of moving his jaw while a razor scraped along it. Still, the man's hands were swift and sure. After a while, Hart's mind began to wander.

Why was Beth so determined that he marry? He had no doubt she held a high opinion of matrimony. Look at how she'd married off her brothers. And he supposed she valued the opinions of the Literary Society. Still, she wasn't the sort to posture and impress. She could have told the ladies to leave him be. It was as if she wanted him married to someone else besides her.

The seat seemed to tighten around him, and he shifted. The barber frowned. Hart made himself freeze. Perhaps he'd better think of something else besides Beth Wallin.

There was always his work to consider. Things had been quiet overall lately, but even with time to spare he'd learned nothing more in his investigation of the gang. He'd followed his hunch and ridden past the seam-stress's shop several times a day, to the point at which she'd taken to waving at him from the window as if they were old friends. But outside a high volume of customers, he'd spotted nothing unusual. And though her brother had encouraged him to visit, he didn't come out of the shop to greet Hart, staring at him mournfully from inside.

He'd never found it so difficult to extract information on his quarry. The gang members chose their victims with care—men who, because of embarrassment over being gullible or fear of reprisal, were hesitant to speak to the law. The two victims who had talked to him gave vague answers that led nowhere. All he knew was that two men were involved plus whoever was leading the victims from the docks.

Bobby Donovan's face came to mind. He seemed a little old for the trick, but then Scout Rankin had ful-filled the function for his father until he was eighteen. Still, why would a newcomer to Seattle like Bobby, brother of a seemingly prosperous business owner, be involved with such thugs? Was he that lonely for com-pany? Or had someone coerced him?

Ganzel stepped away to fetch his scissors, and Hart rubbed his smooth chin. He couldn't deny the barber had done a better job than he ever had. Maybe there was something to be said for getting a shave once in a while. Saturday afternoon was a popular time, he'd noticed. Gents gussied up for dances that night and services on Sunday, trying to gain a lady's favor.

He had no call. He'd gotten out of the habit of attend-ing services, and he had no lady to impress.

The barber moved around him as if studying him

from every angle. "Your hair's already fairly short," he said. "I'm not sure what I can do with it."

Ganzel's gaze went out the front window as if he was thinking. Then, to Hart's surprise, he nodded. He started for one side, then stopped, scissors moving left, right in the air as if he remained unsure where to begin. But still he didn't seem to be looking at Hart's hair.

Involuntarily, Hart glanced out the window, just in time to see pink skirts fly out of sight.

His clean-shaven jaw hardened.

"Trim it up over my ears and above my collar," he told the barber, facing front. "And don't do anything fancy."

"Yes, Deputy. Of course." The scissors clicked as the barber set to work.

A short time later, Hart paid the fellow and left. Beth was nowhere in sight. He thought about ignoring the appointment she'd made with the tailors, but he supposed it wasn't fair to keep the men waiting if Beth had sent them a note ahead of time as well. He headed for the next street down.

The tailor's establishment bore a distinct resemblance to Mrs. Jamison's shop. Bolts of fabric, in colors more understated, were neatly stacked on end along one wall. A big mirror stood opposite. The smell hinted more of leather than roses, but the effect was the same. Perhaps that was why Beth looked so much at home.

She was standing by a set of shelves that held gentlemen's accessories—gloves, handkerchiefs, suspenders—and was deep in study over a pair of leather gloves that might have been big enough for one of her brothers. Her pink skirts twitched as if she was tapping her foot, and her gray-veiled hat was slipping just a trifle on her curls.

She didn't even turn her head as he entered, but he was certain she knew he was there.

Mr. Black and his partner hurried forward. The two older men were recent additions to Seattle, having come up from San Francisco like Mrs. Jamison a few months ago. Both were short and slender. Mr. Black's brown hair receded from a well-shaped face, while Mr. Powell had a generous mane of silver-gray hair and heavy jowls. Both were a credit to their profession with their navy coats and pinstriped trousers. He doubted he'd ever knot a tie so well.

Of course, it wasn't often he needed one.

"Deputy McCormick," Mr. Powell said, "such an honor. How might we assist you today?"

Hart glanced toward Beth. "To be frank, I'm not sure."

She had a tie in her hand now, raising it as if to hold it against the light. "My brothers all needed a coat, trousers and waistcoat for church," she told no one in particular.

"Seems I need a coat, trousers and waistcoat," Hart told the tailors.

Black clapped his hands. "Of course! I have just the thing for the coat. A nice, durable brown with wide lapels. Ready-made. Inexpensive."

Beth coughed.

The two men exchanged glances. "Excuse me," Powell said and hurried to her side.

"Or perhaps an understated plaid," Black went on. "I can see a gentleman of your bearing wanting something sturdy, not necessarily fashionable."

Beth dropped the tie and glared at him. Powell drew her back for a hushed conversation. Hart might have thought they were discussing something as important as the pay wagon's route from the docks instead of men's clothing.

Black pulled a tape from the pocket of his coat. "I'll just take your measurements."

"Not yet," Powell said, striding back to join them. "Miss Wallin is of the opinion that we are recommending the wrong designs to Mr. McCormick."

Black's look her way was positively frosty. "Is she indeed?"

"I wouldn't argue with her," Hart advised him. "It never works."

The tailor raised a brow.

As if she took that as a sign of encouragement, Beth swept closer. "If you wouldn't mind? Wide lapels will only draw undue attention to his shoulders, making him look top-heavy. You want narrow lapels on the coat, to emphasize his height."

Black rubbed his chin. "Hmm. You may have a point."

"And not brown. It will wash out his coloring. In addition, you want something with a nap, because rough material has a way of making the skin look clearer." She glanced around, then went to select a bolt of nubby gray wool that reminded Hart of the waters of Puget Sound during a rainstorm. "This," she proclaimed, pressing it against his shoulder. "See how it makes his eyes sparkle?"

"The look in my eyes has nothing to do with the color," Hart informed her.

She blushed, lowering the fabric. "Forgive me, sir. I didn't mean to interfere. I'm just enthusiastic about fabric."

And everything that went with it.

Powell regarded her fondly. "It is refreshing to find a young lady so knowledgeable about gentleman's fashions."

"Well, when you have to help five brothers look presentable, you learn something," she demurred. She leaned closer. "Black for a waistcoat, I think. Silver shot, perhaps."

"Brilliant," Powell breathed reverently. He nudged Black with his elbow, and his partner went to fetch more fabric.

Powell strode across the shop for the accessories. "And this for the tie."

As he returned with a scarlet bow tie with long ends, Beth threw her arms around him for a hug. "Perfect."

The tailor's jowls were a pleased pink as she released him. Hart had a feeling he'd look just as pleased after one of Beth's hugs.

But then, he wasn't willing to put himself in a position to earn one.

"Are we done?" he asked.

"Now, now," Beth said as the tailor's smile faded. "Mr. Powell and Mr. Black will need to take your measurements, schedule a fitting or two since they will be tailored just for you." She must have read the look on Hart's face accurately this time, for she stepped back. "I should be going. So much to do. Thank you, gentlemen."

Powell watched her go. "What a remarkable young lady."

"Indeed," his partner agreed. "She'd make some man an excellent wife."

They both looked to Hart.

"No," he said. "Not me. Now, if you're going to measure me, let's get on with it."

The men set to work, positioning him in front of the mirror, muttering to themselves as they determined the size of his neck, the length of his arms. Hart stood still, counting off the minutes. But in the mirror's reflection, he spotted the flutter of pink skirts past the window and knew he was only prolonging the moment he'd have to have another discussion with Beth.

It took longer than she'd expected for Hart to be measured. Beth paced up and down the block several times before the door opened and he came out. He stopped for a moment, blinking, as if the sunny day was too bright after being indoors so long. That gave her time to reach his side.

"You didn't let them talk you into brown, did you?" she asked.

He eyed her. She'd always considered him striking, but his smooth chin and fashionable haircut lent him an air of sophistication, power. She couldn't wait to see how he'd look in his new clothes. The ladies of Seattle would be swooning.

Not her, of course. She was beyond that.

"I don't usually let anyone talk me into anything." He turned toward Mill Street, and Beth fell in beside him.

"You have somewhere else you expect me to be?" he asked with a glance her way.

"Not today," she said. "Feel free to do whatever you'd like."

"Generous of you to leave me time to myself."

Beth shook her head. "Oh, come now. This is for your own good. I never knew a gentleman who didn't appreciate a good shave, a new suit."

He snorted. "In gray."

"Surely you could see the wisdom of the gray material. It's as durable as brown and more suitable to your coloring."

"So you said. Never gave the color I wore much mind."

"That's why you have me," Beth assured him. "When did they want you to return?"

"Two weeks."

Beth pulled up. "Two weeks! What nonsense. Why, Nora could have the fabric cut and marked in two days, besides doing her other chores. I have half a mind…"

Hart caught her arm before she could head back to the shop. "I told them there was no hurry."

Beth frowned at him. "Certainly there's a hurry. You need those clothes before Easter services, and I was hoping to show you off at one of Fanny Morgan Phelps's performances before she leaves town the end of the month."

"Show me off?"

Anyone else might have quailed under those narrowed eyes. Beth refused to be cowed. "Yes. Surely you know Seattle has been visited by its first truly professional theatrical troupe." Joy pushed her hands together in front of her bosom. "Just think—thrilling melodramas like *The Lady of Lyons*, moral lessons like *Uncle Tom's Cabin* and, wonder of wonders, Shakespeare."

"Shake what?"

Beth dropped her hands. "Shakespeare. Surely you've heard of him. He's the most famous English playwright ever. I thought everyone had read at least one of his works in school."

He started off once more, stride lengthening. "Never finished school."

Her heart went out to him. She'd loved school—literature, history, science, even arithmetic. "Didn't they allow orphans to take part? That seems unwise and unfair."

Without the stubble on his chin, she could see it grow tighter as he walked. "They sent us to school. I liked learning, but school mostly taught me my place."

Her own jaw tightened. "Small wonder you didn't finish. I'm very glad you didn't take that to heart. No one can define your place except you."

"So I understand now." He cast her a glance. "But I didn't understand until I ran away."

"Really?" She could picture the defiant boy, determined to make his own way in the world. "Where did you go?"

"As far as I could get from St. Louis. Which, in my case, was only the Ohio Valley."

"And what was it about the lovely Ohio Valley that made you want to stay?"

He didn't answer immediately. Beth glanced at him to find him staring down the block. She followed his gaze, but didn't see anything among the wagons and pedestrians that would warrant such a fierce look.

"This Shakespeare," he said. "I take it you've read his work."

"Oh, certainly," she assured him, twitching her skirts around a rain barrel. "I especially like his sonnets. 'Shall I compare thee to a summer's day? Thou art more lovely and more temperate.'"

If Shakespeare had seen Hart's frown, he might have rethought his poetry.

"Well, not everyone likes sonnets," she allowed. "Levi favors the dramas—all that murder and mayhem."

His steps slowed as if he was allowing her to keep up. "Murder?"

Trust a lawman to find that interesting. "Yes, but don't get your hopes up. I understand Fanny Morgan Phelps tends more to the comedies, which I love. *The Tempest, A Midsummer Night's Dream.*"

He made a noise that sounded suspiciously like he was gagging. Beth nudged him with her shoulder. "You'll like them, I promise. I just have to see when tickets might be available."

He sighed. "I'll take an extra shift to cover the costs."

Beth waved a hand. "No need. I'll pay."

Once more he stopped, and this time she did quail.

"A gentleman," he said, "does not allow a lady to pay his way."

"I'm not a lady in this case," Beth countered. "I'm your matchmaker."

"And only the fine ladies of the Literary Society are aware of that," he reminded her. "To everyone else, it will look as if Beth Wallin is cozying up to the deputy sheriff."

Her cheeks flamed. "Perhaps I could give you the money, and you could buy the tickets."

"Perhaps you could keep your money, and let me buy the tickets."

Stubborn. Beth sighed. "Very well. But I don't intend to bankrupt you with new clothes and entertainment. You will shortly have a wife to support, after all."

He raised a finger, ready to tell her off, no doubt, when a man stumbled out of the alley just ahead of them. Both hands cradled his head, and blood dripped between his fingers.

Beth gasped. No time to think. She grabbed Hart's hand and darted forward. "Hurry! He needs our help."

Chapter Seven

Hart had little doubt he was looking at the latest victim of the gang. Two ships had docked earlier in the day. He had thought the passengers wouldn't disembark until the evening tide and had planned to meet them even though it was his afternoon off, but at least one must have been in a hurry to reach town.

"*Ach, mein kopf,*" the fellow moaned, staggering forward.

Beth brought herself under one arm to steady him. Even though she prized her gowns, she seemed heedless of the potential damage from the blood. How could he not admire a woman like that?

As Hart stepped forward to help her, the man flinched away. "*Nein!* Nothing have I left. Leave me be."

Hart touched the badge on his chest. "We mean you no harm. I'm Deputy Sheriff Hart McCormick. What happened?"

The fellow moaned again, clutching his head. A short, stout man, his light blond hair hung limp around his round face, and a thick mustache drooped on either side of his mouth. Hart had the odd thought that Beth likely wouldn't approve of the rusty color of the man's rumpled coat.

"Easy, sir," Beth said in a soft tone. "We are friends. We only want to help."

The man lowered his hands cautiously, then his bleary blue eyes widened as he stared at the red stain across his fingers, and what color he had fled. Hart caught his elbow as he swayed.

Beth's eyes were just as wide. "Oh, you poor man. Let's get you cleaned up and comfortable. There's a chemist just down the way."

Hart had a dozen questions he wanted to ask, but he knew Beth was right. The man would be in no state to answer until his wounds had been tended.

Yet even though Beth had offered help in such a caring manner, the stranger hesitated, gaze darting between them. "You are friends with the *polizei*?" he murmured to Beth.

"*Polizei*, police, yes," Beth assured him, moving forward and forcing him to keep up. "And we have medicine, this way."

He stumbled along beside her.

Confident they would make it past the next few shops, Hart took a moment to glance in the alley. He hadn't expected to see anyone—the gang would be long gone with its spoils. The only evidence that something untoward had happened were some overturned empty crates and mud scuffed by boots. At least this fellow had put up a tussle.

Hart caught up with Beth and the newcomer in the store. The chemist Mr. Cassidy had been persuaded to bring out a chair, and the victim, who Beth was explaining was a Mr. Schneider, was sitting on it while Beth cleaned his wounds with a damp cloth Cassidy must have provided. At least their surroundings should have brought Schneider some comfort that he'd be well cared for. Whitewashed shelves behind the center counter held jars of every compound imaginable, the blue-green glass betraying strange shapes and sparkling powders known for their medicinal or chemical properties.

A tall, lean fellow with a narrow face and thatch of graying brown hair, Cassidy leaned closer to Hart, the scent of the men's cologne he sold hanging around him like a cloud. "What's he done that you had to strike him, Deputy?"

Beth must have heard, for she rounded on the chemist. "Deputy McCormick didn't do this."

Cassidy quailed under the fire in her eyes. Hart leaned closer to her and Schneider. "No, I didn't, but I'd like to know who did."

The man winced, but at Hart's presence or Beth's ministrations, Hart wasn't sure. Beth's look hardened, mouth compressing. Likely she thought Hart should wait to interrogate the fellow, but every moment counted when dealing with the gang. More passengers would be arriving soon. Hart didn't want them to be met with the same fate.

"How did you come to our shores, Mr. Schneider?" she asked, patting his face carefully to remove the last of the blood. He'd taken a blow to his eye, breaking the skin along his bone. Hart could only wonder what other bruises lurked under his plaid waistcoat and linen shirt.

Schneider's shoulders came down under Beth's tender care. "From the boat I came."

"A traveler," she mused. "And why did you choose Seattle?"

Hart shifted from foot to foot, but Schneider answered readily enough. "I buy hops from here to take back home."

No need to ask the location of home. It was clear the fellow was of German descent. Some of his countrymen had been traveling to the area to purchase hops from farms to the south of Seattle. More pressing questions needed to be answered.

"Who hit you?" Hart demanded.

Schneider shuddered. Beth frowned at Hart, but she rose and spoke to the chemist, who hurried off. Then she touched Hart's arm, tilting her head to one side. He withdrew with her away from the counter of the little shop.

"Why must we badger him?" she asked. "He's had a terrible time of it."

"He won't be the only one," Hart told her. "I wasn't joking when I mentioned a gang the other day. Someone's been preying on new arrivals, robbing them and leaving them hurting. I can't stop them if I can't get answers."

She hissed out a breath. Then she squared her shoulders. "I understand. I'll do anything I can to help."

She marched back to Schneider with so much purpose Hart could only stride after her, a little afraid she was going to take the German to task herself.

Instead, she accepted the bandage the chemist had returned with and began to wind it around the little man's head. "There, now," she crooned as she worked. "What a terrible time you've had. I simply don't know what the world is coming to that a newcomer would be treated so badly."

She leaned back and smiled at him. The chemist sighed as he watched, doting smile on his face as well.

Schneider was no more immune to her sweet look. "*Danke*," he said, gaze fixed on her like a drowning man a rope. "You are too kind."

Beth patted his hand. "I'm just sorry this was your introduction to our fair city. I'm also sorry we must ask you so many questions, but it's important that we catch these villains. Who did this to you?"

Hart held his breath as the man glanced between her and him.

Schneider dropped his gaze. "Oh, I could not say."

Beth bent closer. "But surely you saw them. Your wounds indicate they struck from the front."

Smart lady. She was right. Hart narrowed his eyes.

The German squirmed. "I saw nothing. I will go now."

Frustration pushed him forward. "No, you won't. Not until we talk."

He blanched. "*Nein*! I will not speak. It is worth my life."

Beth turned to Hart. "It's as if he's afraid of you."

She sounded so puzzled. He could have told her any number of men feared him, for good reason. As one of a handful of lawmen in the entire territory, he stood between them and the crimes they planned to commit. Still, this man didn't seem to be a criminal. He was the victim.

Hart spread his hands, but Schneider jerked away as if he expected another beating.

Beth's brow cleared. "You have no need to fear, Mr. Schneider. Deputy McCormick is a fine man, an upstanding man. A…a…mighty warrior, a knight."

Hart's brows went up. Was that how she saw him? Small wonder she'd once offered undying devotion. Surely she knew better now.

Cassidy smothered a laugh, but Schneider's face brightened in a smile. "I understand, *fraulein*. You trust him, *jah*?"

Beth glanced at Hart. "With my life."

Was he blushing? He willed himself to stand taller. His glare to Cassidy sent the chemist scurrying back behind his counter.

Schneider glanced between them again. "*Ser gut*. I will tell you what I can, then. A lad met me on the path from the boat. He says he knows a clean place to stay with good food."

Just like what had happened to the fellow in the plaid trousers earlier in the week. "Did he tell you his name?" Hart asked.

Schneider fiddled with the edges of his waistcoat. "This I do not recall."

Didn't recall, or wouldn't say? "But you followed him," Hart surmised.

"*Jah*. He says the alley is a quicker way, a small slice."

"A short cut," Beth guessed.

Hart nodded. "Only there were men waiting."

"Two of them." Schneider closed his eyes as if the memory hurt as much as his wound. "The boy told them not to hurt me, but they did not listen. He ran away then. They took all I had—the money to pay for the hops, my travel expenses." He sank his head into his hands again. "I am ruined. My employer will discharge me. I cannot even pay my way home."

Beth put a hand on his shoulder. "I belong to a group

of civic-minded women, Mr. Schneider. I'm sure we can find a way to help."

Schneider raised his head. "*Vas?*"

Beth nodded. "Have no concern. For now, answer Deputy McCormick's questions. It may be he can track down those brigands and get your money back."

She put a lot of faith in him. But as she looked his way, compassion and pride melding in her gaze, he found himself unwilling to deny her.

And that worried him as much as the gang.

Beth kept her hand on Mr. Schneider's shoulder as Hart questioned him, interjecting when needed if the deputy's words made the poor man shudder. Even with her here, he seemed hesitant to deal with Hart. Very likely it was the trauma of the moment. How horrible— to come to a new town, full of purpose and hope, only to be met with cunning and violence. She was certain Allegra, Mrs. Wyckoff and the other members of the Literary Society would be willing to help.

So would Hart. She could almost see the thoughts shining behind his dark gray eyes as he listened to Mr. Schneider's story. Mr. Cassidy offered to pay for a night in the Occidental Hotel for the man, and the two went off to make arrangements after Beth promised to call on the wounded man soon.

"I'm very glad we happened along when we did," she told Hart as they left the store together.

"So am I," he answered. Hand to her elbow, he guided her toward the corner. "Thank you for your help. Even if he couldn't seem to describe his assailants, this is the most information I've heard from one of the victims."

"How many others have there been?" She cast him a glance as they turned onto Mill Street. His face was set, his steps firm.

"Enough to concern me."

He wasn't going to share. He was trying to protect her, just like her brothers.

Annoyance pushed her head up. "Someone must know who's in this gang."

"Very likely."

"I could ask around," she suggested.

"You will not."

Now, there was some force. "Why not? I know nearly everyone in Seattle."

"You know all the nice people. These are not nice people."

She'd give him that. When she thought of the blood on Mr. Schneider's face, she shuddered.

He mistook her reaction. "It's all right, Beth. I won't let anything happen to you."

She knew that. Whatever their differences, he was a hero, and heroes protected people. Still, nothing said she couldn't ask a few questions. What was the harm?

"I can see you'll be busy the next day or so," she said as they reached the bottom of the hill. "I won't disturb you. The next phase in our plan to find you a bride will be to show you to advantage. I would have liked to include your new suit, but I suppose we'll simply have to make do for church."

"Church."

He said the word as if pronouncing someone's death. Beth giggled.

"I didn't mean for a marriage ceremony. Just for

Sunday services. Do you generally attend the Brown Church or the White Church?"

"Is there a difference, besides the color?"

She'd always thought it funny that the two main churches in Seattle were named after their paint rather than something more inspiring. "I favor the Brown Church," she told him. "The Reverend Mr. Bagley is such a dear. I imagine Allegra and Clay will want to leave by half past nine. You can walk with us."

His mouth twitched, as if he was struggling with his response.

Beth sighed. "Forgive me. Faith is so important. I wasn't trying to make light of it. If you'd prefer to worship alone, I'll quite understand. I'm just so used to worshipping with my brothers. It will feel odd to have only Allegra and her family in church beside me."

"I'll be at the door of the house at a quarter past."

Relief flooded her. Goodness, was she homesick already? She'd only been in town two days. But the thought of sitting in a pew without her family was suddenly daunting. That Hart would be beside her made everything much better.

But Hart wasn't the only one interested in escorting her to services, she saw Sunday morning. She was standing on the drive in front of Allegra and Clay's house, waiting for him, when a buggy rolled up. Even now, the things were rare enough to turn heads, but even if they had been more common on the few roads around the area, people would have stopped to stare at this one. Painted a buttercup yellow with cocoa-colored silk fringe on the top and leather upholstered seats, the four-wheeled carriage was driven by a set of dapple gray horses with high heads, as if they were proud of what they carried.

Scout grinned at her from behind the reins. "I thought you might need a ride."

Beth grinned back. "Even if I didn't, I'd take you up on the offer. What a beauty."

Scout ran a gloved hand over the polished wood front board. "It was shipped up from San Francisco."

"And an excellent investment," Clay said, coming out of the house with Allegra on one arm, their children right behind. The Howards made quite the pair in their fine clothing, him fair and her dark. He caught Georgie with his other hand before the boy could dash any closer to the team. "Easy there, my lad. You'll scare the horses."

"Oh, Mr. Rankin, what a wonderful carriage," Gillian said, eyes glowing.

Scout inclined his head. "Thank you, Miss Howard. Perhaps you'd like to ride in it with me and Beth. There's room for four."

"Then Deputy McCormick can join us too," Beth said as Gillian begged her parents' permission.

Scout's face clouded. "Oh, is he going to church?"

Beth nodded, glancing around the side of the house. Surely it was after a quarter past. Where was he?

Just then he rounded the corner. He'd brushed off his duster and wore black trousers instead of his usual denim, but the dark color still made him look lean and strong. She swallowed, then chided herself, putting on a smile.

"Look who came to drive us to church," she told Hart as he joined them.

He eyed the buggy. "Mighty fine outfit, Rankin."

Scout thawed. "Thank you, Deputy. If you'd help Miss Howard and Miss Wallin to their seats?"

Beth didn't wait. She scrambled up beside Scout as Hart helped Gillian up.

"Sure there isn't room for five?" Georgie wheedled.

"Next time," Scout promised.

"Be careful," Clay warned as Allegra gathered her son closer, apparently concerned he'd try to climb in anyway.

"Always, sir," Scout assured him. With a flick of the reins, he urged the team around the curve of the drive and back onto the street.

"When did you learn to handle horses?" Beth asked as they started down the street, Gillian gushing at Hart.

"I drove a six-horse team for a time at one of the gold camps," Scout told her. "You have to do something to eat when you don't find gold."

Beth thought she heard Hart *humph*.

Gillian rested her arms on the bench, golden head poking up beside Scout. "But Papa says you found gold, Mr. Rankin. Lots of it."

Scout colored. "Enough to keep me comfortable. But it took a while, and I had to pay my way in the meantime." He glanced over his shoulder. "I didn't fancy turning out like Pa."

Beth knew he was addressing that to Hart instead of Gillian. She glanced back as well. Hart's arms had been crossed over his chest. Now he lowered them with a nod.

"Doesn't look like that will be a problem," he said to Scout.

She thought Scout sat a little taller.

The area around the church was crowded as they approached—wagons, horses and a few buggies jostled for space with the resultant rattle and clank of tack and grunt of horses. Scout found a place to leave the buggy and tie up the horses. Then the four of them joined the others climbing the stairs.

The vestibule was lit only by the sunlight trickling in through the open door. Just beyond, dark wood box pews, nearly full, stretched out on either side of a center aisle that led up to the altar and a bronze cross. As if trying to decide where to take a seat, a woman with a flowered hat and a young man stood blocking the way forward. Something white fluttered to the floor.

Hart frowned at it as if expecting it to leap up and draw on him. Beth touched his arm, and his frown eased.

Scout bent and picked the thing up. The square of linen was edged in fine lace and embroidered on the corner with roses. So that was the game. Before Beth could stop him, he touched the woman's sleeve. "I believe you dropped this, ma'am."

The owner turned, and Beth recognized Mrs. Jamison. How disappointing that the lady would need to resort to such tricks. Whose attention had she been trying to attract? She barely knew Hart and probably had never met Scout.

Still, she had obviously dressed to impress. Her raven hair was piled up under the hat to fall behind her. Her lavender jacket and sweeping skirts were as fashionable as they were unpractical for the wet Seattle weather.

"Why, how kind," she said with a winning smile as she took the handkerchief from Scout, brushing her fingers against his. "I don't believe we've been introduced."

"Mrs. Jamison," Beth said, duty bound, "may I present

my good friend Thomas Rankin and Miss Gillian Howard. You remember Deputy McCormick."

Hart inclined his head, and Gillian bobbed a curtsey.
Scout seemed to be frozen in his tracks.

The seamstress fluttered her dusky lashes. "Mr.
Rankin, Miss Howard, a pleasure. Nice to see you
again, Miss Wallin, Deputy. This is my brother, Robert Donovan."

The dark-haired lad was staring at Gillian. "Miss
Howard," he murmured. Gillian blushed.

Mrs. Jamison had turned her attention to Hart. "I
haven't seen you the last couple of days, Deputy. I hope
nothing untoward has happened to keep you away."

The last two days? Had Hart been calling on the
lady? Beth forced the frown from her face.

"Just busy, ma'am," he told her. "Best we find seats
now."

"Of course." She smiled at Scout. "Perhaps we'll
have time to become better acquainted after service."

"Yes, ma'am," Scout stammered. "Thank you,
ma'am." His gaze followed her swaying progression
down the aisle, her brother at her side. Beth thought a
starving man might have looked that way at a haunch
of venison. She waved a hand in front of Scout's face,
and he started.

"Sorry." He sighed. "*Mrs.* Jamison, eh?"

"I hear she's a widow," Hart put in.

Smiling to himself, Scout went to take a seat at the
rear of the church.

Gillian hurried to where her parents and brother sat
near the front. Hart looked as if he would have preferred
to join Scout, but Beth led him down the aisle and slid
in behind the Howards. So many questions, and no time

to ask. She had barely composed her thoughts when the Reverend Bagley entered, and service began.

She'd grown up worshipping in the front room of the family cabin. She wasn't entirely prepared for the formality of the service, the solemnity. Still, there was something fine, something warm about voices joining together in song and recitation.

Wallin Landing had built a church about a year ago. Her brother Levi's sermons there tended to be more casual. Reverend Bagley had a pedantic way of speaking, yet his theme, designed to fit in with the Lenten observance, was fitting. He talked about the woman who had broken the alabaster jar and poured out costly perfume on Jesus to prepare him for his death.

"We are reminded that we must live as extravagantly," Mr. Bagley said, gazing around the congregation through his silver-rimmed spectacles, bushy brows coming down. "We must pour out all we have in His service."

All she had. It wasn't much. She'd spent most of the money Ma had left her to bring a piano to the Wallin Landing church. The future of her claim was more precarious than she wanted to admit, and the land would go toward expanding the town, at any rate. She couldn't see how God could use her wardrobe, which was more extensive than most on the frontier.

All that was left was her character. Her family said she was enthusiastic. Certainly she loved them and her friends.

She couldn't help glancing at Hart. His gaze was on the minister, his eyes narrowed, as if he wasn't any surer about what he was supposed to do. Ever since he'd rejected her, she'd refused to think about marrying, about letting herself love. Would there ever be a time she'd be ready to open her heart again, to love as extravagantly as Reverend Bagley suggested?

Chapter Eight

Hart shifted on the pew, trying to keep his gaze forward. Still, his shoulders bunched. Why did he feel as if he wore a sign reading *sinner*? If the good people of Seattle knew the life he'd once lived...

He forced his shoulders back, his chin up. He owed no one an explanation. He'd paid for his crimes, as surely as if he'd been sent to prison. He'd dedicated his life to keeping others from the same pain. He had every right to sit in this pew, listening to Mr. Bagley drone on.

Watching the emotions flicker across Beth's face.

She was so intent, drinking in every word. The light in her eyes said she understood, she approved. What had the minister said? God expected everyone to pour themselves out for others.

Once that would have been impossible for him. Growing up in the crowded orphanage in St. Louis, he'd had to snatch and fight for every morsel of food, every inch of blanket. No one, from the overbearing woman in charge, to her frightened and scurrying assistants, had stood up for him. If he was going to survive, it was all up to him. That was one of the reasons he'd run away, headed east when he was about Bobby Donovan's age.

His experience had taught him much. He'd become stronger, more determined. More ornery, some might have said. But he'd also learned that life came at a price. And those who loved must be willing to pay it.

His uneasiness stilled as he considered the matter. He'd always thought he wasn't good enough for God. Maybe it was his time in the orphanage. Maybe it was the way he'd failed his sweetheart Annabelle. But if Mr. Bagley was right about the good Lord's expectations, the Almighty ought to be rather pleased with Hart for dedicating his life to the law.

Do You listen to folks like me, Lord? Am I doing what You want?

Something drew his gaze to Beth again. Now, how could God be anything but pleased with her? She was bright, she was happy, she lavished her love on anyone who came near. She must have caught him looking, for she turned and smiled at him. Suddenly he was certain he was right where he belonged. He was still smiling when he followed her down the aisle at the end of the service.

The look must have encouraged the other members of the congregation, for several came forward to shake his hand, let him know they appreciated his work. Hart thanked them, but tried to find a way to extricate himself quickly. Praise was fine, but close encounters could only lead to personal questions he didn't feel comfortable answering.

Beth swished her blue skirts. "See?" she whispered between acknowledgements. "I knew this would work."

He'd forgotten he was supposed to be on display.

His smile must have slipped, for the next lady hurried to excuse herself.

Beth linked arms with him. "Never mind her. You're doing splendidly."

He wasn't sure whether to preen or protest.

"I have a question for you, though," she continued as the other members of the congregation strolled past. "Have you decided to court Mrs. Jamison?"

Hart stared at her. "No. Of course not."

Her smile nearly blinded him. "Oh, good. Because I would not advise it as your matchmaker."

Relief vied with curiosity. "Why not?"

She sniffed. "A lady has no need to resort to artifice to attract a gentleman. Her character should be sufficient."

Hart eyed her outfit with its white piping outlining her figure. "No doubt that's why women spend so much time getting gussied up."

"Nonsense," she said, rapping him on the arm with her free hand. "I don't dress up for men. I dress up for me."

Just then he caught sight of Mrs. Jamison and her brother exiting the church. He'd decided not to talk to her before services, despite her evident interest, because he knew enough not to arrive late. But this was the perfect opportunity to check on the pair, so long as he didn't give Beth any ideas.

"Listen," he said, watching Mrs. Jamison and Bobby, who were moving closer. "I promised myself I'd keep an eye on Mrs. Jamison's brother."

Beth frowned, glancing their way as well. "Do you suspect him of something nefarious?"

"Not yet, but I'd like to be sure. And I have a feeling

he needs a friend. Come on." He took Beth's arm and moved to intercept them.

"Ma'am," he said, removing his hat with his free hand. "Donovan. Glad you could make services today."

Mrs. Jamison smiled, but her brother dropped his gaze and shuffled his feet. "I believe this is the first time I've seen you here, Deputy," the seamstress said. "Was there a particular reason you graced us with your presence?"

Those dark lashes were fluttering again. Did she expect him to say he'd come hoping to see her?

Beth stepped into the breach. "Deputy McCormick is often on duty on Sundays, alas. I'm just glad he could be here today."

The seamstress's smile remained pleasant. "Did you enjoy the service, Miss Wallin?"

"Very much," Beth assured her. "What of you, Mr. Donovan?"

Bobby glanced up, meeting her gaze, and color flamed into his cheeks. "Yes, ma'am." His voice squeaked.

Oh, but Hart remembered being that young and unsure. He'd wanted friends, someone he could count on, and his desperation had led him to the wrong people. The Cathcart gang had already made a name for themselves, robbing stages and outlying farms, before they'd welcomed Hart to their band. Their wild camaraderie had spoken to his troubled heart. He'd realized the cost too late. Unless someone acted, Bobby Donovan could fall into the same trap.

Hart tipped his chin toward a group closer to the lad's age, including Gillian Howard and Ciara O'Rourke, Maddie Haggerty's sister, who had gathered under a fir at the edge of the yard. "Have you met some of our young folk, Donovan? I'd be glad to introduce you."

Beth caught his eye and smiled, then turned to Bobby. "So would I. Nothing like making friends to make you feel more at home."

The lad followed Hart's gaze toward the group. He smoothed back one side of his dark hair.

Mrs. Jamison put a hand on her brother's arm. "Bobby's just a bit shy. Perhaps another time." She beamed a smile at Hart. "Don't forget your promise, Deputy."

Hart frowned. "Promise, ma'am?"

"To send me your sweetheart for her wedding gown." Her smile to Beth could have cut through a bull's hide.

The color vanished from Beth's cheeks, but she kept her smile in place. "I'll be sure to tell the lady when she and Deputy McCormick have agreed to wed. Come along, Bobby. I'll stay with you until you're comfortable."

Mrs. Jamison frowned, but Bobby broke away from her hold and followed Beth to join the others. Coming out of the church, Scout headed in that direction as well.

"How kind of her," the seamstress said, but the words remained as sharp as her smile. "But I appear to have misspoke. I take it Miss Wallin doesn't intend to have you court her."

"No, ma'am," Hart assured her, glad he hadn't had to report the fact in front of Beth. "I've known her family for years. I'm just looking out for her while she's in town."

"That shouldn't be difficult. She appears to be well known and well liked." She nodded to where Dexter Horton, Seattle's first banker, and Mayor Yesler had stopped to pay their respects to Beth, who quickly turned to introduce them to Bobby and Scout.

"She is that," Hart agreed. "Your brother could be as well, if he'd put himself out a bit."

She sighed, gaze lowering. "Poor Bobby. We lost our parents when he was only ten. Even though I married young, my husband was like a father to him. When he died as well, Bobby was devastated." She took out a lacy handkerchief and dabbed at her eyes.

The situation with her brother was worse than Hart had thought. "He needs friends, upright and kindly, to help him find his way. Aiden O'Rourke would be a good choice."

"O'Rourke?" She cocked her head. "An Irishman?"

Her skepticism betrayed her prejudice. "Brother of the owner of the Pastry Emporium. Fine lad."

She made a noise that committed to nothing. "You are well informed about the local population, Deputy. What do you know about Mr. Rankin?"

Horton and Yesler had moved on, and Scout had stepped closer to the others under the tree. Though he was the eldest of the group, he joked around with Aiden, setting Maddie's dark-haired brother to laughing. Hart could have told the seamstress any number of unsavory stories, but perhaps he ought to let Scout prove himself. Hart had been given the opportunity, after all.

"He's made something of himself, no doubt," he told Mrs. Jamison.

"A businessman, then?"

"No, ma'am. Gold fields."

Her look didn't change, but something about her brightened.

Beth came hurrying back just then, eyes shining and

cheeks pink. "We've been invited to a picnic this afternoon up on the knob. Please say you'll come, Deputy."

"Donovan invited too?" he asked.

She glanced at Mrs. Jamison. "Yes, as a matter of fact. I do hope you'll let him join us."

Mrs. Jamison pursed her lips. "I wouldn't want to impose on the deputy to keep an eye on him. Will there be other adults present?"

Beth looked puzzled. "Mr. Rankin and I will be there as well. My friend Ciara O'Rourke is close to reaching her majority."

Mrs. Jamison inclined her head, making the flowers on her hat bob. "Very well. My brother has my permission."

Beth turned to Hart. "Deputy?"

What could he say? He wasn't normally the type to picnic, especially with a bunch of youth. He ought to be cleaning his gun, exercising Arno, polishing his boots. But he found himself hesitating to make the excuse.

Perhaps it was all the memories of his past. Perhaps it was the look in Beth's deep blue eyes. He found he couldn't refuse her.

"All right," he said. "I'm in."

It was a merry group that clustered around Beth as they gathered at the Howard house. She'd known all of them except Bobby Donovan most of her life. At sixteen, Aiden was more arms and legs than body, his black-haired head sticking out of a shirt and coat Maddie had already let out twice. His older sister Ciara's brown hair was still braided down her back as it had been eight years ago when Ciara and Beth had first met, but she was taller than Beth now, and no one would doubt her a woman in that pretty cotton frock embroidered with daisies. Scout and Bobby were already laughing together as if they'd known each other fifteen years instead of fifteen minutes. Even Hart had a smile tugging at his mouth as he watched them.

Allegra's cook had been persuaded to fill a wicker hamper. Scout and Aiden took the handles to carry it up the hill to the meadow that lay at the top. Ciara and Gillian followed with jugs of apple cider and cups. Bobby carried an umbrella Allegra had insisted upon to shade the ladies. Beth walked with Hart, blankets bundled in her arms.

Hart glanced down at the stringed rackets she'd handed him. "What did you say these are for again?"

"Battledore and shuttlecock," Beth explained, detouring around a root on the path. Already the trees were becoming thicker, shadows crossing the path and blocking the sunny sky. "Allegra taught Gillian, and she taught us. I'm not tremendously good at it, yet, but Ciara's excellent. I'll teach you, if you'd like."

He grunted. Very likely, when one was used to defeating villains, batting a feathered cork back and forth was far too tame.

Still, he was good about helping spread the blankets when they came out of the trees. A few brave wildflowers dotted the waving grass of the clearing at the top of the hill, and Gillian set about picking them to weave into crowns. Ciara was busy unpacking the hamper, Bobby helping. Aiden and Scout had been exploring the edges of the clearing.

"Plenty of downed wood if we want to start a fire," Aiden reported, returning to throw himself down on one of the blankets.

"No fires," Hart ordered. "Even with the recent rains it would be too easy to get away from you."

The others looked disappointed, but Beth could only commend his good sense. A forest fire was one of the biggest dangers of living in the wilderness. Aiden might not realize that, having grown up in cities or towns, but she'd lived with loggers and farmers too long not to fear the consequences.

"Ah, well," Aiden said with a good-natured shrug. "What's to eat?"

Allegra's cook had packed cold chicken, biscuits, dried apples and cookies. Everyone tucked in, laughing and talking. At one point, Aiden challenged Scout to a duel over a cookie, and the two leapt to their feet, brandishing drumsticks. Ciara, Gillian and Beth cheered them on.

Hart chuckled. "Why do I feel old?"

Beth pulled the crown Gillian had made for her off her head and draped it around his. "There. That should help."

His look, one brow raised, flowers bright against the dark of his hair, set off peals of laughter.

Beth managed to compose herself. Rising, she held out her hand. "Come on."

He looked so skeptical she nearly laughed again. But he accepted her hand, and she drew him out onto the meadow.

"Take both my hands," she advised.

He did as she bid.

"Now, turn with me in a circle, like this." She swung to the right, and he mimicked her to the left. Slowly at first, then faster and faster she moved, until her feet skimmed the grass.

"Let go!" Beth cried. He did, and she flew back to land on the soft grass. Dizzy, she lay still a moment, savoring the warmth of the sun on her face, the caress of the breeze, the scent of the grass.

Hart knelt beside her, face pale. "Beth! Are you all right? Did I hurt you? Speak to me!"

Beth sat up. "Well, I certainly would if you'd let me get a word in."

Something flew through the air and bounced off Hart's shoulder. He shot his gaze across the meadow, hand going to his hip where his holster usually sat.

"Sorry!" Aiden called. "Got away from me."

Beth put her hand on Hart's, finding his fingers stiff, tensed. "It's all right, Hart. There's no danger here."

He blew out a breath and pushed himself to his feet. "So it seems. I should go."

"No, wait!" Beth clambered to her feet. "Please stay. I haven't shown you how to play battledore and shuttlecock yet."

He eyed Aiden and Scout, who were batting one of the feathered shuttlecocks between them. Bobby and Gillian were doing the same while Ciara kept count in the shade of the umbrella. "You sure?"

"Absolutely." She tugged him back to a blanket and picked up the last two rackets and one of the feathered corks. "The goal," she said, handing him the racket, "is to keep the shuttlecock in the air the longest."

Ciara nodded. "Scout and Aiden managed eight times just now."

He turned the racket as if studying it. The curved wood stringed with gut looked small in his capable hands.

"I'll start," Beth offered. She moved away from the

blanket, tossed the shuttlecock in the air and struck it with the racket, lobbing it in his direction. It fell at his feet.

"Probably easier to shoot the thing, eh, Deputy?" Scout called.

Hart scowled. He picked up the cork, tossed it in the air as Beth had done, and struck it hard.

It bounced off her chest.

He took a step forward. "Did I…"

"I'm fine," Beth assured him. Why was he so determined to see harm? Was he so used to fighting he couldn't enjoy peace? How sad!

She bent to pick up the shuttlecock and tried again. This time he got under it and sent it back her way. Beth returned it.

"The number to beat," Ciara announced, "is now ten. Beth and Deputy McCormick are at two. Gillian and Bobby have three. Scout and Aiden are at five, no, wait. They must start over."

Hart tapped the cork, hands swift but gentle, and it arced toward Beth. She shifted to get under it and sent it back.

"Four for Beth and the deputy. Five for Gillian and Bobby. Three for Scout and Aiden."

"We don't have to work too hard," Aiden bragged, sending a grin Beth's way. "We hold the record so far. Oh, rats!"

"Six for Beth and Deputy McCormick," Ciara said with a laugh. "Seven for Gillian and Bobby. Scout and Aiden start over."

Beth focused on the feathered cork, fluttering down from Hart's serve. She tapped it, and her stomach sank. She'd struck too lightly. The shuttlecock was heading for the ground. Hart dived under it, pushed it higher and back toward her. With a grin, she returned it.

"Nine for Beth and the deputy," Ciara sang out. "Nine for Gillian and Bobby."

Scout and Aiden must have stopped to watch. Beth didn't dare spare them a glance. Her world had shrunk to Hart's determined face as he lobbed the shuttlecock toward her. She returned it.

"Eleven for Beth and Deputy McCormick!" Ciara cried.

Hart struck the cork back toward her with a grin. "How much longer do you want to go on?"

"Until no one can possibly catch us, of course." Beth returned his grin along with the shuttlecock.

They sent the feathered cork back and forth three more times before a stray breeze caught the thing and pushed it beyond Beth's reach.

"Fifteen times!" Ciara cried, clapping with the others as Scout went to retrieve the shuttlecock. "Well done!"

The flush in Hart's cheeks, the gleam of his eyes, told Beth he was pleased and not a little surprised by the approval.

"That twist you did with your wrist," Bobby said, edging closer to Hart. "Can you show me how to do it?"

Scout and Aiden gathered near as well.

"Boys," Ciara said with a shake of her head as Beth joined her on the blanket. "Next thing you know they'll be asking how many notches he has on his gun belt."

"Hopefully none," Beth told her friend. "I don't remember hearing that he had to kill anyone in the line of duty."

Ciara nudged her. "Only broken a few hearts, it seems."

Beth started. She had never told her friend how Hart

had rejected her. All Ciara knew was that Beth no longer fancied him.

"Hearts?" she asked, voice coming out higher than usual.

Ciara raised a brow. "Oh, come now. It's written on your face. You still like him."

"Certainly I like him," Beth protested. "He's an old friend."

Ciara's smile was knowing. "So you say. But I have a feeling he's won more than this contest. If you don't watch out, Beth, he's going to win your heart all over again."

Beth must have shaken her head too vehemently, for Ciara's smile faded. "Beth? Don't you want to fall in love with Hart McCormick?"

Her hands were so tightly knit she could feel all her bones. "Oh, Ciara, no. He doesn't care about me."

Ciara put a hand over Beth's. "I think you're wrong, but if you ever have questions about him, talk to Maddie. He's more open with her than anyone, or at least he was before she married."

Beth nodded, but she didn't think she could take her friend's suggestion. She could just imagine what Hart would think if she went behind his back and investigated him.

Chapter Nine

Hart found it difficult to ease back into work on Monday. As he waited for the telegraph operator to send a query to San Francisco about a man charged with petty theft, he remembered the grin on Beth's face when they'd won at battledore. Why was it one look from her brightened his life?

"This must be important," the telegraph operator said, handing him back the note. "I've never seen you smile like that."

Hart schooled his face. "Every case is important." He tipped his hat and strolled out of the office.

But he couldn't seem to focus on patrolling either. Monday and Tuesday he generally kept close to town. Several of the larger businesses moved money those days, and supplies arrived from the south. Good time for criminals to strike. Wednesday and Thursday he rode around the county so he could be back in Seattle for Friday and Saturday, when the sawmill, Seattle's biggest employer, paid its men and the dance hall was full.

Today, however, Beth's face superimposed itself everywhere he looked. Her rapt expression as she sang a hymn, her concentration as she listened to the minister, her giggle at the picnic, the feel of her hand in his.

When he saw her, late-morning, standing on the boardwalk in front of Kelloggs', he almost rode past, sure she was just a figment of his imagination. Her determined wave made him realize his mistake.

"Good morning, Deputy," she said with her usual smile. Today she was all business in a tailored dress the color of forget-me-nots with a white collar, white parasol and white gloves. "We have work to do."

Hart pushed his hat back off his brow. "I have work. Did you need my help?"

A dimple appeared in her cheek, drawing his gaze to her lips. They were the prettiest pink, like the inside of one of the seashells on the Sound. He forced himself to meet her gaze instead. There was a decided twinkle in the blue of her eyes.

"We're going to look for a new house," she announced.

Hart frowned. "You moving to town permanently? I thought you filed a claim at Wallin Landing."

Her laughter floated on the breeze as she twirled her parasol. "Not a house for me. A house for you."

Hart leaned back in the saddle. "There's nothing wrong with my house."

"For a bachelor, likely not," Beth agreed, parasol stilling. "Allegra tells me that cabin has two rooms and a fireplace to cook in. But you have to admit that's a little cozy for a wife and children."

His face felt hot even though the breeze was cool. "Miss Wallin, I am not planning to take a wife and beget children anytime soon."

"Hush!" She darted forward and laid a hand on Arno's muzzle as if he'd been the one to make the statement.

"You promised me you'd go courting, and I promised the ladies of the Literary Society I'd help."

Hart sighed. "You don't need to find me a house, Beth. And today's not a good day in any event. I'm scheduled to work until sundown."

"You *were* scheduled to work until sundown," Beth replied, stroking Arno's nose. "I talked with Mrs. Wyckoff, and she talked with her husband the sheriff, and you have the rest of the day off. You can thank me later." She released his horse with a fond pat, and Arno, the rat, whickered his thanks for the attention. "Now, stable this dear beast and let's be off."

Arguing, he was learning, would get him nowhere. Then again, his investigation into the gang was going nowhere as well. Schneider steadfastly refused to tell him anything more, and no ships were due in until tomorrow. At least in looking around the area he might spot a stranger he hadn't noticed before.

He rode Arno back to the Howard house and let him loose in the pasture behind the stables, then returned to Kelloggs', where Beth was waiting. She stood humming to herself, rocking aimlessly side to side, her parasol twirling once more.

"Surely you have better things to do," he said as he joined her.

"They're already done," she assured him, lowering her parasol. "I advised Gillian on what to wear to interest the young man who's caught her attentions, accompanied Scout to Messieurs Black and Powell for a new suit for Easter, urged them to finish yours sooner—you have a fitting at two, by the way—and made sure Mr. Schneider was comfortable at the Occidental."

"Schneider." He seized on the name as she turned

the corner and started up the hill toward the residences. "Did he say anything more about his ordeal?"

"Not much. He seems embarrassed about the whole thing, poor dear."

"So did the other victims."

"Were there three or four? I forget."

"Four."

Her sweet smile warned him of his error. Why did he keep forgetting to watch his tongue with her? That innocent look made it far too easy to share confidences. "Keep that to yourself," he warned.

She nodded, smile fading. "It's simply terrible. Of course you must catch the villains. I'm almost sorry to pull you away from your duties today."

"Almost?" He couldn't help the tease.

She shot him a grin. "I am not entirely altruistic."

That he found hard to believe.

She stopped beside a clapboard house two blocks up from the business district. One of the more recently built houses, it had obviously been put up hastily, and Hart wasn't sure whether it was the steep slope or the frame of the house that made it lean.

Taking a paper from her little bag, Beth frowned down at it.

"Mr. Denny gave me a list of houses available for rent or purchase. I don't much like the look of this one."

Neither did he. "Even if it stood up straight, it has too many windows. You'd be hauling coal or wood for days to heat the place, and how would you defend it?"

She cast him a glance. "Expecting a siege, are we?"

He chuckled. "I hope not, but you never know."

"Hmm. Well, let's see if the next is any better."

It wasn't. A two-story affair, every edge and cornice

dripped bric-a-brac. He thought Beth would admire it, but she wrinkled her nose. "What was the builder thinking? A stream of lace is fine, but you certainly don't want to drown in it."

She was equally unimpressed with the next two houses. Her parasol drooped at her side unless she was using it as a cane to push herself higher on the hill. "The last one is out a ways. We'll have a bit of a walk."

"You don't have to do this," he said as they neared the top of the hill.

"Yes, I must," she insisted. "You cannot see these places as a woman would. You need my perspective."

He couldn't argue with that.

"I also did what I could about this gang problem," she continued, twitching her skirts away from the damp grass that verged the road, which was dwindling to a path. "I asked Allegra, Clay and Mrs. Wyckoff about Mr. Schneider's case. They were unaware of the situation with the gang, but Clay said he'd ask his business partners."

The entrepreneur had his hand in more than a dozen businesses in the area. "I'll thank him when I see him next. I never thought about asking the business owners. They usually come forward if they have a problem."

"Of their own," Beth pointed out. "They may not think to alert you if they find someone hurt behind their establishment. They'd assume the injured party would come to you directly." She glanced his way. "I take it they don't come so readily."

Hart shook his head. "They seem to be as embarrassed as Schneider, and none of them will describe their assailants."

"Perhaps they fear reprisal."

"But if they gave me the information to catch the criminals, there would be no reprisal."

"There is that." They must have reached the last house on her list, for she drew up before one. It was solidly built, two stories high, with a deep porch wrapping around it and a stable behind.

"Oh, Hart, it's perfect!" She picked up her skirts and climbed to the porch to peer in the front window. "There's a darling parlor with room for a table, and I can see the handle of a pump in the kitchen. *Inside* the kitchen. Can you imagine?"

Few homesteads in Seattle boasted indoor plumbing, of any kind. The house must be situated near its own spring. He glanced around the side of the house. "Pasture out back too—room for Arno, maybe a milk cow."

Beth bounced off the porch in a flurry of blue. "Mr. Denny said several houses on the list had at least three bedrooms and a cellar. I can assure you any lady in Seattle would approve of this one." Hands on her hips, she turned to eye the place again. "I can see you here."

So could he. Lounging on the porch, his feet up on the railing, keeping an eye on the city below. Sitting down to dinner with his wife and children around him, a wife with sunny curls, blue eyes and a smile that brightened his life.

Hart turned away from the place. "It's a fine house, but it's not for me. Now, I need to get back to work."

Oh! Honestly, sometimes she just didn't understand him. She'd seen his eyes light as he'd looked over the house. Now he stomped down the hill as if she'd taken him on a snipe hunt rather than to a perfectly acceptable home.

She glanced back at it one last time before following him. It really was perfect. She could imagine living there, sewing lacy curtains for the windows, setting rose-patterned china on the table to welcome family and friends. She could build a house just like it on her claim, or rather her brothers could, but this one tugged at her heart.

All the more reason to leave it be.

He must have slowed, because she caught up to him easily. "You promised to procure tickets to one of Fanny Morgan Phelps's performances," she informed him, striding past.

"Can't see how that does me any good," he grumbled as he lengthened his stride to pace her.

"I told you—attending a cultural event will show the ladies of Seattle you have refinement of spirit. If you will not look for a home, at least you could go to the theatre."

The idea seemed perfectly logical to her, but he cast her a look as if she had suggested that he ride Arno to the moon. She made her face as stern as possible.

"Tonight, then," he said. "I'll stop by the Occidental and get tickets. I can look in on Mr. Schneider at the same time."

Beth glared at him. "You were supposed to have this afternoon off."

He met her glare with one of his own. "The law doesn't take an afternoon off. Neither do criminals."

"Oh! Hart McCormick, you are the most provoking man. I begin to believe the ladies were right to avoid you."

"Good. Then we can stop this."

"Fine. Only you get to tell Ursula Wyckoff."

He stopped, and she nearly collided with him. He caught her shoulders as if to steady her. Her parasol bumped against her leg.

He lifted it aside, touch gentle and smile wry. "Sorry."

Was he apologizing for the quick stop or his argumentative behavior? The skin had tightened across his cheeks, as if something tightened inside him as well.

Beth stepped back, gathering her composure. "Are we proceeding with this plan or not?"

His hands fell. "We'll proceed. We'll give them a show until they get tired of the drama and turn their attentions elsewhere."

So, that was his game. "It's no good, you know," she said, falling into step with him as they headed into town. "They won't give in so easily."

"Neither will I."

He left her at the Howard house and promised to retrieve her by six for the play. She wasn't even sure if he could get tickets so close to the performance. It wasn't every day one of the premiere acting companies from Victoria chose to go on tour. The troupe had been quite well received. But she was ready by half past five just in case.

Ever since she'd had charge of her own wardrobe at eighteen, she'd saved, studied fashion plates, watched for sales on material and helped Nora sew until Beth had a decent collection of gowns. Her brothers teased her that some were too fancy for the frontier, but none were completely impractical. Besides, just because she lived an entire continent away from sophisticated New York didn't mean she couldn't turn herself out smartly.

She generally reserved her best gowns for worship

services and special occasions. A night at the theatre—
oh, very well, Yesler's Hall that had once been his cook-
house—surely counted as the latter. Accordingly, she
pulled on a sky-blue matte satin gown with a curved
neck and puffed sleeves, put her hair up high and fixed
it in place with mother-of-pearl combs and draped a
white wool shawl about her shoulders.

"Too bad the flower crowns faded," Gillian said as
she helped her. "You'd look like a fairy princess."

She felt a little like a fairy princess as she came
down the stairs to wait for Hart. But when she opened
the door to his knock a short time later, she found she
was accompanying a prince.

Messieurs Black and Powell had managed to finish
the waistcoat and trousers, doing a superb job of fitting
them to Hart's lean frame. The gray material outlined
long legs and a slender waist. The pattern of the waistcoat emphasized the breadth of his chest. Instead of the
suit coat, he had donned his leather duster, the length
of which made it appear as if he was wearing a kingly
robe. It was almost as if he'd come courting.

No, not that. She wasn't ready to allow any such acquaintance, especially not with him. She was helping
him attract a suitable wife, and it would not be her. Her
heart gave a painful thump as if it agreed.

She put on a smile. "Mr. McCormick. I take it you
were successful in procuring the tickets."

He nodded, then offered her his arm. "It's not far.
Can you walk in that getup?"

"Why, such compliments. You quite turn my head."

"I was more worried about you turning your ankle."

Beth laughed despite herself. "I'll be fine. Shall we

go? I wouldn't want to be late." She put her hand on his arm and let him draw her from the house.

The sun had just set beyond the Olympics on the other side of the Sound, leaving the mountains silhouetted against a rosy orange sky. Already the temperature dipped, and she was glad to have Hart's warmth beside her as they headed down the hill.

"So, what shall we have the pleasure of watching tonight?" she asked as the lights from the buildings along Mill Street began to glow.

"One perfectly suited to you," he promised. "*The Taming of the Shrew.*"

Beth blinked and glanced his way, but she couldn't make out his face in the growing dark. "I beg your pardon. Did you just call me a shrew?"

"No. You said you liked the funny ones. The clerk at the Occidental said it was a comedy about courting."

Beth smiled. "Then I'm sure I'll enjoy it."

She thought his arm relaxed under her hand. "Good."

They had been alone on the hill, but the closer they drew to Mill Street, the more people crowded around, gentlemen in top hats, ladies in fine wool cloaks. Excitement hung like a silvery moon in the air. Beth shivered with it, smile growing.

The sturdy wood building was awash in lights as they entered. Young Billy Prentice, the porter from Lowe's hotel, grinned at her as he took the tickets. Then, as if remembering he was supposed to be a fancy usher in the tailcoat that sat too loose on his frame, he schooled his face and offered her his arm to lead her to their seats.

The first couple rows held padded chairs, but the rest of the hall was filled with simple wood benches. Billy took her and Hart to seats about halfway back.

"Enjoy the show, Miss Wallin, Deputy," he said before hurrying to assist the next couple.

Hart glanced around. "Looks like they fancied up the place."

As much as they could. The long, single-roomed hall had been used for everything from civic meetings and community recitals to Yesler's annual Christmas party for his men. The space still smelled faintly of sausages. The biggest change was the wide raised platform on one end, lanterns all along the foot. Partitions on either side would allow the performers to wait until their cue. The painted backdrops must have come with the troupe itself, for she was fairly sure no one in Seattle would have any idea how to represent an Italian villa.

"So many people," she murmured to Hart, glancing around. Voices rose and fell like the waves on Puget Sound as the seats filled. While most of those attending were couples or bachelors, she sighted several of the women she had once hoped to match to Hart. At least one was keeping an eye on him. Better and better. Even Mrs. Maynard, one of the Literary Society members, glanced their way with approbation.

Then the play started, and she could think of nothing else. Fanny Morgan Phelps captured her imagination immediately. A tall woman with a buxom figure, her voice was commanding. Beth completely commiserated with the fair Katherine's plight.

"Obedience," she complained to Hart as they made their way toward the exit at the end of the play. "Is that the be-all and end-all of a marriage? If my husband attempted to starve me and deprive me of clothing to make me obey him, I'd have a thing or two to say about the matter."

"What about that Bianca girl?" he countered. "Playing her suitors off each other. Mighty high-handed, if you ask me."

"I grant you that was ill done. Oh, the entire lot of them have no sense whatsoever. If I had been matchmaking, I would have found someone much less wily for Katherine, someone who would dazzle her with romance, not attempt to master her."

He cocked his head. "Dazzle her with romance?"

Her face was warming. "Yes, you know. Bringing her flowers."

"Flowers."

How could one word hold such skepticism? "Yes. Reciting poetry, singing under her window."

He choked. "Singing?"

Beth swatted his arm. "Do not make light of it! It's highly romantic. You should read the books Pa left us— now, those are heroes."

He eyed her as if wondering, but Beth's surety was growing. She grasped his arm. "Of course! I don't know why I didn't think of it before. Poetry! The Literary Society is going to discuss the works of Vaughn Everard, a dashing English poet from early in the century. I take it he was quite the romantic figure. All the ladies at Wallin Landing adore him. Read his works, and you'll know just what women want. If you follow his example, the ladies of Seattle will be following you in droves!"

Chapter Ten

Poetry? He'd been ridiculed growing up for his craving for reading. Books had been an easy target for theft and destruction at the orphanage. Certainly Jake Cathcart had had a good laugh.

"Dime novels?" the outlaw leader had scoffed when he'd caught Hart reading at the hideout they'd built in a wooded area. "You don't need to read about outlaws, boy. You are one." He'd taken the book and thrown it in the fire while the others cackled. Hart had been careful to hide the stories ever since.

But Beth had no such trouble. She'd laid out an entire curriculum by the time they reached the street through the crowds. "And *The Courtship of Miles Standish*, though you must take his approach as a cautionary tale."

Apparently, Mr. Standish had done poorly in his courtship. That one might be worth reading for ideas on how to thwart the plans of the Literary Society. He was just glad none of the members in attendance tonight had approached to pressure Beth or him.

Beside him, Beth stiffened. "When did that happen?"

Hart followed her gaze to where Scout was helping

Mrs. Jamison up into his buggy. The lady's raven locks sparkled with jewels, and her evening gown was cut to emphasize her graceful curves. A diamond necklace adorned her throat.

A diamond? In Seattle?

Beth grabbed Hart's arm and all but dragged him toward the carriage. "Scout! Thomas! Wait!"

Hands on the reins, Scout smiled at her from the seat, though his look cooled as Hart drew up beside her. "Beth, Deputy, nice to see you."

Hart inclined his head. "Rankin. Mrs. Jamison."

The lady's smile was nearly as cold as the stones around her neck.

"Did you enjoy the play?" Scout asked.

"Tremendously," Beth assured him for her and Hart. "I wish I'd noticed you. We could have sat together."

"Mr. Rankin thoughtfully procured seats in the front row," Mrs. Jamison said with a devoted look his way.

So, that was how the wind blew. Beth must have realized it as well, for her gaze veered from Scout to the lady beside him. Hart struggled to see the two of them as a couple. For all her beauty and sophistication, Mrs. Jamison had to be at least six years Scout's senior, with experience not only in matrimony but also in business. There had to be more seasoned men who would be glad to court her.

Scout shrugged, pink tingeing his cheeks. "I thought the view would be best from up front. But it was hard to see anyone except the players." He grinned at Beth. "Who would have thought, eh, Beth? Us, at a Shakespearean play."

Beth giggled. "At least it wasn't *A Midsummer*

Night's Dream. Remember when Rina made you read Puck?"

Hart wasn't sure what a puck was or why Scout would want to read it, but her friend laughed. "I could barely recognize the words in my head, let alone sound them out."

Mrs. Jamison shivered, a delicate movement that set the bobs at her ears to swaying.

"Oh, forgive me," Scout said. "You're probably cold. I should get you home."

She favored him with a smile. "Nonsense. It's a lovely night for a drive."

Hart could see it coming. As soon as Scout left, Beth would either lecture Hart on the ungentlemanly behavior of keeping ladies out in the cold or demand that he go shopping for a buggy. To his surprise, she moved closer to the carriage and set a gloved hand on the yellow-lacquered side, her face glowing in the light from the lantern affixed to the front of the buggy.

"Say, Scout, would you mind terribly giving me and Deputy McCormick a ride back to the Howards' after you drop off Mrs. Jamison? I wore fancy shoes, and my feet are protesting."

Funny. She had laughed off Hart's concerns about walking earlier.

"Not at all," Scout assured her. "Do you need help climbing up or..."

"I'll help her," Hart said. He bent closer to Beth and murmured, "What are you doing?"

"Assisting a friend in courting," she murmured back, but she accepted his hand to step up into the rear seat.

Why did she think Scout needed help? Against all odds, he was escorting one of the prettiest ladies in Seattle. And if Beth thought he'd be too shy, giving him an audience wasn't likely to increase his courage.

Puzzled, Hart climbed up beside her, and Scout set off. By the stiff way Mrs. Jamison held her head, she was not amused to find herself with two chaperones.

"Yes, I quite enjoyed that," Beth was telling no one in particular as Scout maneuvered the vehicle through the dispersing crowd. "Though I'm sure it was quite plebian compared to some performances you must have attended in San Francisco, Mrs. Jamison."

The seamstress bestirred herself, turning just enough in the seat so that she was facing Scout. "The plays there were marvelous. I imagine those in New York and London would be even more so. How I long to visit someday."

"You should go," Scout told her. "A lady like you would be welcome everywhere."

Her smile thanked him. "But I'd be alone. And I find entertainments so much more enjoyable in congenial company."

Scout ducked his head as if honored by the statement.

"What a shame your brother couldn't join you," Beth said.

"Oh, forgive me, Evangeline!" Scout said with a troubled glance her way. "I should have asked about Bobby."

Once more Beth stiffened, and Hart thought he knew why. It generally took a bit before a lady allowed a gentleman to use her first name. Mrs. Jamison and Scout had only met last Sunday. It seemed Scout didn't need much help courting after all, if he'd so endeared himself to the lady in such a short time.

Mrs. Jamison laid a hand on Scout's arm. "Not at

all, my dear Thomas. Bobby wouldn't have been able to join us. He had schoolwork. His studies are very important to him."

Now, how could that be? Spring term didn't start until after Easter. If she'd managed to enroll her brother early, Bobby surely would have known Aiden and Gillian before the picnic on Sunday. They attended the North School.

"Maybe next time," Scout said.

"And next time consider a chaperone as well," Beth told him. "You wouldn't want to jeopardize Mrs. Jamison's reputation."

That set up more apologies from Scout and assurances from the widow. By the time they quieted down, Mrs. Jamison had convinced him to take Beth and Hart to the Howards' first. Beth slumped back in her seat.

But only for a moment.

"And how is your latest creation coming along?" she asked the seamstress. Before the widow could answer, Beth reached out to tap Scout's shoulder. "Mrs. Jamison's designs are published in *Godey's*. Did you know that, Scout?"

Scout glanced at his companion. "No indeed. Impressive. Beth's been a devotee for years."

"*The Ladies' Monthly Magazine* from London is more respectable," Mrs. Jamison said. "But one does what one can in the wilderness."

Beth drew in such a deep breath, shoulders rising, that Hart had the odd notion that she was set to explode. Time to change the subject.

"Have you had any trouble since arriving?" he asked Mrs. Jamison, who was fluttering her lashes so vigorously Hart wondered whether Scout felt the breeze.

"Trouble?" Her voice sounded higher than usual. "Why, whatever do you mean, Deputy?"

Scout's voice was harder. "Deputy McCormick looks for trouble. That's his job."

Beth roused herself. "And he's very good at it. Why, right now he's on the trail of a vicious gang that robs newcomers."

Hart clamped his mouth shut. While he had made no secret of pursuing the case, announcing the fact to all and sundry didn't seem like such a good idea. Seattle was still a small town, and gossip spread.

Mrs. Jamison pressed a beringed hand to her cheek. "How awful! Oh, at times like this I fear that a mere woman and child could scarcely survive in this world."

She could have gone onstage with Fanny Morgan Phelps. Hart half expected her to swoon against Scout's shoulder. Beth's *humph* beside him told him she also recognized a performance when she saw one.

"Now, then," Scout said, edging closer to Mrs. Jamison on the bench. "You aren't alone. You have any number of friends in Seattle."

Her eyes were dark pools in the lantern light. "I hope I may count you among that number, Thomas."

"Of course you can," Beth put in brightly. "Scout's friends with everyone."

Mrs. Jamison twisted to face directly ahead, and Hart wouldn't have been surprised to hear her grinding her pearly white teeth.

When Scout drew up before the house, Hart jumped down and came around to help Beth. "Thanks for the ride, Rankin," he said. "Mrs. Jamison, always a pleasure. Give my regards to your brother."

The lady smiled. "I will do that, Deputy. It's so kind

of you to escort the younger generation like Bobby and Miss Wallin."

It was a deliberate hit. Beth sucked in a breath beside him, but Scout was already turning his team to start back down the hill.

"And to think I admired her," she muttered. "I begin to believe she made up that story about having designs in *Godey's*."

He'd heard her mention the word enough times over the years, often in tones of reverence, that he knew how high she held the lady's magazine.

"She was trying to put you in your place, no doubt," Hart said. "Perhaps she's jealous."

Beth turned to him, skirts swirling. "Jealous? Why? I don't have half her talent."

"But twice as much respect, I warrant. A seamstress wouldn't normally move in high circles. She's probably used to fighting for her place. Maybe she didn't realize you were just being friendly."

"Not friendly enough," she said, watching the carriage lamp fade in the darkness.

He cocked his head. Something else was bothering her, besides Evangeline Jamison's cutting behavior. "You don't like the idea of Scout courting her."

"Not in the slightest."

He should have known. Scout and Beth had grown up together. It was only natural that they form an attachment now. In many ways—wealth, youth, outlook—Scout was a better match for her than Hart would ever be.

But he didn't deserve her.

"I understand. You should tell him how you feel."

She squared her shoulders. "Oh, I intend to. At first

opportunity. I should have realized that his income would attract the unscrupulous, but I truly had a higher opinion of Seattle's female population. I must find another lady to vie for his attentions. A shame Ciara and Gillian are still too young." Her fingernail flashed in the moonlight as she tapped her chin.

Hart felt as if he had started up the Duwamish without a paddle. "Wait, you want Scout to court another woman?"

Her finger fell. "Certainly! Scout deserves a wife who loves and respects him. I highly suspect it is his money and not his character Mrs. Jamison finds fascinating. After all, she hasn't had the opportunity to get to know him yet. And he certainly knows nothing about her outside her dreams of visiting London one day."

Relief was like cool rain in the heat of summer. "So you're not interested in Scout."

"Of course I'm interested in Scout's well-being! He's like a brother to me."

He should not be this pleased. The entire affair had nothing to do with him.

So why was he glad that another fellow hadn't staked a claim on Beth's heart?

Beth pulled the brush through her hair that night, trying not to cause more snarls. Why did the men of her acquaintance need such help in matters of romance? Her brothers had had excellent examples of what to do and what not to do from their father's adventure novels, and they'd still needed cajoling, encouragement and, at times, downright scolding to win a wife. Hart fought her at every step, as if he had no idea how important a wife could be. Now here Scout went falling for the first pretty woman to glance his way.

Beth certainly believed in love at first sight, but that usually involved people of great beauty and nobility. Mrs. Jamison was certainly beautiful enough to turn heads, but Scout, bless his heart, was neither handsome nor noble. He was an acquired taste, and Mrs. Jamison had not taken the time to acquire it before attaching herself to him. That alone made the seamstress suspect.

Beth fully intended to discuss the matter with Scout the next day, after she attended to her other duties. She still thought a course of reading might help Hart see the value of a proper courtship. She hadn't brought any of their family's books with her to town, being engrossed in one Maddie had lent her about a family of four sisters in England all trying to attract gentlemen, but she needn't have worried about getting a message to her family. Her brothers had no intention of leaving her alone in Seattle.

Simon stopped by the next day. He claimed to have come in for the mail, but her second oldest brother didn't fool her. Simon was efficient to a fault. He generally had more important things to do, especially this time of year with the fields to prepare for planting, than to drive in to Seattle for the mail.

"They seem to be treating you well," he said, glancing around Allegra's elegant parlor as if expecting to find her in chains.

"A bed and room of my own," Beth told him. "They even feed me on occasion."

He looked her up and down as if he wasn't too sure of that.

"How much longer?" he asked. "Nora misses you."

Beth thawed. "And I miss her. I miss all of you. But things are progressing slower than I'd hoped. I could use your help."

His light green eyes brightened. That was one thing about her family—they were always ready to lend a hand.

Still, it took some work to convince him that all she needed were books. In the end, he promised to send them with the next Wallin who came in for the mail.

His brow furrowed as he rose. "You will be careful, Beth."

She smiled at him. "Yes, Simon, I promise. Give everyone my love and assure them I'll be home for Easter."

She was still thinking about her family when she left Allegra's copy of Vaughn Everard's poetry at the door of Hart's cabin. There was no sign of Arno in the pasture beside the little house, which probably meant Hart had already ridden out. Funny—Simon worried about her safety. She didn't worry about Hart's. She knew he was more than a match for any criminal.

But, just to be helpful, she went to the Occidental to check on Mr. Schneider.

The German buyer had nearly recovered from his wounds and was set to journey south to see about his hops.

"Though who will extend me credit I do not know," he lamented to Beth as they sat on two of the crimson upholstered chairs in the little lobby. "Not a penny have I left. I pay my bills here thanks to your friends."

She was glad to have helped him recover. His coat had been cleaned and pressed, and the bandage had been removed from his head. He looked perfectly respectable to Beth, his mustache bristling with pride, his head high.

"Perhaps Mr. Horton can help," she told him. "He's planning on building a fine bank, the first in Seattle. If you show him your credentials, he might take a chance. I could give you his direction."

Mr. Schneider thanked her profusely, bowing over her hand as she prepared to take her leave. Suddenly, he dropped her fingers and paled.

Beth put a hand on his arm. "Mr. Schneider, what is it? Are you ill?"

"*Nein.*" He shook himself and gave her a sheepish smile. "I think I see one of the men who attacked me, but I must be mistaken. Such a villain would not come into this fine hotel, *jah*?"

She certainly hoped not. Beth glanced around, but she didn't notice anyone looking particularly nefarious. "Can you describe him?"

He dropped his voice. "*Nein.* When they finished with the beating, they tell me that they will find me if I speak. They will finish the job." He swallowed.

Oh, if there was anything she hated it was a bully. "Nonsense, Mr. Schneider. The more Deputy McCormick knows about these men, the more likely he is to catch them and put them away behind bars where they cannot hurt anyone. You must speak with him before you leave."

He leaned closer, blue eyes heavy. "I tell you, Miss Wallin, because you have been good to me. The men who robbed me said I should not go to the police."

"Because they hoped to frighten you," Beth assured him.

"*Nein.*" His voice was choked, and perspiration stood out on his brow. "Not for that reason. They say I must not go to the police, for the police support them."

Beth recoiled. Hart, in league with villains? She would sooner believe Father Christmas a thief, George Washington a traitor. She squared her shoulders.

"You can tell me, Mr. Schneider. I promise you only the most trusted, most heroic of our lawmen will hear of it. Whatever we do, we cannot allow those creatures to continue preying on travelers."

Reluctantly, Mr. Schneider agreed, going on to describe the two men who had attacked him. Beth pulled a pencil and the house list from her reticule and took notes on the back of the paper so she wouldn't forget anything.

"I don't recognize anyone from your description," she said as he finished and she tucked the paper and pencil away. "But I'm sure it will help. Safe travels, sir." She wrapped her arms about him for a hug.

Beaming, Mr. Schneider thanked her again and hurried for the stairs to his room. Clutching her reticule close, she left the hotel. A glance at the sky told her it wasn't quite noon. If she was fortunate, she might catch Hart riding down Second Avenue.

She started up the street, dodging between the men moving among the shops. Oh, but Hart would be pleased with the information Mr. Schneider had given her. He kept an eye out for shady characters. Surely he'd recognize the villains from the descriptions. Those men were as good as jailed.

She had just crossed Mill Street, skirts bunched in one hand to keep them out of the mud, and stepped up onto the boardwalk when a man jostled her.

"Terribly sorry," Beth started, but the fellow grabbed her arm and yanked her around the corner of the building into the alley. In the shadows of the buildings on either side, she could just make out height and breadth.

He shoved a finger at her face. "You're sticking your nose where it doesn't belong. Go home, stay there and keep your mouth shut or you won't like what happens next."

She didn't like what was happening now. She had no doubt she was facing one of the men Hart was after. What was to keep him from striking her down as he'd done Mr. Schneider or one of the other victims? Very likely he knew she'd spoken to Mr. Schneider. He was determined to keep her from telling Hart what she'd learned.

But she wasn't about to do as he asked—go home, stay there or keep her mouth shut.

She stepped back out of reach, opened her mouth and screamed at the top of her lungs.

Chapter Eleven

Over the clatter of wagons and the call of men's voices, a woman's scream pierced the cool spring air. The sound froze Hart's blood. He urged Arno into a gallop, scattering other riders before him.

A crowd at the edge of Mill Street told him the location. He reined in, jumped down and drew his Smith & Wesson as he landed. People scrambled out of his way.

The sight in the center of the group stopped his breath. Mrs. and Mr. Denny were helping Beth to her feet. Her skirts were covered in mud. The jaunty little hat she favored had slipped down onto one ear. He holstered his gun and stepped forward.

"Are you hurt?"

Beth made a face, going a long way toward reassuring him. "No. But the miscreant stole my bag."

A thief who favored women's purses? That was something new for Seattle. There weren't enough ladies to make it worth the time.

"I insist you apprehend the fellow, Deputy," Mrs. Denny said, nose high.

"This is an outrage," Arthur Denny agreed. "Young

ladies like Miss Wallin should be safe strolling our streets."

They should be safe in their family's barn too, but that hadn't stopped an outlaw from gunning down Annabelle.

The dam holding back the memory threatened to breach. Hart held it by force of will. Bending, he scooped Beth up in his arms.

"I'm fine," she insisted. "Please, Deputy, put me down."

"Not until I'm sure," he said, striding out of the alley, her rescuers giving way before him. Out of the corner of his eyes he saw Denny tying Arno to the hitching post.

Hart headed around the corner for Doc Murray's, bumping through the door to the fellow's office. In the act of peering into a boy's ear, Doc looked up, brow raised.

Hart set Beth down on the high table the room boasted. "Miss Wallin was attacked."

The mother cried out and clutched her son close. Doc straightened. "How awful. Where are you hurt, Miss Wallin?"

Hart crossed his arms over his chest. "That's what you're going to tell us. Hop to it, man."

The doctor nodded. A younger man, he'd come to town shortly after that old rascal, Doc Maynard, had gone to his just reward. Murray had inherited his patients as well as many others who had struggled with Maynard's unorthodox ways. Now the dapper man with his neat brown mustache gathered up some instruments and moved to Beth's side, not nearly fast enough for Hart. The mother bustled her boy out the door as if concerned Beth's injuries might be infectious.

Murray asked Beth some questions, requested that she turn her head this way and that, raise her arms, stand on her own. Hart stayed close, ready to catch her if she swayed.

"Truly, Doc, I'm fine," she assured him with a frown to Hart.

Doc tsked. "So it would seem. Still, you've been through an ordeal. I suggest rest for the remainder of the day, perhaps laudanum for the pain."

"There is no pain," Beth said with a pointed look to Hart before giving the doctor a smile. "Thank you for your concern. I'll let you get back to treating those who actually need it."

Gathering her skirts, she swept from the office.

Hart was hard on her heels. "I'll escort you to the Howards'."

Beth stopped, holding up one hand. "No, you will not. You've already wasted enough time on me today. Besides, you'll have work to do once you hear what I learned."

Hart cocked his head. "What *you* learned?"

She nodded. "I stopped by the Occidental to check on Mr. Schneider and convinced him to describe his assailants to me."

Hart frowned. "How? He couldn't seem to manage it before."

"For good reason." She glanced either way, then drew him farther from the doctor's door. "Hart, the villains told him it was no good going to the law, because the law was in on it."

Hart drew himself up. "That's a lie. Wyckoff's integrity is unassailable."

"As is the town marshal's and the constable's." She

shook her head, and her hat slid to her shoulder, along with a coil of platinum hair. She set about repairing the damage. "And it goes without saying that your reputation is spotless."

Not as spotless as she thought. If anyone besides the sheriff looked into his background, they could well wonder if he was being paid by the gang to look the other way. "So, you think it's a lie, to scare the victims into silence."

"Exactly. Intimidation seems to be their best weapon. Well, it won't work with me." She patted the last hair in place. "I didn't want to miss a word of Mr. Schneider's description, so I wrote everything on the back of the house list."

Hart held out his hand. "I'll take it from here. I don't want you any more involved."

"Too late, I'm afraid. The bully stole my reticule with the paper in it. That's how I fell, trying to pull it out of his grip." She glanced down at the clumps of black mud, the dull damp circles spreading from them. "I only hope I can save this dress."

"Forget the dress." His words must have betrayed his fears, for her head snapped up and her eyes widened. Hart seized her by the shoulders.

"Do you have any idea of the danger? He could have slit your throat and left you to bleed to death."

She shuddered. "Now, there's a horrid picture."

He gathered her close, chest hurting. "I can think of several just as bad. You have to stop trying to help, Beth. I can't lose you."

For a moment, she nestled against him, her arms around his waist, her head resting on his chest. Her soft sigh was muffled by his duster. He couldn't seem to let go.

She pushed him back. "Now look at what you've done. I just fixed my hair. I suppose it's fallen again." She started fussing with her hat, all busyness, but her fingers were trembling. He only wanted to hold them close, keep her safe.

He had to get a grip on himself. "Beth, as deputy sheriff, and your friend, I insist you stay out of this. I'll speak to Schneider, get the details."

"Too late," she said around the hairpin sticking out of her mouth as she used both hands to sweep up her hair. "He's traveling south today. Oh, this is impossible!"

She threw up her hands, and her hair tumbled down about her shoulders, like a pile of gold.

He couldn't stop himself. "Let me." Stepping behind her, he gathered up the tendrils, each strand like silk. She smelled like vanilla, and he nearly brought the curls to his nose to inhale more of the sweet scent.

"Pins," he said, holding out one hand.

She dropped them meekly into his palm. He supposed he ought to be glad she didn't jab one in his finger.

He gently inserted them into the pile, careful to support the heavy coils. Then he stepped back. The hold of the pins was as precarious as the hold on his feelings. He stood behind her a moment, counted to ten, took a deep breath. This fear, this yearning, could only be caused by the memory of Annabelle. And Annabelle was gone.

As he came around in front of Beth, he kept his face impassive. She dropped her gaze nonetheless, cheeks pink.

"Do you want me to walk you home?" he asked.

"Yes, er, no. I'm fine." She collected herself, raising her gaze. "Thank you for the help. But Hart, I can't step aside. The villain may have stolen the descriptions, but I still remember what Mr. Schneider said. I'm your best chance of catching these criminals."

He didn't like it. Beth could see that. His dark brows drew down. That chin was growing firmer by the minute. But he wouldn't argue with her. He wanted to stop these villains too much.

He put a hand on Beth's elbow. "Doc said you should rest. We can talk about this later."

Beth allowed him to steer her around the corner for Second. "I don't need to rest. But I'll go back to the Howards' to change. I'm a sight."

"Pretty as a pig in mud," he assured her.

Beth giggled. "I see we still have to work on compliments. Read that book I left you. It should help."

"I'll consider it."

Had anyone ever sounded more doubtful?

"Oh, come now," Beth said. "It's as good as your dime novels. I promise."

"I'll take your word for it."

But no one else's. His gaze moved from person to person along the street. His scowl said he suspected each of them of some foul crime. The way he hustled her along, they probably thought *she* was a criminal.

But she couldn't forget the way he'd held her a few moments ago, as if she were precious, so very dear to him. She'd once dreamed of him holding her like that. His strong hands had caressed her hair almost reverently.

He'd just been helping. Like her brothers, he didn't seem to think she could manage on her own.

"I don't see why I can't tell you as we walk," she said as they reached the end of the block and started up the hill toward the residences.

His grunt was the most encouragement she was going to get.

"As you know, two men were involved," Beth said, determined to share. "I'm convinced the fellow who took my bag was one of them. He certainly matched one of the descriptions. I got a good look at him when he grabbed my bag. Tall, whip thin, with short dark-blond hair. Deep, sunken brown eyes. Mole on his right cheek. Inferior wool coat of an unflattering cut."

"Schneider never said that last part."

Beth grinned at his skepticism. "No. It is my own observation. He was surprisingly clean, though. I would think villains wouldn't want to spend time or funding on laundry and bathing."

He rubbed his chin, and she tried not to think about how that hand had felt in her hair. "Interesting. Schneider bled. One of them might have caught a few drops on his clothes in the process."

"And blood is terribly hard to remove," Beth told him, lifting her sodden skirts out of a mud puddle. "One of the laundresses in town might remember the stains. I'll ask around."

He dropped his hand. "*I'll* ask around. That's my job, remember?"

He was right. There was no reason he couldn't handle this. "Sorry. Where was I? Oh, yes, the other one. He was short and stout, with a receding hairline, oily brown hair and bloodshot eyes. I certainly don't recall meeting anyone who met that description. Do you?"

"No, but I'll keep an eye out for the pair," Hart said

as they neared the Howard house. "Now, promise me your investigating is done."

Beth dropped her skirts. "Oh, I can't promise that. You never know what might need to be investigated—a woman who shows excessive interest in Scout, a lady who shows undue interest in you."

He stopped her at the foot of the steps leading up to the front porch. "I thought you wanted me to marry."

At the moment, her resolve was sorely tested, but she refused to admit that to him. She wasn't about to go through that rejection again. "Only to the right woman," she told him. "I just wonder when our plan will bear fruit."

"Your plan," he corrected her. "And it's already bearing fruit. Dried apples, to be exact. I found pies from two different women waiting for me at the office this morning."

Beth's smile deepened. "Did you now?"

He didn't look the least pleased. He'd widened his stance, and the handle of his revolver stuck out as if in defiance. "Invitations too. Seems several mamas of eligible young misses want me over for dinner. Showing civic pride to support the law, they said."

At last! The women of Seattle had finally recognized him for the gentleman he was. She couldn't help a sense of pride herself, followed by a decided lowering of her spirits.

"How nice," she made herself say. "And which have you decided to accept?"

"None." He bent to meet her gaze. "I have work to do."

A shiver of pleasure ran through her. Silly! She wasn't his work. He was hers.

"That will never do. One of them must interest you."

He straightened. "Not a one. I already looked up their menfolk and told them as much."

"Oh, Hart, you didn't!"

He seemed almost pleased about it, as if he hadn't just committed the social blunder of the year. "I did. All except the Widow Dunbar. I'll have to speak to her directly."

So Mrs. Dunbar was regretting her hasty decision. Too late. Beth had already decided the lady wasn't the bride for Hart. "I'll speak to her if you'd like."

He shook his head. "No matchmaking, Beth. I won't have her."

Curiosity got the better of her. "Why? She's pretty and bright."

"And bossy and opinionated. That's not what I want in a wife."

The words stung. "I see. I thought you wanted a woman with spirit."

He bent his head again. "I want a wife who'll stand on her own two feet, not walk all over mine."

"Oh." She shifted, afraid of what her face might reveal. "Well, I can certainly appreciate that. I'd like the same sort of husband, if I was interested in marriage."

He snorted. "You're a matchmaker. Of course you're interested in marriage."

She decided not to argue. The discussion could go down too many paths she no longer wanted to walk. "It's settled then. I'll tell Mrs. Dunbar you're not interested, and you'll accept the next invitation you receive."

He stepped back. "I never agreed to that."

"Oh. Well, in that case, I'll tell her you can't wait to dine with her."

"Beth Wallin…"

"That growl may frighten the criminals you chase, but it won't work on me. I have too many brothers. Do we have an agreement?"

"I ought to lock you up for safekeeping."

Beth pressed a hand to her chest. "Me? Sweet little Beth Wallin? The entire city of Seattle would be in shock."

"And your Literary Society friends would march around the office until I let you out."

"If my brothers didn't batter down the door first."

"I'd rather take my chances with your brothers."

Beth giggled. "Clever fellow. Hatpins can be deadly, you know. Oh, come now, Hart—one invitation. Is it really so much to ask?"

He cocked his head. "I'll make you a deal. I accept the next invitation, you fend off Mrs. Dunbar and you stay away from my investigation of the gang."

"That's two for one," Beth protested.

"Take it or leave it."

If she didn't take it, he might never give a lady a chance. Worse, Mrs. Dunbar might set her cap at him. That might frighten off other contenders.

"Done," she said, sticking out her hand.

He took it, hand dwarfing hers, and gave it a shake. "And remember this: If you go back on your word, I *will* lock you up, despite the Literary Society and your brothers."

Chapter Twelve

Stubborn, opinionated woman! Hart strode down the hill, away from the Howard house and a certain lady who was severely cutting up his peace. Why had she questioned Schneider? Didn't she realize she could make herself a target? Men who preyed on other men didn't often scruple about harming women as well. She could have been killed.

Stars exploded on the periphery of his vision. He made himself stop, take a deep breath. The fear of loss overwhelmed him. He could see Annabelle's face, the color waning as the light from her blue eyes faded, until he held only a husk. She'd been all of eighteen, a dreamer like Beth, seeing only the good in the world. He'd run away again, from the gang this time, sick at heart over what he'd become. He'd snuck into her father's barn, intent on getting a good night's sleep before he left the area. She'd discovered him when she'd come to do the milking.

One look in those sky-blue eyes, and he'd realized he still had some good in him because all he wanted to do was prove himself to her.

"Don't be afraid," he'd said, taking the buckets from her unresisting grip. "I would never hurt you."

And yet, knowing him had led to her death. She'd been everything he could have asked—sweet, kind, generous, loyal to the very end. She'd convinced her father to hire him as a farm hand, made sure he got more than his fair share of vittles from the cook. She'd taken him to church, introduced him for the first time to a God who could love someone like him. Maybe that was why he hadn't railed at God for taking her.

Besides, he knew Jake Cathcart had pulled the trigger, getting his revenge on Hart for alerting the local lawmen to the gang's whereabouts. God didn't enter into an outlaw's thoughts very often.

He was just starting to enter into Hart's thoughts again.

But will the pattern be any different this time, Lord? I couldn't protect Annabelle then. How can I protect Beth now? How can I keep her family from feeling that searing pain of loss?

How can I keep from feeling that pain again?

Something slid over him, warm as a coat on a cold night. Certainty? Assurance? His shoulders came down, breath came easier. All he knew was that he had work to do. With a nod, he started down the hill once more. Beth had given him a lead on the gang. He'd be mad not to take it. And by catching them, he kept her and the other citizens of Seattle safe. That was where he needed to focus.

Over the next two days, he stayed in town. He had a local draftsman make charcoal sketches based on Schneider's descriptions, nailed up wanted posters all over town, and showed them to the owners of the various businesses. Unfortunately, no one claimed any knowledge. He didn't think it was fear clogging their memories. Everyone knew everyone in Seattle. That the gang members were unknown meant they were new to the area, like the people they robbed. Still, they had to eat, had to sleep. Someone must have seen them. He kept looking.

A handful of ladies and gentlemen took in laundry for a price. Hart also checked with them, holding his breath each time, expecting them to say Beth had been there before him. She seemed to be keeping her word, however, for none reported he was the second to ask them about cleaning blood off clothing. He tracked the two instances to their source and found only mill workers who had gotten into a scuffle over a game of cards. It seemed every hint led him nowhere.

When he wasn't investigating or patrolling, he did his best to lay low. It made him a less obvious target for Beth. Besides, he'd promised her he'd accept the next invitation he was given. If he didn't open the notes left for him at the office or allow himself to be close enough to any lady while he was out, he wouldn't be invited. It was as simple as that.

With Beth, he was coming to learn, nothing was that simple.

"There you are," she proclaimed as he came out of the cabin on Thursday. "I need your help in a noble cause."

His face must have betrayed his suspicions, for she trilled a laugh. "Nothing onerous, I promise. Mary Ann Denny is hosting a gathering in her garden about a civic matter, and she requested that each of us bring a gentleman along."

So Beth wanted an escort. Hart sighed. "I'm not the tea and cookies sort."

She pressed a hand to her chest. "Who would ever refuse cookies? Come on, Hart. You never know. Maybe she's plotting sedition. I'm sure Sheriff Wyckoff would want you to be sure."

Somehow he doubted Mrs. Denny was up to anything illegal, but most likely the sheriff would encourage him to attend. His superior kept on eye on local politics. The Dennys' influence in the city was well established.

"I'll stay a few minutes," he told her. "Then I need to get to work."

"Of course." She linked arms with him as they started the short distance to the Denny house. "So, whose invitation have you decided to accept?"

"No one's," he told her. "I haven't received any."

"What! Well, I'll have to speak to Seattle's ladies. They can do better. Which would you prefer—a dinner engagement or a walk through the woods?"

"Either could get me killed."

She squeezed his arm. "Come now. The woods can be very picturesque, and our ladies don't cook so badly as to endanger your health."

"You haven't tried the pies they left. Sheriff Wyckoff is using one as a doorstop."

She laughed again. Funny how much he enjoyed that sound. It was bright, clean, filled with joy. He couldn't help smiling along.

His smile faded when he heard Mrs. Denny announce the purpose of the meeting.

"Women's suffrage?" he murmured to Beth as they stood with a dozen other people in the rear garden of the

Denny's home, surrounded by carefully tended flowers. The other women must not have been as persuasive, or as secretive, as Beth, for Hart was the only man besides Arthur Denny in attendance.

"Can you think of a nobler cause?" she murmured back. "The territorial legislature has voted it down twice, but by a narrow margin. Mary Ann feels now is the time to see it through."

Indeed she did, for the dark-haired lady went on at great length about the rights of women and their place in history, her husband nodding his bushy-haired head dutifully beside her. By the time she was done, Beth's eyes positively glowed with fervor.

"Very good to see you here, Mr. McCormick," their hostess said as she made the rounds after her stirring speech. "I find it highly encouraging that our local lawman supports our cause."

"Never really thought about it before," Hart admitted. "But if idiots are allowed to vote, I don't see why women should be denied."

Mrs. Denny blinked, mouth hanging open, and he realized how that must have sounded to her.

"I meant no disrespect, ma'am," he told her. "It's just that I've watched over any number of elections. Some of our finest citizens exercise their right to vote. So do young men with no experience and little learning, old men who have forgotten much of what they knew. Then there are the crooked types hoping to vote in someone who will do their bidding for a price. It isn't their gender that should make them eligible to vote. It's their character, their loyalty to the country they love."

Beth was staring at him now, and he had a sudden urge to bolt. Who was he to spout off? His character had once been black enough that he ought to have been banned from civic functions entirely.

"Nicely said, Deputy," Mrs. Denny replied with a nod. "A shame more gentlemen don't take the opportunity to consider such matters." She cocked her head to look up at him. "I don't suppose you'd be willing to speak at our next meeting."

Him? He glanced between her and Beth, who was so puffed up she might float off the ground like a balloon.

"Surely you have someone better," he protested.

"I think it's a marvelous idea," Beth said, as if her beaming smile would have left any doubt. "We had Susan B. Anthony and Abigail Scott Duniway visit a few years ago. Their speeches were quite inspirational, but they look at things from a woman's point of view. I think we'd highly benefit from hearing a gentleman's perspective."

He'd had to patrol the area around Sarah Yesler's house when she'd hosted the controversial suffragettes. The territorial newspapers hadn't been kind, and the sheriff had feared some citizens might show their displeasure through violence. Hart still didn't understand why the men fussed. Anyone who had braved the wilderness knew that women did as much if not more than the men. Why shouldn't they have a say in who ran things and which laws were passed?

"If you could schedule the meeting on my day off, I'll attempt to come," he told Mrs. Denny. "Just know I'm not much for speaking."

She smiled. "I agree with Miss Wallin, Deputy. We would be most interested in your thoughts. And I have been eager to hear about your progress in choosing a bride. Is a proposal imminent?" She glanced between Beth and Hart.

"I'm certain the ladies will be lining up when they hear how he supports suffrage," Beth assured her.

"That wasn't why I agreed to speak," he told Beth as the meeting began to break up.

"I know," Beth said, strolling along beside him as he walked her back to the Howards'. "But you have to admit it's a happy consequence."

Nothing happy about it. "You took me there under false pretenses," he accused her. "You didn't need my help. You were just trying to show me off again."

Her skirts were swinging. "Not entirely. Mary Ann Denny did ask us to bring along gentlemen who would support the cause. It's not my fault you were the only one in town brave enough to accept the ladies' offer. Besides, if I can't get you to buy a respectable house, the least I can do is involve you more in the community."

He had no idea how the two related, but she glanced up at the blue sky and spread her arms. "Oh, isn't it a glorious day?"

"You aren't going to give up on this, are you?" Hart asked.

She lowered her arms. "About women's suffrage? No. It's too important. And so are you." She shot him a grin. "Race you back." Picking up her skirts, she pelted ahead.

Hart watched her a moment. The veil streamed behind her, her hair glinting in the sunlight.

How did anyone stay angry with her?

He darted after her.

"Winner!" she declared, coming to a halt in front of the porch steps.

"You had a head start," he reminded her.

"Then I'll agree to a rematch. Perhaps after dinner tonight, when your work is done?"

He supposed he could have counted that an invitation, but since Allegra had offered to let him dine with the Howards whenever he liked, he really couldn't call it the "next" invitation he received. So he agreed.

With Allegra a member of the Literary Society, Hart was a little concerned Beth might mention the progress on his courtship, but she was good throughout the meal, urging Georgie to tell Hart about his new kite, Gillian to reveal her role in the school theatrical, Clay to share his latest investment and Allegra to explain the projects the Literary Society was supporting. He'd dined with the family any number of times, but he'd never had them speak so freely about their activities. Perhaps his questions sounded too much like an interrogation. How effortlessly Beth made everyone feel valued and important.

Though Beth offered to help clear the table, Allegra shooed her away. So, Beth linked arms with Hart and drew him out onto the front porch. The night was cool. Lights sparkled in the city below, brighter than the starlight peeking through the clouds. It had rained earlier, and everything smelled clean.

The light from the parlor bathed her face and set her hair to glowing. He tried not to remember how it had felt in his fingers.

"Too dark for our race, I fear," she said, turning from the view to face him. "How goes the investigation?"

He shrugged, not wanting to admit to the slow progress.

"Mr. Weinclef told me you were circulating drawings," she said. "That was very clever of you."

He fought the urge to preen. "Much good it did me. No one claims to have seen the men."

"No one?" Her exasperation matched his. "Why not?"

Mindful of Gillian and her brother in the parlor just inside the open door, Hart lowered his voice. "That's what I wondered. They may be newcomers, unknown to the rest of us, but they have to be staying somewhere in town to be able to intercept passengers from the ships so easily."

She nodded. "Newcomers, of course. No one in Seattle would be so despicable. Yet they must be conducting some sort of business in town. They've been robbing people. Surely they'd want to spend their money."

"So you would have thought. But I've checked everywhere men generally outlay cash, even the shadier places, and no one will admit to seeing them."

She leaned against the porch rail. "They must be hoarding their ill-gotten gains like a dragon his loot. But even if they're camping out and hunting for food, they'd have to replenish their ammunition. What did the laundresses say about bloody clothing?"

"All accounted for to my satisfaction. These men are invisible."

She started and put a hand on his arm. "Hart! Not invisible. Someone must be sheltering them—getting them food, doing their laundry."

She was quick. "If that's the case, it will be all the harder to find them."

"Not necessarily," she argued. "There are only a half-dozen grocers in the city. We should ask each of them if anyone seems to be buying more than the amount of food needed for the number of people in that household."

Hart eyed her. "Good idea. I'll start tomorrow, which means you don't have to."

"Oh!" As if she realized her mistake, she held out her hands, wrists up. "You caught me, Deputy. I'm ready to go peaceably."

Hart shook his head. "I'll let you off with a warning this time, Miss Wallin. Leave the investigating to me."

She laughed, but he couldn't believe she'd give up so easily, promise or no. He almost expected to see her standing at the counter when he went to talk to Weinclef at Kelloggs' the next day about people buying food.

The fastidious clerk put his long nose in the air. "We at Kelloggs' do not indulge in gossip about our clients, Deputy."

Hart affixed him with his best stare. "Talk."

Weinclef flinched, then he leaned closer and lowered his voice. "One customer has been buying a lot more than usual, but perhaps he's merely stocking his cellar. I heard he was courting."

The store seemed to be growing darker. "Who?" he asked, afraid he knew the answer.

Weinclef's Adam's apple bobbed as he swallowed. "Scout Rankin."

Hart's suspicions came flooding back. Scout's place was plenty big enough to hide two men and a boy. He knew all about victimizing others. They had only his word that he'd earned his money on the gold fields. His partner Levi Wallin had returned poorer than when he'd left.

The evidence against him was mounting, with only one thing on his side.

He was Beth's friend.

Even that might not have been enough to keep Hart

off his trail if it hadn't been for the fact that no new reports came in of newcomers being lured away and robbed, even though several more ships had docked. It was as if the gang had gone to ground or moved on.

He was considering the matter as he prowled around his cabin late Saturday night. He'd eaten dinner, including a slice of the strawberry pie that had been left at the office by another of Seattle's eager ladies, and was pleased to find the usual end-of-the-week festivities quiet when he'd ridden down Mill Street. Now he noticed the book Beth had left him earlier in the week.

"The Complete Works of Vaughn Everard, Famed Poet and Duelist," he read aloud from the cover page. Duelist, eh? Wonder who had put him in jail for the crime. He flipped to the first poem and started reading. Then he sat in the chair.

The sound of church bells ringing raised his head. Midnight? He should have ridden out an hour ago to check the town again. He closed the book and stared at it with new respect. How strange that the words of an aristocrat born nearly one hundred years ago would speak so strongly. It was as if the fellow had been sitting beside him, feet stretched to the fire. He seemed to understand how Hart felt, the hole that gaped inside him, the need to make things right, if not for himself then for others.

The words remained on his mind as he saddled Arno and headed down to the more boisterous parts of town where already raucous music played and voices rang out. Everard had written of a return to faith, a renewal of love. He'd obviously suffered loss. What had convinced him to try again? What had made him willing to risk the pain?

Beth's face came immediately to mind, eyes bright and grin conspiratorial. She'd once claimed to care for Hart. What would it be like to accept her love, to give his in return?

The sky opened, and rain fell hard. Hart pulled up his collar and tugged down his hat. He didn't need nature to confirm the feelings that shook him at the thought of letting Beth into his heart. He'd captured bandits, stopped vandals and settled disputes with hostile natives. Who would have thought the one thing to terrify him was the thought of loving a pretty woman named Beth Wallin?

Chapter Thirteen

The matter bothered Hart over the next few days. Fear was an old foe, one he'd thought he'd defeated. At times he'd feared for his life at the orphanage. Before he'd joined the gang, he'd feared he was destined to be alone. After he joined the gang, he'd feared he'd become hardened like Jake Cathcart, caring for no one but himself. In all circumstances, he'd fought the fear and found his way to the other side.

But he could see only two ways past his fear of loving Beth—drawing closer or pulling away, and neither was tenable.

He could only hope his concerns weren't written on his face when Mrs. Wyckoff caught him outside the office on Friday.

"And how are you and Miss Wallin getting along?" she asked, pausing on the boardwalk beside Arno, her yellow skirts settling about her ankles.

"Fine," Hart said, turning to check the cinch on Arno's saddle. He'd tightened it himself not an hour ago, but she wouldn't know that. So long as he kept himself busy, he might not give himself away.

"Mrs. Denny tells me you are to speak at the next women's suffrage meeting," she said. "I didn't realize you were interested in community affairs."

He checked the saddlebags as well. "Everyone ought to be interested in community affairs, ma'am. A bird knows to feather its own nest."

"Indeed it does. But I feel as if you've changed, and I can't help thinking it may have something to do with your association with Miss Wallin."

"Wouldn't surprise me," Hart allowed.

"She is a wonder," Mrs. Wyckoff mused. He heard a tapping sound. Her boot against the boardwalk?

"She's already volunteered to help Mrs. Maynard stock the shelves of her reading room, gather donations for those affected by the windstorm, and start a program to help the mill workers learn to read and write. Louisa Denny hopes to convince her to join an amateur theatrical troupe, and Mrs. Dunbar intends to ask her to join the Ladies Sewing Circle. You've known her longer than I have, Deputy. Can she do all that?"

Hart smiled as he closed the flap on the saddlebag. "Very likely. She always was a bundle of energy."

"But will she still have time to fulfill her obligation to you?"

Hart turned to face her. She was leaning forward, as if she'd been trying to catch a glimpse of his face, and her eyes were eager and bright.

"Beth Wallin is spending more time than she should on me," he told her. "She thinks that highly of you and the other ladies in the Literary Society. If you aim to blame someone that I'm not hitched yet, blame me."

Mrs. Wyckoff's mouth twitched as she straightened. "No need for blame, Mr. McCormick. We knew this would be a difficult assignment. It seems Miss Wallin is making headway. I'll ask her assessment of the situation."

She sailed off down the street. He ought to feel relieved. Instead, once more, he felt as if danger was closing in.

"Best we find Beth before she does," he murmured to Arno as he swung up into the saddle.

It took a little investigating, but he located her at the North School. A single story with an attic, the white block of a building had narrow windows and a narrow stoop, as if it held the knowledge gained there close. As he reined in at the door, Beth came out in a swish of pink skirts.

"Deputy McCormick," she greeted him as if mindful of the faces crowding at the windows. "I just finished introducing Gillian's class to the wonders of fashion. Were you scheduled to speak today too?"

Hart tipped his hat in the direction of the watching children. "I've had the pleasure of addressing both classes before. I came to speak to you."

She approached Arno, stroked his long nose. "You've accepted an invitation, is that it?"

She sounded almost disappointed.

"No invitation," he assured her. "I came to warn you. Mrs. Wyckoff wants a report on how I'm doing courting."

"Oh." She paused, and Arno bobbed his head to encourage her to keep rubbing. She smiled at him before raising her gaze to Hart's. "I'll tell her we have made great progress. It's only the truth. You've considered a new home, improved your social standing. The foundation is laid."

And it was up to him to build on it.

"She's not going to let up on you, is she?" he asked.

Beth spread her hands, earning her a snort of protest from Arno. "I expected this to be a test. She wants to be certain I have what it takes to join the most prestigious women in Seattle. I am well aware I'd be the youngest. It's a great honor."

An honor he could cost her. Yet how could he take a wife? He wasn't ready.

"I'll talk to Allegra," he said. "Maybe she can convince Mrs. Wyckoff to leave us be."

"No need," Beth said. "We'll find you a bride, Hart. It's just a matter of patience."

He'd learned to be patient over the years, hunting criminals, searching for evidence. Outwitting this frontier matchmaker would take more than patience.

It would require the commitment of his heart.

Beth congratulated herself as she got ready for church that Sunday. All in all, it had been a productive week. She'd learned more about Mr. Schneider's attackers, and Hart was on their trail. She'd contributed a few of her own ideas, which she had every hope might help him. She'd spoken with Ursula Wyckoff, who seemed satisfied with Hart's progress. Even though he'd refused to look at any more houses, he had gone with her to the suffrage meeting and even agreed to share his thoughts. Surely some lady would embolden herself to make his acquaintance, perhaps even at services this morning.

She'd also talked Mrs. Dunbar out of pursuing Hart by emphasizing the dangers of his position. She felt a little guilty about that conversation, for the lady had turned teary-eyed. She should have known that a discussion about burying a husband would raise too many memories. Not that she thought Hart was in any danger of succumbing. In the ten years she'd known him, he had resolved any number of crimes and had never been shot in the process.

She'd also fended off another attempt by her family to bring her home. This time it had been John. They couldn't have picked a better emissary. John was a favorite among her family, perhaps because he most resembled their mother with his auburn hair and forest-green eyes. He was also the most reasonable and understanding, making her feel a little guilty about arguing with him.

"You know I have the utmost respect for the ladies of the Literary Society," he said as he and Beth stood on the Howard porch and he delivered the books she had requested Simon send. "They helped fund the library at Wallin Landing. But surely whatever cause they're supporting now doesn't take all your time."

"Enough," she told him, fingering the worn leather covers of the books. "And I'm helping Scout as well."

John's smile was commiserating. "You're a good friend, Beth. But Scout's a grown man. He's been to the gold fields and back. He can take care of himself."

Beth shoved the books onto the porch rail. "And I can't?"

He spread his hands. "It's more a case of we can't. Without you, Wallin Landing is a mess."

Her stomach knotted. "Oh, no! What's happened?"

His answers were vague and did nothing to still her rising concern. Finally, he hung his head. "It's Dottie," he confessed. "She's never been through a Wallin Easter. She's not prepared for all the traditions. You'll know how to help her feel more at ease."

Figure on John to focus on his wife. The two had married less than a year ago, after Beth had brought the mail-order bride to Seattle. They were devoted to each other and Dottie's toddler, as Beth had known they would be.

"Callie's new too," Beth reminded him. "And they're both smart. If you and Levi explain things to them, I'm sure they'll be fine."

John rubbed the back of his neck. "Maybe. But you're so much better at this. When you're home, we can just leave things to you."

"Then perhaps it's a good thing I'm not home," Beth told him. "You were becoming entirely too dependent. Now, tell me how things are really going."

She'd been able to draw from him a full report of how plans were progressing for Easter. It didn't sound like such a mess to her. Just in case anyone needed her advice, she sent a list of reminders home with him.

The one task she had been unable to accomplish was to talk to Scout about Mrs. Jamison. It wasn't generally proper for a lady to visit a bachelor at home, but this was Scout! She'd stopped by several times, but no one had answered her knocks. And she hadn't been able to locate him in town either.

She mentioned the matter to Hart as he walked with her to church that morning. Allegra and Clay were just ahead, holding hands in such an endearing manner that Beth could only sigh at the sweetness of it. Gillian and Georgie were even farther in front, obviously hoping to reach the churchyard in time to meet friends before services.

"Odd," Hart said, gaze going off to the town spread below. "The gang seems to have disappeared as well."

Beth gasped. "You don't think they took Scout, do you?"

The dark look he shot her told her everything. "Hart McCormick! Don't you dare assume Scout is involved. He'd never harm anyone."

"I want to believe that," he said slowly with a grimace, "but he was an accessory to his father's crimes."

"That was a long time ago," Beth said primly. "And Scout only did that under duress. His father beat him if he didn't comply. That's how he got that broken nose, you know. He wouldn't let Drew's wife, Catherine, treat it even though she's a trained nurse. He was so afraid of how his father would react."

Hart said nothing, and Beth glanced over at him. Both hands had tightened at his sides. The tailors had finished his new coat, and the gray fabric did indeed bring out the depth of his eyes. The look in them made her catch her breath.

"You didn't know. I'm sorry, Hart, but it's true. Scout was as much a victim as the men his father made him lure in. He wouldn't be involved with the gang. He couldn't."

He nodded. "I hope you're right. It seemed to me he'd changed. And Mrs. Jamison certainly finds him a gentleman worth pursuing."

Now it was Beth's turn to scowl. "That's what I'd like to discuss with him." She stopped at the edge of the churchyard where she'd hoped to waylay Scout. Several other men were loitering just outside the gates, as if waiting until the last minute to meet with their Creator. A few cast her glances. One went so far as to wink. Beth put her back to them.

Just then she spotted the yellow carriage coming up the hill. She waved to Scout as he reined in. Tying his horses, he approached with a smile. The tailors had been busy, for they'd also finished the navy wool suit she'd picked out for him. Both the color and the styling made him look polished, confident. She hated to darken his mood, but he needed to understand the situation before Mrs. Jamison convinced him to do something he would later regret.

"Scout, I must speak with you," she said, taking his arm. Hart moved a little away from them as if to give them privacy.

"What's wrong?" Scout asked with a frown. "Has something happened to Levi or the rest of your family?"

"No, but I fear something will happen to you. What possessed you to start pursuing Mrs. Jamison?"

Color flashed into his narrow cheeks, making his scar stand out. "Why shouldn't I pursue her? She's beautiful, and sweet, and kind, and she's all alone in the world, like me."

Beautiful, perhaps, but Beth would have called her cunning instead of kind. And she wasn't alone. She had Bobby.

"Mrs. Jamison could snap her fingers and have a dozen men jump to her call. In fact, that's just what she did last week when she dropped her hanky."

He stared at her. "What are you talking about?"

Beth sighed. "It's a known gambit to get a fellow's attention. I wasn't sure who she was after that day, but apparently, you've piqued her interest. Here, I'll show you." She pulled her handkerchief out of the reticule she'd made to replace the one she'd lost and lifted it high with two fingers. Releasing it, she watched it flutter toward the ground.

"Oh, dear," she said, raising her voice. "I seem to have dropped something."

The world exploded. One of the fellows loitering nearby rushed forward only to bump heads with his comrade who must have had the same thought. A third bent for the hanky while a fourth shoved him aside. The first two got into fisticuffs, while the second two said a few choice words that she was sure should never be uttered in the presence of a lady. Scout clutched her arm and drew her back from the melee.

A shot rang out. Beth gasped, people closer to the church ducked for cover, and everyone else froze.

Hart lowered his gun. "Enough. I ought to arrest the lot of you for breaking the peace."

The men lowered their gazes, shuffled their feet, muttered apologies that seemed more directed at Beth than the lawman.

"Get inside and thank the Lord for my patience," Hart ordered them. "And ask Him for the sense to make better decisions," he added as they hurried past.

Scout shook his head, releasing her arm. "You made your point, Beth. But you've forgotten something. Mrs. Jamison wouldn't drop her hanky to attract my attentions. I'm nothing special."

Her heart hurt for him. "Yes, Scout, you are. You're kind and loyal and hardworking. My point is she hadn't known you long enough to realize all that before furthering your acquaintance, which makes me afraid she's interested in something else entirely."

His brow cleared, and he looked away. "Of course.

The money. I should have realized. I just thought she didn't know about Pa, so she might like me for me."

"And so she should!" Beth wanted to grab the lady and shake her until her fancy hairpins fell.

"And so she might," Hart said quietly, moving closer. "Only time will tell, Scout. You can give the lady that much."

Beth frowned at him, but Scout nodded. "Good advice, Deputy. Thank you both for your concern." He pushed past Beth for the church.

Beth sighed. "You didn't have to defend her."

"I didn't intend to. Scout Rankin never struck me as stupid. Maybe he could figure things out on his own."

John had said something similar. Was she becoming so used to matchmaking she'd overstepped?

"I just want him to be sure," she told Hart. "He doesn't have to jump at the first woman to look his way. Any number of young ladies would be pleased to have Scout court them."

"You sure about that? He's right. Anyone who's lived in Seattle longer than five years will remember his father, and not kindly."

"But Scout isn't his father. He shouldn't be judged by the man's deeds."

The church bell began ringing. Beth grabbed Hart's hand. "Hurry! We're late!"

"Hold on." He pulled her up short and held out his free hand. "You forgot this."

In his fingers was her handkerchief. She took it from him, searched his face. Something softened those hard gray eyes, warmed his smile. He turned and strode for the building as if to hide the emotion from her.

Beth stared after him. He had to have heard Scout's

comment. He must know a gentleman returned a lady's handkerchief to indicate she'd succeeded in attracting his attention.

What was he trying to say?

Chapter Fourteen

Hart found it a little harder to focus on Mr. Bagley's sermon that Sunday. Beside him, Beth had sung with her usual enthusiasm and bowed her head to pray with the same devotion, but at odd moments she glanced his way with a frown, fingers clutching her handkerchief. Did he have dirt on his face? He surreptitiously rubbed at each cheek just in case, but her looks didn't cease.

Still, the minister's words poked at him. Love again. It was almost as if the Almighty was trying to tell him something. As the congregation followed Mr. Bagley in prayer, he reached out.

Lord, You know how much I regret what I've done, how it ended. I've tried to be a better man since then. But love, real love? I don't know if I'm ready.

A verse popped into his head. *Greater love hath no man than this, that a man lay down his life for his friends.*

He'd heard that said before, at Annabelle's funeral. She'd certainly lived its truth. Could he?

The service seemed to have set Beth to thinking as

well, for her head was down, her steps small and determined as she walked beside him through the churchyard.

"We in a hurry?" he couldn't help asking.

She slowed as they reached the street. "What? Oh, no. No hurry."

He didn't believe her. "Something bothering you, Beth?"

She shifted on her feet, gaze shooting past him. He didn't have to follow it to know when she spotted Scout with Mrs. Jamison. Beth's mouth tightened, and her eyes narrowed.

He'd seen the pair the moment he and Beth had left the church. Even though Beth was annoyed with the woman, he'd thought she would go into raptures over the fancy gray dress trimmed in black and white, the white net fluttering around the seamstress's feathered hat. With Bobby at her elbow, Mrs. Jamison and Scout were now conversing with Mr. and Mrs. Arthur Denny, with the Hortons waiting their turn nearby.

"The cream of Seattle society," Hart remarked. "Scout's making his mark."

Beth started, and pink flushed her cheeks as if she was embarrassed to be caught staring. "Yes, I suppose it is good that Scout is being accepted at last."

"But…" he pressed.

She looked at him with a smile. "But I would appreciate it more under other circumstances."

She surely had it in for the seamstress. Hart glanced at Scout again. The fellow had ducked his head respectfully to listen to something the railroad president was saying. The same pink tinged Scout's cheeks.

"I need to know more about Mrs. Jamison," Beth

murmured. "It would either assure me of her intentions or give me something to convince Scout to leave her be."

"You want the best for Scout," Hart told her. "She's pretty and likeable, and it seems her husband didn't leave her well enough off because she's still working. Scout's not the shiniest penny in the bunch, shy and wealthy. Why shouldn't they make a match?"

Beth rounded on him. "First, Mr. McCormick, a lady's attributes go beyond her looks. Second, one can use one's talents with or without income from another source. Would you expect Rockefeller to retire after he made his first hundred dollars? Samuel Colt to stop refining his revolver?"

She had a point. "Very well. Mrs. Jamison is dedicated to her profession. She might also have money of her own. So, why do you think she's after Scout's?"

Her gaze returned to the other couple. "Because she seems more interested in how being with him could improve her life than how she might improve his."

Sacrificial love, as the minister had said. It was a high ideal. No doubt Beth expected it in her romances. But having seen it in action, he wasn't sure he agreed that the other person was always better off for the sacrifice. There had been a time he would have done anything to change places with Annabelle, to lose his life instead of losing her.

Scout must have finished his conversation with the Hortons, for he led Bobby and Mrs. Jamison their way. The widow's smile didn't falter, but he thought he saw a tightening around her eyes as they approached.

"Lovely day for a stroll," Scout said with a nod to Beth and Hart. "I thought we might stop at Kelloggs'. They have a new ice cream churn. Care to join us?"

Hart thought Beth would perk up at that. It wasn't

easy to come by the treat in Seattle. Instead she put her hand on Scout's arm. "Not today, thank you. But Scout, I just realized I hadn't invited you to spend Easter with us."

Scout glanced at Hart. "Us?"

Beth seemed oblivious to the undertone. "Yes, all of us at Wallin Landing. I confirmed plans with John just this week. We'll have a wonderful feast with some of your favorites. I know how you like Levi's biscuits."

Scout's smile widened. Hart understood why. The youngest Wallin brother was famous for baking biscuits light enough to fly.

"There will be a special service too," Beth continued as if encouraged by Scout's reaction. "Callie and Simon are playing a duet. Nora organized the egg rolling. And Rina has a school recital scheduled for the evening, with the community invited to share talents as well. Please say you'll join us."

His eyes lit. "I wouldn't miss it. I know you'll enjoy it, Evangeline."

The seamstress batted her eyes at him, but Beth dropped her hand. "Oh, I'm not sure our little get-together would interest Mrs. Jamison."

She turned her smile on Beth. "You'd be surprised what interests me, Miss Wallin. Unfortunately, I really should stay in town with Bobby. I'd hate to leave him alone for the holiday."

Bobby's smile was even more strained. "You could go, Evie. I'll be fine. Maybe Deputy McCormick and I could keep each other company."

Him? Hart peered closer at the boy, noting his pallor, the way he edged back from his sister.

"Don't be silly," Mrs. Jamison said with a stern look

Bobby's way. "Deputy McCormick has more important matters to attend to." She turned to Hart. "Have you caught that horrible gang yet, Deputy?"

The question was all soft inquiry, but he felt the heat behind it. Was she worried the danger might approach her door?

"Just about, ma'am," he said. "Thank you for asking."

"You see?" she told her brother. "We have no need to fear when Deputy McCormick is on duty." She aimed her smile at Scout, hand stroking his arm as if she were petting a tabby. Hart had never seen the motion so proprietary. Maybe Beth had the right of it after all.

"You must accept Miss Wallin's kind offer, Thomas," the widow murmured. "I wouldn't dream of depriving you of time with your friends. All I ask is that you bring me back tales of your triumphs."

Hart wasn't sure church services and egg rolling constituted triumphs, but Scout smiled fatuously, promised to join Beth for Easter and excused himself to stroll off with his lady, Bobby following, after a forlorn look in Hart's direction.

"Well," Beth said.

Hart raised a brow. "I thought you'd be pleased. You managed to separate them."

"And made her a martyr in the process." She shook her head. "I almost wish she had agreed to come. Nothing shows up tin like true silver."

"I'd like to see her up against all the Wallin ladies," Hart agreed. "But you'll probably have more fun without her."

"There is that." She put her hand on his arm and gave it a squeeze. "Why don't you join us, too, Hart? My whole family adores you."

He found that hard to believe. All her brothers were upstanding gentlemen. What need did they have for someone like him? Of course, none knew about his past. Maybe they saw the badge and assumed the man wearing it had a character as bright. He started to demur, when an idea struck.

He cocked his head. "Is that an invitation?"

"Of course it is." Her smile brightened as if to prove it.

"In that case, I accept."

"Good. You might want to ride out early that morning to be in time for service. I'm sure you could bunk with the logging crew so you could stay for the concert."

"Wise plan," Hart said.

She frowned. "Why are you smiling like that? Are you so pleased with the festivities?"

"Your family knows how to enjoy a holiday," he assured her. "I'm glad to be invited to join."

"Oh." She relaxed. He ought to leave well enough alone, but he couldn't help adding, "After all, I promised to accept the next invitation I received."

"Oh!" Her head came up, eyes blazing. "Hart McCormick, you know what I meant. This doesn't count."

"First invitation from a lady," he replied. "That's the first invitation, and I'll jail any man who claims you aren't a lady."

She shook her head. "You are impossible. Is one dinner, one promenade too much to ask to become better acquainted with a lady you might want to court?"

He crossed his arms over his chest. "Yes. I'm not going courting."

"Why are you so pigheaded?"

They were attracting attention. Heads turned their

direction, frowns began to form. Hart took Beth's arm and led her away from the church. "You know where I stand on the matter. I don't see why my refusal is such a surprise."

"What's a surprise is your determination. I thought with the right lady, the right circumstances…"

"I'd give in. I won't, Beth. Not now, not ever."

Her jaw moved back and forth, as if she were fighting to keep words inside. Finally, she squared her shoulders. "Very well. Have your fun. Just remember two can play at this game."

He was certain a cloud crossed over the sun. "Now, Beth…"

Her sweet smile didn't reassure him. "Never fear. I already spoke with Mrs. Dunbar and warned her off your trail. No, I had something else in mind."

"Like what?" he asked, not sure he wanted to hear the answer.

"Perhaps it's time I started my own investigation."

She had the satisfaction of seeing his face darken like a thundercloud. "You gave me your word."

"And I intend to keep it," she told him. "I promised not to investigate the men who hurt Mr. Schneider. I never said I wouldn't look into anyone else."

"Beth Wallin…"

"Hart McCormick." She pulled out of his grip. "Thank you for your escort to church. I have plans for the rest of the day. I hope you enjoy yours." She sauntered up the street. A quick glance back showed her he was following her. Did he intend protection or deflection? Either way, she wasn't about to gratify him. She walked straight back to the Howard house and shut the door behind her.

Oh, but she had an idea. Could she follow through on it? He had certainly paled when she'd mentioned an investigation. She wasn't going to do anything rash or dangerous. Very likely he thought she meant to investigate Mrs. Jamison, which she fully intended to do. But his continued refusal to take even the smallest steps toward matrimony was beginning to concern her.

She'd become so accustomed to having him a part of her life—always in the background, a dependable force for good, a legendary figure—that she'd never really questioned what she knew of him. Now she understood he'd been raised in an orphanage, which meant his parents had passed on. It sounded as if he didn't remember either of them. How sad. She'd been four when Pa had died. All she had of him were stories. But Ma had been a big part of her life, guiding her, encouraging her. She couldn't imagine having no one.

Still, his barren upbringing hadn't stopped him from forming attachments. Sheriff Wyckoff and his wife had only the highest regard for him. He and Clay had long discussions about politics and world affairs. She saw them out at the paddock from time to time. He treated Georgie and Gillian kindly, and he was trying to encourage Bobby Donovan. Her brothers relied on his judgment. What had she missed?

Ciara had said that Maddie knew more about Hart. Perhaps it was time Beth learned more as well. She waited at the upstairs window until she saw him ride out on Arno. Then she hurried back downstairs and headed across town.

Maddie Haggerty generally took Sundays off. She

and her family had originally lived in a four-room flat above the bakery. Her husband, Michael, had built them a bigger house on Fourth Avenue a few years ago. With bric-a-brac around the roofline, and white and yellow paint, it resembled some of the cakes Maddie made.

The Haggertys were delighted to see her when Beth showed up at the door. She had known Maddie since the Irishwoman had arrived with the second Mercer Expedition in 1866. Michael had arrived a year later, escorting Ciara and Aiden out from New York to live with their sister. The burly longshoreman-turned-blacksmith and the outspoken baker had fallen in love. Their son Stephen was now six years old. He had his father's thick black hair and his mother's shining brown eyes.

But as cute as Stephen was, Beth had come to see Maddie. It took a little maneuvering to get her alone. After all, they expected she'd come to see Ciara. But a whispered conversation with her friend was enough to convince Ciara of Beth's need. Accordingly, Ciara chivied the rest of the family into the rear yard to play battledore.

"Was there ever anyone more devoted to the game?" Maddie remarked with a shake of her red head as she poured Beth another cup of tea. "How is it you're immune, me darling girl?"

Even after more than two decades in America, Maddie still hadn't lost the lilt of Ireland in her voice. Beth leaned closer where she sat on the rose-patterned sofa in the parlor. "I'm as competitive as the rest of them, I fear. But today, I have another task in mind. Maddie, Ciara tells me you know more about Deputy McCormick than most of us. I need your assistance. You see, I'm trying to find him a bride."

Maddie's eyes widened. "Why would you be doing that?"

She willed her cheeks not to heat. "The Literary Society asked me to lend a hand."

Maddie leaned back. "What a kind, sweet girl you are to agree. I'd have told them to mind their own affairs."

Beth chuckled. "I probably should have done the same. But if I didn't agree, they'd have found someone else who might not have had his best interests at heart. Deputy McCormick agreed to let me try."

"Did he now? That surprises me."

Beth raised her chin. "I can be very persuasive."

"Of that I have no doubt. So, he agreed to let you match him. Why do you need my help?"

"Because he fights every step. I thought at first he was just like my brothers. You know how they hesitated, until they met the right woman."

"Ah, but they were no proof against your cozening ways," Maddie said, shaking a finger at her. "Hart McCormick is used to being the one in command."

"I've noticed. Yet it seems to be more than that. It's as if something is holding him back. He simply refuses to court."

Maddie's fingers cradled the delicate china of the tea cup. "Are you certain the problem lies with him?"

"Yes," Beth insisted. "It's not the ladies. I assure you, they're quite interested now that I've drawn him to their attention."

"As well they should be. He's a fine figure of a man, established in his career, respected."

Beth nodded. "My assessment exactly."

"Sure-n but you've always had a soft spot for the fellow."

She flinched, and Maddie's sharp eyes narrowed. She should have realized she'd have to share a confidence to get one.

She glanced out the parlor door, but saw no one. A call from outside assured her the others were involved in their sport. She drew in a breath and met Maddie's gaze.

"Very well. I will admit that I thought I loved him. It was merely a silly schoolgirl infatuation. I asked him outright whether he might want to court me. He sent me off with a curt word."

"Ah." Maddie's look softened, and she set down the cup. "It's sorry I am to hear that. You might have made a fine pair."

She wasn't sure whether to feel vindicated or depressed. "It doesn't matter. My proposal to him was more than a year ago. It should have no bearing on his current feelings toward marriage. And if it was only me he objected to, he wouldn't be fighting my matchmaking now."

"I still don't understand why you're so set on finding him a bride," Maddie said. "Tell the Literary Society he'll have none of it and leave the man be."

Beth sagged. "But Maddie, doesn't he deserve a happily-ever-after?"

Maddie's face crumpled. "Ah, me darling girl, of course he does. Only I'm thinking he had all that and lost it."

Beth stared at her. "What?"

Maddie rose to her feet and set about pacing the room, emerald skirts belling around her. "'Tis a tale of woe, to be sure, and I'm not thinking he'd thank me for the sharing of it."

"That bad?" Beth bit her lip a moment. Did she really

want to know? Did she have a right to know? Yet how could she help Hart if she remained ignorant?

"Truly, Maddie," she said, "I won't tell a soul."

Maddie's gaze was hard on Beth's. "I'll have your promise on that. If I hear the story from another, I'll know where it came from."

"Maddie." Beth tried not to look as hurt as she felt. "People tell me all sorts of things in confidence. I'm no gossip."

Maddie's smile was comforting. "No, but you have been known to shout out your thoughts. This one you'll likely have to take to your grave, for it could not only cost Hart his position but his friendship with you."

Beth felt as if the walls pressed closer, yet she could not back away, not now. "I understand, Maddie. Tell me. Why is Hart so set on remaining a bachelor?"

Chapter Fifteen

Maddie went to close the parlor door before returning to Beth's side on the sofa. Her brown gaze was troubled.

"I only learned of Hart's story by accident," she murmured. "It was when Michael and I were courting. You remember when there was trouble for the Irish in Seattle."

Beth nodded. A sympathizer for a dreaded Irish gang in New York had arrived in Seattle and begun to stir up sentiments. Stores had been robbed, buildings vandalized, and Maddie's first bakery had been burned to the ground before Hart and Sheriff Wyckoff, working with Michael and the other Irish, had stopped the villain.

"Hart had always been kind to me," Maddie went on with a smile. "Sure-n but I think he liked the fact that I wasn't afraid of his dour looks. But he suspected Michael of being part of a gang because he wanted the Irish to band together and protect our families. Hart was wrong, of course, but I couldn't seem to get him to see that. He and I had words, and I accused him in front of the sheriff of not understanding what it meant to protect those he loved."

"Oh, you must have been angry with him," Beth said. "You know he fights for justice, for those who have been hurt. But of course you had to stand up for Michael. What did Hart say?"

Maddie's smile turned rueful. "He walked out on me. Sheriff Wyckoff told me the truth of it. I'm thinking he didn't want me to have the wrong impression of his deputy. He admires Hart a great deal."

"So does his wife," Beth assured her.

"Then you can understand it took a lot for the sheriff to be telling me what he knew of Hart. You see, Hart used to ride with an outlaw gang."

Beth surged to her feet. "That's not true!"

"Would you be calling me a liar, then?"

Maddie's quiet voice was nearly as challenging as Hart's. Beth forced herself to sit. "No, of course not. I'm sorry, Maddie. It's just…an outlaw?"

Maddie nodded. "You can see why some might not take too kindly to the notion. Their deputy, the man they rely on for protection, on the other side of the law?"

She could certainly see the point. Small wonder Maddie was careful to whom she told the tale. Some of Seattle's more militant citizens might call for his resignation, or worse.

"But why would he be an outlaw?" Beth protested, fingers pleating the material of her skirts. "That goes against everything he stands for."

"Sure-n, it goes against what he stands for now," Maddie agreed, watching her. "But he wasn't always as you know him. You heard he was raised in an orphanage?"

Beth nodded. "He told me he hated it so much he ran away."

"When he was about thirteen," Maddie confirmed. "He was likely on his own for a bit. Sure-n but he must have been lonely, maybe even hungry at times. I'm thinking a gang of outlaws might seem like a family of sorts to a lad like that. That's how the gangs recruit in New York, preying on those who feel like outcasts."

Beth twisted the handle on her teacup, rocking the china left to right and back again. She could imagine Hart as a defiant, lonely boy, looking for something better, not unlike Mrs. Jamison's brother Bobby. Thinking he'd finally found approval from men who would only use him. After reading about adventures, he would have wanted some of his own.

"Sheriff Wyckoff didn't say why," Maddie continued, smoothing down her emerald skirts, "but Hart gave up on his thieving ways and left the gang behind. I'm thinking it's because he fell in love."

The words felt like a slap. "He was in love?"

"So the sheriff said. But the outlaws were none too pleased with his leaving, and they came looking for him. His sweetheart tried to protect him and was killed for her trouble."

Beth gasped. The shock was almost as if she had been shot herself. She should jump to her feet again, run from the house, find Hart and beg his pardon for trying to force a wife on him. Yet she couldn't move. What pain he must have endured to watch the woman he loved die for him. She didn't know her name, but she mourned her loss, knowing how Hart must have mourned.

How he was still mourning.

Was this why he insisted on dark colors for his clothing? It was said Queen Victoria still wore the black, fifteen years after her husband's death. Was Hart wearing the black for his lost love?

"You see why he might not be so willing to try again," Maddie said, voice gentle.

"Of course," Beth murmured. Having loved and lost, he had no room in his heart for another. What woman in Seattle could possibly compare to his martyred sweetheart?

How could she possibly compare?

"You'll remember your promise, now," Maddie said, gaze once more watchful. "You'll be telling no one, not even the good deputy."

Beth stared at her. "Not even Hart? How can I look at him the same way again? He'll notice."

Maddie made a face. "Perhaps he will at that. But I doubt he knows the sheriff confided in me. He'll not react well when he realizes others have heard of his pain. Have you not seen he's a private sort?"

"Yes, but I thought it was because of his work. You really shouldn't tell other people that you suspect one of their friends of a crime."

"True," Maddie allowed. "He volunteers little about his work. Less about himself. We should be respecting that, Beth."

Beth frowned. "If we are his friends, shouldn't we help him carry his burdens rather than pretend they don't exist?"

Now Maddie frowned. "'Tis a fine thought, to be sure. But I'm thinking the deputy would tell us if he needed our help."

"He wouldn't," Beth said with certainty. "He values his privacy, as you said. And he would bear up under any pain alone. Anything else opens your heart too much."

Maddie's face puckered. "Oh, but you're right there, me girl. Yet I'm thinking your own heart's the one touched. You said you were no longer infatuated with him, Beth, but sure-n I'm finding it hard to believe you. Are you still pining for the fellow?"

She opened her mouth to deny it, then closed her lips. In truth, she wasn't sure how she felt about Hart. At the moment, all of her hurt for him. Was that a sign she still loved him?

She wasn't about to share her doubts, with Maddie or him. "Perhaps I'm a private person as well."

Maddie laughed, a lighthearted sound that made Beth smile despite herself. "Oh, no, me girl, it's too late for that. You've never been private. What you think, what you feel, shines from your face for all to see."

She certainly hoped Maddie was wrong. Or at least that she'd matured to the point where she could control her face, hide herself from hurt.

"Then I suppose it's impossible for me to keep my promise to you," she told Maddie. "If my face betrays me, I'll never be able to keep Hart from guessing I know about his past."

Maddie sighed. "That's only the truth. I should have thought of it before telling you. Still, I can't regret you knowing. If you need to be discussing the matter with him, for his good, not your own, then I'll absolve you of your vow to keep silent in front of him."

"Thank you," Beth said. She wasn't sure why she felt so relieved. She would not enjoy the conversation. How was she to find the courage to even broach the subject?

How did you discuss a death so personal? How did you commiserate about such a tragedy?

On the other hand, how could she keep quiet, knowing that the pain was what likely kept him from finding love again?

Hart had thought when Beth had declared her intentions of mounting an investigation that she would go after Mrs. Jamison. He wasn't sure what she could learn on a Sunday afternoon, with some businesses and the telegraph office closed and many families spending time together. When she'd stayed in the Howard house longer than he'd expected, he'd hoped Allegra and Clay had pulled her into their family activities. Mounting Arno, he'd ridden down into town. A quick sweep assured him that everyone was behaving, so he'd returned the horse to pasture in time to see Beth heading down Fourth. The finest houses, the finest families, were situated along the hillside. Even in his fancy new suit, he looked like a hawk among doves as he followed.

She was well known by most of the families, but he wasn't entirely surprised to see her make a beeline for Maddie's. Yet if Beth was intent on investigating, what did she think the Haggertys could tell her about the seamstress? As far as he knew, neither Maddie nor Ciara frequented Mrs. Jamison's establishment. And he hadn't seen either with the lady socially. What was Beth up to?

Her countenance when she left an hour later was so subdued he nearly banged on the door to demand what had happened. Her bowed head, her slow walk, told him she carried a heavy burden. She didn't even notice him.

Had something happened to a member of her large family? Why would Maddie know before Beth did?

He followed her at a discreet distance, but she only returned to the Howard house. Though he remained on duty in the area for another hour, she never stepped out again. The smoke from the chimney assured him Allegra and Clay were home. Were they comforting her?

Why did he feel that should be his role?

At length, concern propelled him to the door. Clay invited him in, bid him make himself comfortable by the fire in the parlor, but he caught no sign of Beth. When he went so far as to ask, Clay informed him that Beth had retired to her room, pleading a headache. He didn't see her again that evening.

Over the next few days, he expected her to approach him at the house or in town. Very likely, she'd argue further with him about the Easter invitation, perhaps trot out another lady or two for his approval. But she seemed to be busy with other matters.

"You angry with me?" he asked when he spotted her coming out of the house Tuesday morning.

Her smile was as bright as usual. "Not at all. But you should know Mary Ann Denny is talking about a women's march after Easter. You might want to alert the sheriff."

"I'll do that," he said, but she sailed past before he could question her further.

Why hadn't she asked about his investigation? He'd come to enjoy talking about the case with her. She always had something to contribute that got him thinking. Why hadn't she pressed her case about courting? He couldn't believe he'd finally convinced her to give up her quest to find him a bride. She'd been determined when she'd left the churchyard. The change in her had come after she'd talked with Maddie.

He stayed in town Wednesday, telling himself he should keep an eye out for the gang. The only suspicious person he saw was Bobby Donovan. He spotted the youth lounging outside Kelloggs', gaze on the passing horses.

"Shouldn't you be in school?" Hart called, urging Arno closer.

Bobby straightened. "Evie hasn't enrolled me yet. Are you looking for someone?"

He wasn't about to go into details. "Always."

Bobby's smile hitched up. "It must be fun being a lawman."

"I wouldn't call chasing dangerous men fun," Hart countered. "But there's a certain satisfaction to it. Come down to the office sometime. The sheriff would be happy to talk to you about the profession and your future."

His eager look evaporated. "Evie wouldn't like it."

Hart nodded. "She'd worry about you, no doubt. But you have to do what you're meant to do. It's up to you to decide where your path leads. Just pray about it, and see that it points toward something worthwhile."

Bobby nodded. "Yes, sir. Thank you."

"Any time." He turned Arno and eyed Bobby over his shoulder. "And Donovan? I mean that. You need anything, you let me know."

"Scout and Aiden said the same thing," Bobby assured him. "It's nice to know I have friends."

With a tip of his hat, Hart rode on. A shame he and Beth couldn't talk so easily at the moment, but there were too many concerns, on both sides.

By Thursday, he had had enough. Something had happened, and he needed to know what if he was to protect Beth. So, he stopped by the bakery. Ciara was at the university, but the young lady who was acting as counter clerk let him through the curtained doorway to speak to the baker herself.

Maddie's bakery had expanded over the years. Three worktables stretched out in front of the brick ovens, heat radiating around the room as Maddie's four assistants, all of them women, prepared for the next round of baking. Cloth-draped trays waited with rising dough. Sugar and spice scented the air.

Maddie was bent over a rack of cookies, piping on icing. She straightened at the sight of him and raised her hands. "Sure-n you caught me, Deputy. I'm guilty of putting icing on this morning's cookies for me own family."

"It's rare you don't sell out," he answered with a smile. "I imagine your family will be glad for the excess." Moving closer, he lowered his voice. "I need to talk to you. I'm worried about Beth Wallin. Do you know what's troubling her?"

Maddie picked up a cloth and busied herself wiping her hands. "She's probably just deep in plans for Easter. The lady's never been one to let grass grow under her feet."

Hart watched the color climb in her cheeks. She was hiding something. "You're sure? She seems to have changed since she came to see you Sunday."

Maddie gazed up at him, head cocked. "And how would you be knowing that, unless you followed her?"

Hart stepped back. "Just keeping an eye on the town. That's my job."

"To be sure. But she's not the girl you met eight years ago. Beth Wallin can take care of herself, from my way of thinking."

"Most people can take care of themselves until disaster strikes."

Maddie chuckled. "Disaster, it is now? Flood, famine or fire, Deputy?"

Hart shook his head. "Make light of it if you will, but you know Seattle can be a dangerous place."

Her smile faded. "Indeed I do. It can also be a carefree, warm and loving place. I'm thinking you need reminding of that."

"All I need right now is to know that Beth Wallin is fine."

Maddie shrugged. "Then it's Beth Wallin you should be asking, not me."

He couldn't argue with that. Excusing himself, and accepting her offer of a cookie for his trouble, he headed back onto the street.

Beth had been staying close to the Howards, so he tried the main house first. He was rewarded with news from the housekeeper that Beth and Allegra were out back with Arno. He found the ladies standing beside an empty patch of ground stretching from the house toward the stables. They made a fine picture, Allegra's dark, sleek head close to Beth's bright curls.

Allegra spotted him first. "Deputy," she greeted him. "Come join us. We were just discussing what vegetables I might plant once the risk of frost is past. What do you think—Windsor beans or carrots?"

"Always partial to carrots myself," he offered, but his gaze was drawn to where Beth was studying the rocky soil. She was wearing one of her pink dresses today, but the ruffles seemed to be sagging with her spirit.

"That was Beth's opinion as well," Allegra said, brushing down her own violet skirts. "I have seeds from the apple tree your mother put in, Beth. I thought a row of trees would do very nicely there." She pointed to the end of the garden.

Beth raised her head and eyed the spot. "Better to plant them at the north or south rather than the east or west. Otherwise, as they grow, they'll shade the garden a good part of the day."

Allegra laughed. "And that's why I need your help. Being raised in Boston, what do I know about growing fruits and vegetables?"

It wasn't Boston as much as the Howard family and her family's wealth that had kept her out of the dirt. The death of her first husband, Clay's younger brother, had encouraged her to try elsewhere, to be her own person, she'd claimed. She had only bloomed in confidence since coming to Seattle.

"But surely you didn't seek us for my pitiful farming skills," she told Hart now. "How can we help you, Deputy?"

"I have a few questions for Miss Wallin," he replied.

Beth immediately perked up. "Questions? About your investigation?"

"I'll just pace off the plot," Allegra told them, moving away. He could only appreciate how she gave them privacy while still honoring her role as chaperone.

"What happened?" Beth asked, closing the distance between them. Her blue eyes were wide. "Was someone else attacked? Did you capture one of the men?"

"No," Hart said, feeling suddenly foolish for being so concerned.

She frowned. "But you said you had questions for me."

He spread his hands. "Well, you've been too quiet lately."

Now her brows shot up. "Me? Too quiet? No one's ever complained about that before."

"I just wanted to make sure you were all right."

"Oh." She dropped her gaze, pink skirts swinging as she must have shuffled her feet. "I'm fine. You needn't worry."

But he had been worried, and that fact in itself frustrated him. When had he become so attuned to her, the way she shifted, the way her breath hissed past her lips?

How soft her lips looked.

"Did you do as you threatened?" he pressed. "Did you start your own investigation? Did you learn something that troubled you?"

She shook her head, and he almost let himself relax. "But something's concerning you," he insisted.

She sighed. "Why do I bother trying to hide anything from you? You are simply too good a lawman to be fooled."

Hart widened his stance. "So, what happened? What did you discover about Mrs. Jamison?"

She glanced up, eying Allegra at the far side of the patch. "I haven't learned much about Mrs. Jamison yet. Something else is troubling me. I can't talk further here. Meet me tonight at eight, by the gate to the pasture."

He glanced at Allegra as well. Surely nothing Beth had discovered touched the Howards. But the fact that she felt she must protect them from the information tightened his gut.

"Make it six," he said. "And don't be late."

Chapter Sixteen

Beth slipped out into the twilight, pulling her coat close in the growing cold. Clouds made the sky heavy. She felt just as heavy.

She'd avoided Hart most of the week, afraid by word or deed she'd blurt out what she now knew. Allegra and Clay had commented on her reticence. Gillian and Georgie tiptoed past the guest room as if afraid she had some dire disease. She couldn't tell them it was her heart that hurt.

Even now, her feet dragged as she approached the pasture gate. Easy to make out Hart's silhouette against the green. He stood still and tall, gaze moving back and forth. She felt it narrow in on her.

"Talk," he ordered as she stopped next to him.

Despite herself, Beth raised her chin. "Well! I like that. Not even a 'how are you' or 'fine weather we're having.'"

"You're too quiet, and it looks to be coming on rain," he returned, voice sounding rougher than usual. "What have you got yourself into, Beth?"

She pressed a hand against her chest. "Me? Nothing, I promise you. This has to do with you."

He stiffened. There was no way around the matter now. She might as well go straight through the middle. She lowered her hand and lay it on his arm. "Hart, I know about your past, the death of the woman you loved. I'm so sorry."

He recoiled, pulling away from her touch. "Who told you?"

"Does it matter? Rest assured few know the tale, and I promised to speak of it to no one but you. That's why I wanted to meet you privately."

He was no more than an outline now in the shadows. "Thank you for that. I doubt Allegra would want me living here if she knew I was once an outlaw." His booted foot scraped at the dirt. "What exactly were you told?"

Was there more than Maddie had let on? Beth licked her lips. "You ran away from the orphanage and fell in with a gang. But you soon regretted it and left."

"Not soon enough. People were hurt. I robbed banks, Beth, held up stages. I was the sort of man your brothers help me hunt down and bring to justice."

Was he determined to make her think badly of him? "But you've changed. Now you uphold the law."

"Now I uphold the law," he repeated, as if by repeating it he made it true. "What else were you told?"

Beth blew out a breath. "After you left, the gang came looking for you. They killed your sweetheart. Oh, Hart, I can't imagine."

"I wouldn't want you to imagine." His voice was sharp. "I don't want anyone to feel that pain again."

Yet he felt it now. "That's why you won't marry, isn't it?" Beth murmured. "You're still mourning her."

He shook his head, and her heart jumped.

"I'm not mourning Annabelle, Beth. She died more than ten years ago, and I know she's in a better place."

Annabelle. She even had a romantic name. Beth could picture her—flaxen hair, cornflower-blue eyes, adoring smile. How she must have loved him!

"Tell me about her," she said.

He took a step back. "Why?"

Because she wanted to know, because she needed to know. "It might help."

She felt his sigh. "She was the prettiest gal I'd ever met, and the sweetest and kindest. She had a way of looking at me that made me want to move mountains. She convinced her pa to let me hire on at their farm, helped me dream of being something more than I was. And when they came for me, she stepped in front of a bullet so I'd have time to defend myself."

Tears were hot on her cheeks. "What courage."

"What a loss. I should have been the one to die."

"No." The word flew out of her. "No, Hart. Neither of you should have had to die. It was a terrible tragedy, but you can't let it stop you from living."

"I am living," he spit out. "I'm working to be a better man. I vowed that day that no family would suffer the way hers did because of an outlaw's deeds. I can't stop every criminal, but I stop as many as I can."

"And look how many you've stopped. That hateful man who nearly roused Seattle against the Irish, the villain who tried to kidnap John and Dottie's son. I know there have been others. You're a hero, Hart."

"No, I'm not. If you can't see that, you don't really know me."

Beth peered closer, trying in vain to make out the

expression on his face. "Yes, I do. You're set in your ways, opinionated and stubborn. You're also courageous, hardworking and determined. If you can't see that, maybe you should look in the mirror more often."

He shook his head again. "Will nothing make you give up?"

Beth sighed. "Not likely. I'm convinced having a wife would be a benefit to you, Hart, an encouragement, a helpmate."

"A wife," he said, "would only get in my way."

Beth gasped. "For shame, Hart McCormick! Do you think so little of women? Was your Annabelle nothing but a nuisance?"

"My Annabelle," he said, turning away, "is dead. Because she had the misfortune of loving me."

Beth darted in front of him, touched his arm again. "You can't blame yourself. The villain made his choice, and so did she."

"And now I've made mine. I'm not marrying, Beth."

Stubborn, annoying… Beth made herself count to ten. "She sacrificed herself so you could live. You owe it to her to move on."

He grabbed her shoulders. "You don't know what you're asking. It's a story to you, like the dime novel adventures, like those books your pa left you. It's not a story to me, Beth. I lived it. I'm still living it."

Hurt wrapped around her, for him, for what might have been. "I still say the right thing is to let her go."

He let Beth go instead. "We're done talking. And I'm done with courting. I don't need a matchmaker. Go home for Easter. I'll stay in town and keep looking for the gang."

"Oh, Hart, no!" She clasped her hands together to keep

from touching him again. "I understand now why you won't marry. I'll speak with the Literary Society, convince them the case is hopeless. With all the other things I've been doing, perhaps they'll admit me regardless. And my invitation stands. My family would enjoy having you with us for Easter. Please don't let this conversation stop you."

He was still again, as if weighing his options, weighing her. Then he snapped a nod. "All right. But don't build up castles around me, Beth. I'm just a man, and a flawed one at that."

He strode off for his cabin then, before she could tell him the truth. Two years ago she had held out her heart, seeing only a heroic figure, someone larger than the life she'd led. Now she saw him, his pride, his fears. She saw all his flaws.

And she cared about him anyway.

It seemed her matchmaking was over. She didn't have the strength to find a woman for Hart, not when he was so very hurt. It wasn't fair to the lady or to him. She wanted to hold him close, ease the pain, but she didn't have the right.

She didn't have the opportunity either. He avoided her the next few days. She couldn't blame him. Knowing she was privy to his darkest secret, every time he looked at Beth he must remember Annabelle's death. She almost wished she hadn't asked Maddie about his past.

Still, she found it hard to simply leave Seattle. There was so much to do and see here, so many friends to visit, good work to do. And there was still the matter of Scout and Mrs. Jamison. She'd spotted them around town together—shopping, eating treats at the Pastry Emporium, strolling along the boardwalk. Mrs. Jamison was so busy courting she couldn't possibly be fulfilling the commissions she must have taken. Did she intend to rely on Scout's money to pay her bills instead? It was up to Beth to prove the lady wasn't worth his time.

Or prove to her own satisfaction that Mrs. Jamison was a suitable bride for Scout.

She started with the Denny ladies, knowing them for some of the seamstress's customers.

"Such a talented woman," Mary Ann Denny maintained as she, her sister and Beth wandered through Kelloggs', looking over the latest fabric and notions. "Did you see her drawings in *Godey's*?"

She'd have to dig through her stacks for the January issue when she was home for Easter.

"I wonder why she came to Seattle," Beth said instead of answering the question. "Anyone who designs for the fashion magazines should be in New York or Boston."

"No doubt the death of her husband drove her to it," Louisa Denny replied, fingering a bolt of cambric. "Some men do not think of the future when managing their financial affairs, another reason women should have more rights."

Their theory matched Hart's, but it offered no proof. If Scout thought the lady destitute, he might propose marriage to rescue her.

If only she knew someone from San Francisco who remembered the widow's time there. Mrs. Jamison must have had friends, acquaintances. Beth tried the postmaster next.

"Mail for Mrs. Jamison?" he asked, scratching his

graying head. "Can't say I've seen any coming in or going out."

How odd. The seamstress hadn't been in Seattle more than a month or two, but surely someone would have written to her, if only to make sure she'd arrived safely. And if she was in correspondence with Mr. Godey, she'd have sent a letter. Or did she have another way to contact friends in San Francisco?

Beth was on the dock waiting when the San Francisco steamer captain came ashore. She'd had to fend off offers of a stroll, a boat ride and a whiskey. The last offer she'd refused with the point of the umbrella she carried. Finally, the tall, spare gentleman set foot on the planks. Captain Tremaine listened to her story as they walked toward the shore.

"Jamison," he said, stroking his brown beard. "Can't say as I recall the name. But there was a Widow Jasson who married one of the prospectors. Poor fellow was discovered dead only a month later. Papers said he was the third husband she'd buried."

Beth thanked him, unable to do more with her mind so full. Could it be the same woman? Was Mrs. Jamison so hardhearted she could marry for money again and again? And had none of her ill-gotten gains satisfied her avarice that she must pursue Scout now?

Hart stood across the street from the docks, watching Beth. On his patrol through town, he'd noticed her waiting on the planks and had stopped to keep an eye on things. He should have known she wouldn't need his help. Any man who had approached her had been dismissed with a word or a wave of her umbrella. What had Captain Tremaine said to her that her usually busy body could stop so long?

He didn't like it. He'd been avoiding her the last few days with the excuse that he had much to do. He'd patrolled the city and county and even checked on Scout's activities, just in case there was any sign of the gang. But Scout seemed completely caught up in courting.

He knew his busyness was only a pretense. The truth was Beth's concern had scraped off the scab over the sore Annabelle's death had left. He wasn't ready to probe the wound further.

But he wasn't ready to see her in danger either. He met her as she crossed the street. "How goes the investigation?"

She blinked, focusing on his face as if returning from a long distance. "Investigation?"

Hart shook his head. "You're not here because you're planning a trip to San Francisco."

"Hmm." She glanced back at the dock. "I suppose that would get me the answers I need, but I really don't want to be gone from home so long, and I'd have to find a chaperone." She made a face.

He took her elbow and led her away from the shore. "So, who are you investigating now? Mrs. Jamison?"

He was almost glad when she agreed. The last thing he needed was for her questions to draw the gang out of hiding. Although he'd relish a chance to take on the robbers face to face, he couldn't chance that Beth might be hurt. She'd already poked the bear once. She might not survive a second time.

And neither would he if something happened to her.

He pushed the thought away. "What did you learn, or should I ask?"

He listened as Beth laid out her theory. It made sense, but it wasn't anything he could act on.

"Pretty thin evidence," he told her.

"Particularly if I'm to persuade Scout," she agreed. "But I'm not sure where else to check."

He didn't want her checking anywhere. If Mrs. Jamison was innocent, asking more questions might jeopardize her reputation and her business. If she was guilty of murdering three husbands, looking more closely might make her select Beth as her next victim.

"I'll telegraph the marshal in San Francisco, see what he knows," Hart offered.

"Oh, Hart! That would be famous!" She threw her arms around him for a hug.

He'd seen her use the gesture a dozen times, with her brothers, her sisters-in-law, friends. It was spontaneous, enthusiastic, all Beth. Yet the feel of her against him raised such a fierce protectiveness that his arms were about her before he thought better of it.

She lowered her arms but didn't move out of his embrace. He should let go, back away, but her eyes were very wide and very blue. He slipped into them, bending his head toward hers, catching the scent of vanilla that whispered of fresh-baked cookies, a loving family, the home he'd never known. His lips brushed hers slowly, carefully. She was soft, tender, sweet, the stuff that dreams were made of.

He made himself pull back. She'd closed her eyes and stood there, lips pursed as if she hoped for another kiss. He very nearly gave her one, but a shout down the street woke him, and he released her and stepped away.

What was he doing? He'd told her he didn't want to marry. She thought he was still mourning Annabelle.

She had every right to expect him to propose, this very moment.

She opened her eyes, relaxed her mouth, and blinked a moment as if orienting herself. "Well, that was unexpected."

Hart rubbed the back of his neck. "You could say that again."

"No, actually, I can't. I find myself rather breathless." She fanned herself with her hand.

He'd heard of women swooning when men took liberties. But surely not the redoubtable Beth Wallin.

"Beth, I…" he started.

She held up a hand. "We will not speak of it. We were merely caught up in the moment. There's no need for you to mention this to my brothers."

"No need at all," he assured her. He didn't like thinking how any of the Wallins would react if they felt he'd trifled with her affections.

She started forward, steps brisk, and he scurried to catch up. "I'll be heading home Saturday afternoon. John is coming to fetch me. Services will be at ten on Sunday. I'll wait in front of the church for you."

She was all business, yet he couldn't help feeling as if something had changed. He wasn't sure what, and he certainly had no idea what to do about it.

But he found himself looking forward to Easter.

Chapter Seventeen

Beth was waiting in front of the Wallin Landing church Easter morning, watching the sunlight filter through the cedar. After so many days in Seattle, her cabin had felt strange, smaller than she'd remembered. Still, all her brothers, their wives and some of their children had checked in on her between last evening and this morning, making her feel more at home. She'd boiled and dyed eggs with her nieces and nephews, giggling over colors and encouraging their creativity. And she'd been able to confirm that everything was ready for the big day and Dottie wasn't feeling nearly as overwhelmed as John had claimed.

Still, knowing that others had largely done all the work felt odd as well. Since Ma had died, planning the family celebrations had fallen to Beth. Easter, Christmas, Independence Day—she had arranged food, drink and activities and had overseen all preparations. She'd felt purposeful, commanding, very much a necessary part of the community. It was a little lowering to realize her family was perfectly capable of making all the arrangements without her.

But it was nice to just join in for once without having to make sure everything was perfect.

She tugged at her sleeves now, settling the pleated white cuffs over her short white gloves. The pink crepe had made the perfect Easter gown, especially with the rosy ribbon and fitted white bodice Nora had added to the pattern. Her hair up under a white straw hat trimmed in pink ribbon and white net, Beth thought she looked rather fine. By the way Drew's logging crew—Harry Yeager, Tom Convers and Dickie Morgan—smiled at her as they entered the church, she wasn't the only one pleased with her looks.

Would Hart be pleased?

Silly! Hart never noticed her clothes. Most of the time she was certain his attentions were elsewhere. Once in a while, she wondered if he even liked her.

Of course, there was that kiss.

She shivered, remembering the feel of his lips, firm but gentle. His hands at her waist had pulled her closer, as if he couldn't get enough of her. She'd wondered what it would be like to share a kiss with him. The reality was so much grander than anything she had imagined, filling her with hope, with longing. When he'd released her, it had been as if he'd taken a piece of her with him.

She realized she'd closed her eyes again at the memory and snapped them open. As if summoned by her thoughts, Hart rode into Wallin Landing.

She wanted to run to him, throw her arms around him again. But that would only be begging for another kiss. Sweethearts or wives might do that, but she wasn't either and never would be. So, she waited while he dismounted, let Arno into the pasture with the horse's old friends Lance and Percy and strode up the hill to the church.

Her brothers had built the whitewashed chapel to inspire. Nestled in the forest, its steeple was the tallest point for miles. But her heart still beat faster when she realized Hart wasn't admiring the church.

He seemed to be admiring her, gray eyes moving over her frame as if memorizing every inch of her.

"Morning," he said, removing his hat. His dark hair gleamed in the sun. "Happy Easter. You look nice. New dress?"

Beth swallowed. Normally, she'd twirl around at such a compliment, show off every angle, extol Nora's inventiveness and detail the source of the pattern. Now she barely managed to thank him. What was wrong with her?

He held out his arm, the gray of his new suit only the slightest bit rumpled from his ride. She took his arm and allowed him to lead her in.

The church was crowded. Besides her brothers, their families and the logging crew, all the farmers, fishermen, loggers, miners and ranchers around Wallin Landing had come in for the service with their families. Nora had saved Beth and Hart places in the middle of the church, on the left side of the two sections that flanked the center aisle. They slipped into the pew to nods of welcome from her sister-in-law and brother Simon and whispered acknowledgements from her nieces and nephews. Little Hannah, Simon's youngest, went so far as to climb up onto Beth's lap. Beth bent her head to rub noses with the sweet-natured two-year-old.

Voices quieted as Callie started playing the opening hymn on the black-lacquered piano Beth had purchased last Christmas with her inheritance. Beth drew in a breath. Their church might be smaller than the Brown Church in Seattle, but the voices rose with even more thanksgiving as all eyes turned to the wood cross behind the simple altar.

Simon rose and squeezed past his family to join Callie for a duet on his violin. Though Beth was used to her brother playing, for church as well as for family gatherings and the local dancers, the music had never sounded sweeter. It swirled through the building, raising heads, brightening countenances. And when her brother Levi went to the pulpit and spoke about how love had triumphed on that day so long ago, Beth reached out and squeezed Hart's hand.

He didn't pull away.

A thrill shot through her. Now, now. Just because he'd noticed her outfit for the first time and allowed her to hold his hand didn't mean he was ready to court her. She wasn't ready to take that chance, was she? Still, she kept her hand on his until the end of the service.

Lars, Nora and Simon's oldest child, nudged in next to her as everyone started to take their leave. His brown eyes sparkled as he gazed up at her. "Are you going to roll eggs with us, Aunt Beth?"

"Of course," Beth assured him with a smile. "I have to defend my championship."

"Championship?" Hart asked as they followed the others out of the church.

"We roll boiled eggs down the hill," Beth explained, lifting her skirts to descend the stairs. "The egg that rolls the farthest wins. My egg has won the last three years."

"Sounds like you have a secret."

She stopped, cheeks heating. Did he know her conflicted feelings? She'd been so careful not to show him the least indication. She searched his face, then forced a laugh. "Oh, you mean with the eggs."

He raised his brows. "You have another secret I should know about?"

She wasn't about to admit it. She took his hand again instead. "Come on. I boiled an egg for you too. Let's go get them."

He didn't protest as she tugged him toward the hall, where she and the others had left the eggs that morning.

A short time later, they stood on the crest of the hill above Wallin Landing, eggs in hand. Catherine and Drew remained at the bottom in the clearing with Nora, Dottie and the children who were too young to take part. Simon and John were standing on either side of the grassy slope to make sure nothing rolled into the trees or over the cliff into the lake. James, Rina and Levi kept the peace at the top of the hill.

Callie sidled in next to Beth. "I understand you're the one to beat."

Beth grinned. Raised on the gold rush camps, Levi's bride was more used to competing than Beth's other sisters-in-law. She was also the closest to Beth in age. After a rocky start last Christmas, the two had become good friends.

"I welcome the challenge," she told Callie now.

Callie grinned back. Though she usually favored trousers or cotton skirts, today she wore the blue-on-blue gown Beth and her sisters-in-law had sewn for her for Christmas. Hiking up her hem, she crouched as if to survey the terrain. "Think I'll try over there. It looks smoother."

Beth shook her head as Callie rose and moved away. "There goes that strategy."

"You have a strategy?" She could hear the amusement in Hart's voice.

"There are three components to a winning run, sir," she informed him as Levi tried to calm Callie's excitable nine-year-old twin brothers Frisco and Sutter, and Rina assembled the rest of the children in an uneven line. "First, the terrain. That side of the hill is a little straighter and, as Callie noted, freer from tree roots and the like."

He edged in that direction, and Beth followed.

"Second?" he asked.

"The strength of the shell. I generally gather the eggs for the main house. I know which hens lay the eggs that are the hardest to crack."

He glanced down at the egg she had given him. It was a pale yellow, hers a soft pink. "I take it these are from that hen."

"Absolutely."

"Take your positions!" James shouted.

Around them, children bent over their eggs, bodies wiggling and voices high. Beth lifted her skirts and squatted on the grass. Hart dropped down next to her.

"What's the third?" he asked.

"On your mark," James yelled.

Beth set her egg on the grass. Hart copied her.

"How well you roll it," she said.

"Go!" James cried.

Beth flipped her egg with her fingertips. Glancing at Hart, she saw his eyes narrow as he mimicked her.

Ten eggs started down the hill. Beth scrambled up, clutching Hart's arm. "Watch!"

The eggs tumbled along. Some stopped after only a few feet. Seven-year-old Victoria, James's oldest, marched up to hers and glared at it as if that might keep it moving. Callie's hit a rock halfway down and struck fast. She rose with a shrug and a smile to Beth. More reached the bottom and rolled to a halt. Frisco and Sutter, Callie's brothers, ran with Lars and his cousins to retrieve theirs.

A few kept rolling, right across the lawn. Tugging on Hart's arm, Beth ran down the hill even as Simon bent and picked up an egg.

"Who had yellow?" he asked.

Yellow? Beth pulled up.

Hart stepped forward. "I believe that's mine."

Simon smiled as he handed Hart the egg. "Then I believe we have a new champion."

James, who had followed them down, tsked. "No, no, no. Like this." He grabbed Hart's hand and held it up in the air. "Ladies and gentlemen, let's have a round of applause for Wallin Landing's newest egg rolling champion, Deputy Hart McCormick!"

He was surrounded. Beth's brothers and sisters-in-law wrung his hand in congratulations, the children hopped up and down and begged to know how he'd done it. He glanced at Beth, wondering how she'd take her dethroning. She was smiling with so much pride he wanted to puff out his chest and crow like a rooster.

All over an egg.

She pushed her way forward. "Mr. McCormick, I demand a rematch."

"Let's do it now," Frisco said, turning as if ready to dash back up to the top of the hill.

Levi caught his arm. "Not so fast. Several of the eggs have cracked. They won't make another run."

"And they won't be any good to eat if we beat them up any further," Catherine reminded him. "Besides, it's nearly time for dinner."

"Food!" Sutter darted for the hall.

"I do feed them," Callie remarked as the rest fell in behind him.

Hart pulled Beth up short as she made to follow. "It was an oddity, you know. I wasn't trying to show off."

She grinned at him, cheeks rosy. "You won, Hart, fair and square. I don't mind. It gives me something to try for next time."

Next time. As if she fully expected him to be at her side next Easter. What surprised him was how much he wanted it too.

But perhaps it wasn't all that surprising, he reflected as he followed them all up the hill toward the hall. He'd always admired the Wallin family. Their father had been dead when Hart had ridden in to Seattle over the Naches Pass trail. Drew, the eldest, had been in charge, even though he was only a little older than Hart. A strapping logger, his blond-haired head towered over most of the others. He'd raised his four brothers and Beth with the help of their mother, who had passed away a few years ago. Now he still sat at the head of the table with his wife, Catherine, and three children at his side in the hall, the main cabin having become too small for the growing number of Wallins.

Simon, nearly as tall as Drew but with a leaner frame, was more to Hart's temperament, logical, force-ful in his opinions. Hart had never been sure what Nora, a gentle seamstress, had seen in him to marry, but the two were clearly devoted to each other, sharing smiles as they helped feed their children.

Then there was James. The pale-haired, slender fellow had an eye for horseflesh, and the people around Wallin Landing relied on his trading post for supplies. He was a wit, teasing his children, his wife, Rina, and anyone else who came to his attention.

Auburn-haired John had always been a studious sort. He'd surprised Hart when he'd agreed to be deputized to help catch the man who had caused his bride Dottie heartache when she and her infant son had first come to Wallin Landing last year. Hart had been glad for the help. He didn't hold with men who preyed on women.

Curly-haired Levi, however, had been even more surprising. He'd been a lad when Hart had first met him, and one determined to blaze his own way. More than once Hart had thought he might have to lock up the boy for driving his wagon recklessly, starting a fight in the street or hanging about with Scout Rankin at the gambling tables. But Levi and Scout had both gone north to pan for gold. While Scout had come home wealthy, Levi had come home with a calling. The minister of Wallin Landing, he seemed to know his own worth now and was happy with his life and his pretty new bride, Callie, her twin brothers and her little niece Mica.

They all seemed happy, in fact, sharing memories along with food around the big table. Beth had been right about the menu—succulent ham, molasses dripping from its sides, potato salad with pearly onions, crisp new carrots, Levi's famous biscuits with apple butter and lemon custard for dessert.

"Too tart?" Beth asked, twinkle in her eyes, as he accepted a second helping from her sister-in-law Nora.

"Oh, don't you like lemon, Deputy?" Nora asked, round face puckering in concern.

"It's more than tolerable, ma'am," Hart assured her, lifting his bowl higher.

Smiling, she spooned him another generous serving.

All in all, it was a lively bunch, the brothers trading quips, their wives interjecting topics of conversation. Comments and questions from the children were met with fond smiles, thoughtful responses. It was a far cry from any Easter he'd spent growing up.

Longing tightened his grip on the fork. This was what he'd been looking for all his life, people who cared, no matter the circumstances. What would it be like to be part of a family?

To have a home, a wife, children of his own?

To give in to his growing feelings and offer for Beth?

A clap on his shoulder broke him from his reverie. The children had left the table to play a game in the yard, and the adults were taking a few moments of much-earned rest.

James grinned at him. "So, champion, what other talents should we know about?"

The others all looked to Hart with smiles of encouragement.

He shrugged. "I can shoot the spade out of an ace at fifty paces, but you probably knew that."

James withdrew his hand. "Actually, I didn't, but I certainly commend the effort. I must ask, though, what crime the ace committed that you felt you had to shoot it."

Beth swatted him away. "Be glad he didn't arrest you for your poor wit."

James put a hand on his chest, reminding Hart of the way Beth used the gesture. "Poor wit? Sister, you wound me."

"Better her than Hart," John put in, with a nod of respect toward Hart.

Beth grinned at Hart. "He's only being modest when it comes to talents. He has quite the taste in literature."

Hart tensed, waiting for her to admit his fondness for dime novels. Surely the fine folk at Wallin Landing read far better.

Beth leaned across the table as if imparting a secret. "He recently read Vaughn Everard's poetry."

The combined sigh of delight from the ladies caused the lamps to flicker.

Hart glanced around at her brothers.

"Everard makes some excellent points," John said.

"You can't refute his logic," Simon agreed.

"Logic?" James staggered. "You see logic in his impassioned poetry?" He righted himself. "I might have known."

"Which was your favorite, Mr. McCormick?" Rina, the local schoolteacher, asked politely.

If he admitted it was the poem about a kiss, the women would all sigh again. Beth might gush, and her brothers might start howling for his head.

"Hard to pick a favorite, ma'am," he told her.

"True," Drew said in his deep voice. "Now, before the children rush back in, when do you need us to haul seats for the concert tonight, Rina?"

Hart relaxed on the bench as the conversation turned to other things.

Beth linked arms with him, lowering her voice to speak to him alone. "I'm glad you enjoyed Mr. Everard's poetry. Ask John to recommend other books while you're here. He loves sharing stories from the library."

The library was the latest addition to Wallin Landing, courtesy of her brother and donations from the Literary Society. A shame the ladies' other worthwhile efforts didn't keep them busy enough that they had to try and find him a bride.

Especially when the only woman he could seriously consider for a bride was sitting right next to him and still beyond his strength to reach.

Chapter Eighteen

It was the finest Easter Beth could remember. The finest day too. Hart fit in so well with her brothers. They shared the same experience of coming to the wilderness and making a way. And they shared a similar love of justice and sacrifice to protect those they loved. Having him beside her made everything more satisfying. She'd even emboldened herself to rest her head on his shoulder as Simon played a stirring song on the violin to open the school recital. When Hart's arm slipped around her waist, she thought she could be content to stay like that forever.

She had promised the Literary Society she'd find him a bride. She now knew his reason for resisting, yet that resistance seemed to be dwindling when he was with her. Was she mad to see interest in those gray eyes, to feel tenderness in the hand that held hers? Hope had a way of rising every time she looked at him. She thought she floated as he walked her back to her cabin that night.

But she wasn't going to be the one to admit her feelings first this time. If he was interested in courting her, he would have to prove it.

She paused at the steps leading up to her door, tingling with the thought that he might kiss her again. Moonlight streamed down through the trees, anointing him in silver. She tipped back her head, drew in a breath, waited.

"Good night, Beth," he said. "Thank you for inviting me."

He remained at the bottom of the steps until she was in the door.

So, what was she to make of that? He'd kissed her on the street in broad daylight, where anyone could have noticed and remarked on it. Why did he hesitate to kiss her in private, where no one but the two of them would know?

Had she misread him, again?

She'd certainly misread Scout. Even though he'd promised to come out to Wallin Landing for Easter, he hadn't arrived. That could only mean Mrs. Jamison had convinced him to stay in town with her instead. Beth had gone so far as to check the back issues of *Godey's* she kept, but she hadn't found a single instance where the seamstress's name was mentioned. Mrs. Jamison was clearly a manipulator, saying what she thought the other person wanted to hear to get her own way.

"Doesn't he realize she has him wrapped around her little finger?" Beth lamented to Hart as he drove them back to Seattle the next morning, Arno tied behind the wagon. Beth had decided to come in one last time and speak to Ursula Wyckoff about Hart.

"Most fellows in love don't realize when their sweetheart orders them around," he said, guiding the horses through a puddle in the road. It had rained that night, and the trees were still dripping.

Beth gathered her coat closer over her pink skirts. "I wouldn't think much of a sweetheart who laid down orders. Marriage should be a partnership. Look at my brothers and their wives."

"Your brothers married fine women, their match in every way. Not every man is so fortunate."

She bridled, then forced her shoulders down. He was right. She'd seen a few uneven marriages in her life, where either the husband or the wife dominated the other.

"That's just it," she told Hart. "I want better for Scout. His father never appreciated him, rarely showed him any affection. He deserves a wife who holds him in the highest esteem."

"Might be hard to find him one in Seattle," Hart pointed out with a look her way. "Too many folks remember his father."

He was right there too. It wasn't fair that Scout was tarred with the same brush, but she'd heard the murmurs, seen the looks. Some of the most established citizens might be seeking him out now, but that didn't mean they wanted him marrying their daughters.

"A mail-order bride, then," Beth said. "I'm sure I can locate one perfect for him. I found Dottie for John."

He shifted on the seat. "As I recall, that almost didn't work out."

"Because I didn't let John know what I was doing. Men can be so stubborn that way. They always want to think an idea is theirs."

"Funny how that works," he murmured.

Was he teasing? Beth shook her head. "I've learned my lesson. This time I'll talk to Scout, make him see reason."

"Beth."

She loved hearing her name in that rough voice. It made her sound strong, sure, wanted. "Yes?"

"Let Scout find his own way."

She threw up her hands. "But he's doing a terrible job of it!"

He cast her a glance, more concern than censure. "That's his business. He doesn't seem to have much confidence in himself. You stepping in isn't going to help."

Why was he always right? Well, nearly always. Beth sighed. "I don't know if I can step aside."

His smile edged into view. "I have complete faith in you."

That was one of them. Between Hart and Scout, she was beginning to feel as if she wasn't as skilled a matchmaker as she'd thought. Still, she'd never failed in work she set out to do. Hart had encouraged her to let Scout discover that Mrs. Jamison wasn't the right woman for him. She'd already voiced her concerns to her friend. Perhaps she should say no more.

Yet when she spotted the yellow buggy outside Kelloggs', she couldn't help but ask Hart to pull in behind it.

He jumped down and came around to help her down. Once more the touch of his hands on her waist made her breath stop. He bent his head, and she raised hers, but still he didn't kiss her.

"Watch yourself now," he murmured. "You don't want to lose a friend."

Beth nodded as he stepped away to untie Arno. He swung up into the saddle.

"Let me know when you head for home."

Annoyance pricked her. "I'm not a child. I don't need your permission."

He chuckled. "And I'm the law. I need to know who's in my town and who isn't." He turned Arno and set off toward the sheriff's office. Likely he hadn't noticed her stick out her tongue at his back.

Beth laughed. And wasn't that just the most mature thing to do? Ah, well. Perhaps she would fare better with Scout.

She found him looking over the tinned goods, paper in one hand.

"We missed you at Easter," she said, moving in next to him.

Scout looked up with a smile. "I missed you, too. But I didn't like leaving Evangeline and Bobby all alone. They don't know anyone else in town."

As far as Beth could see, the seamstress had gone out of her way to make herself known to all the best families in Seattle. But perhaps they wouldn't invite her to dine.

"That was kind of you," she told Scout. "The lady is very fortunate to have such an attentive friend."

He glanced down at the paper in his hand. "I'm the fortunate one."

Beth tipped her head to read the words on the paper. That wasn't Scout's hand, unless he'd learned to add fancy curlicues to his writing while he was on the gold fields. "Oysters?" she asked.

He nodded. "They're Evangeline's favorite. And fish eggs."

Beth wrinkled her nose. "Fish eggs?"

"Caviar," Mr. Weinclef said, appearing from behind the stack of tins. "Imported from Russia. A personal favorite of Mr. Arthur Denny's."

Beth shuddered. "Fish eggs make good bait. I don't think I'd enjoy eating them."

Mr. Weinclef put his pointed nose in the air. "I understand they are an acquired taste."

And Mrs. Jamison had obviously acquired it. "She has you doing her shopping, Scout?"

Scout colored. "I offered. Bobby has quite an appetite, I understand. Growing boy, I suppose. You remember how Levi and I would eat your ma out of house and home."

Beth smiled. "I do. So, what else is on your list?"

Quite a lot. She helped him gather flour, sugar, salt, cornmeal, and assorted other staples, in amounts that would have fed half of Wallin Landing. Mrs. Jamison, it seemed, was stocking up.

And allowing Scout to pay for it.

"Do you have an understanding?" she whispered to Scout as Mr. Weinclef tallied up the supplies. "This seems a large gift otherwise. People will talk."

Scout shrugged. "Let them talk. Why do I have this money if I can't do a favor for a friend?"

"Scout," Beth started.

Scout laid his hand over hers on the counter. "All my life I've had to live on the generosity of others. Don't think I've forgotten the times your family fed me, found 'spare' clothing that would supposedly go to waste if I didn't take it, let me stay the night in a clean bed. It's my turn to help."

How could she argue with that?

She helped Mr. Weinclef and Scout load the goods into his buggy, which sank in the mud under the weight, and watched him drive away. Then she followed the clerk back into the store.

Kelloggs' carried the newspapers from the East Coast that featured advertisements from people seeking spouses. Many of the store's male customers made use of them. She'd posted an advertisement in one when she'd been looking for a wife for John. Like Scout, her most tenderhearted brother had held love high and had needed a little help locating the perfect bride for him.

"But all your brothers are married," Mr. Weinclef protested when she asked for a copy of the newspapers, which were kept behind the counter.

Beth smiled at him. "They certainly are. I'm looking for a friend."

He drew out the sheets so slowly she might have thought he had rheumatism. "I don't think Deputy McCormick would like a mail-order bride."

The very idea made her giggle. "Not that friend."

He lowered his voice. "I hope you aren't thinking of a groom for yourself, Miss Wallin. I know any number of fellows who would be glad to pay you court, at the least encouragement."

Her smile felt tight. "Just give me the papers, please."

He laid them down, and she paid the twenty-five cents and left.

Outside the store, she stopped by the wagon to scan through the offerings. No older widows—Scout needed someone who would match his experience in courting, which was nearly nonexistent, as far as she knew. Look how easily he had been taken in by Mrs. Jamison. And no children—he would need time to accustom himself to the idea of fatherhood. No one who wrote with an overly flowery or highly educated tone—he was a simple man who had barely graduated from Rina's school because Beth had tutored him.

Ah, there was one. "Sweet-natured, shy lady seeks husband out West who will provide safe, stable home."

Just because a lady claimed she was sweet-natured and shy didn't make her so, but Scout could surely provide safety and stability. She'd write for more information before presenting the possibility to him.

She lowered the paper in time to see a man slip back into the shadows of the alley across the way. Something about him was familiar.

Was that the man who had accosted her?

Determination flooded her. Oh, but it would be satisfying to pursue him and give him a piece of her mind. A shame that was out of the question, as it was entirely too dangerous. Better to point him out to the law. She smiled just thinking about how Hart would respond.

Folding the papers, she hurried to the hitching post and retrieved the reins. Even pulling a wagon, Lance and Percy could go faster than Arno's usual stroll through Seattle. There were only so many streets where Hart might be patrolling. She'd find him, bring him back. The fellow wouldn't escape this time. Climbing up on the bench, she slapped down the reins.

Lance and Percy leaped forward with their usual enthusiasm. The wagon didn't follow. Before Beth could grasp what was happening, she was yanked from the box. The ground rose to meet her, and the light snuffed out.

Not a bad day for a Monday. Hart tipped his hat to Mr. Horton, who was inspecting the property where he planned to erect his new bank, the first stone building in Seattle. Hart had been a little concerned that the lack of a visible law presence on Sunday might encourage some of Seattle's citizens to act out or even embolden the gang. But no complaints had been waiting for him at the office, and no one came forward now to share a concern as he rode Arno down Commercial Street.

The quiet gave him time to think about Easter, and Beth.

He'd never considered courting again, and certainly not her. He'd told himself she was younger than he was. She was light to his shadow. She didn't really know him, or she wouldn't have been so quick to claim friendship.

Having spent more time in her company these last few weeks, he could see he had been wrong. She wasn't that much younger than him. Several of Seattle's leading families had a larger age difference between husband and wife, and they seemed happy. While she had a more childlike wonder of the world, he was coming to see the value in not always expecting the worst of people. When he was with her, the darkness abated. And now she knew about his past and still seemed to enjoy his company.

He'd once dreamed of settling down, marrying a woman he cared about, being part of a true family. That dream had died with Annabelle. Could he recapture it with Beth? He couldn't imagine recapturing it with any other woman.

He turned Arno onto Mill Street and around the corner to Second. There was a commotion up ahead, the street blocked, a crowd gathering. He urged Arno forward.

Billy Prentice, the porter at Lowe's Hotel, ran to meet him. "Deputy, come quick. There's been an accident."

He could see that much. A farm wagon stood alone in front of Kelloggs', the horses missing from the traces. Weinclef paced the boardwalk wringing his hands. Hart swung down from the saddle, handed the reins to Billy. "What happened?"

"It just came apart," Weinclef cried, eyes wide. "I always watch when she leaves. She's so purposeful. This time she flicked the reins, and the horses pulled her right off the seat."

All sound shut off. He felt hands on his arm, shoulders bumping his as he pressed forward to the center of the crowd. He shook them off, cold filling him.

Beth lay in the mud, her pretty dress soaked. Someone had turned her on her side, arranged her skirts modestly, but her eyes were closed, her face white. He knew that look. It raised bile in his throat.

"Is she…" He couldn't ask the question, wasn't sure he could bear to hear the answer.

"She's alive, Deputy," Aiden O'Rourke said, face pinched, as he knelt at her side. "But I can't wake her."

"Fetch Doc," Hart ordered, crouching beside him as a wave of thanksgiving broke over him. Aiden rose and ran.

Hart reached out, smoothed the hair from her forehead. Already a bruise was growing, an angry purple, and he had the absurd notion she would be annoyed to find it clashed with her outfit. But now that he was closer, he could see the rise and fall of her chest as she breathed. Was it forced? Had she struck more than her head?

He wanted to gather her close, whisper her name until she woke, but it wouldn't be wise to move her until Doc had determined the extent of her injuries.

"Beth," he murmured, bending over her. "Beth, honey, wake up."

She didn't move. Pain lanced him.

"Deputy." Doc was kneeling beside him. "What happened?"

Hart pushed back his hat, tried to marshal his thoughts. "Some kind of accident with the wagon. I think she hit her head."

"Miss Wallin," Doc called, touching her cheek. "Beth. Can you hear me?"

She didn't respond.

Someone was crying. Hart could hear the soft sob. Others talked in hushed tones, as if she was already beyond their reach. Aiden stared at him as if just as afraid.

Hart straightened. "Billy, I'm commandeering you. Hitch Arno and see if you can find Lance and Percy. Weinclef, Aiden, move these folks along. I'll get Miss Wallin to Doc's."

Doc rose as well. "I don't think anything is broken, but I won't know for sure until I can examine her more closely. If you would, Deputy."

Hart squatted and slipped his arms under her, lifting her carefully. The mud sucked at her body, and her head lolled against his shoulder.

Please, Lord, don't take her. I'll do anything You want. Just heal her.

He carried her down the street, the crowd parting before him, people crying out, asking questions. He paid them no heed. All that mattered was Beth.

Doc directed him to lay her on the tall table in his office. Hart did so and stepped back, feeling empty without her in his arms.

"What's wrong with her?" he asked as Doc set his stethoscope against her chest. "Why won't she wake?"

"Sometimes a blow to the head renders a person insensible," Doc said, repositioning the device. "Give her a bit, and she may come around."

He wanted to believe that. What would the world be without Beth in it? Dark, devoid of joy, an abyss of silence. He'd done everything he could to prevent this kind of loss for others. Now he faced it again.

Once more, he could lose the woman he loved.

And he did love her. He'd fought against the notion, denied it to her face. Yet who wouldn't love her? That infectious smile, that bright giggle. Her enthusiasm for anything, everything. Her faith in her family, in a loving God.

Her unshakeable belief in him.

Choked, he knelt beside the table, his face on a level with her. "Beth, please. Wake up."

Doc pulled back his stethoscope, frowning at Hart. He didn't care. He couldn't lose her. He wouldn't. He took her cold fingers, clasped them close. "Beth, come back to me. I'm only whole when you're at my side."

Her lashes fluttered, and he caught his breath. Her eyes opened, and she blinked, focusing on his face. "I see you've been reading Vaughn Everard's poetry again."

Hart dropped his head to the table, fingers tightening on hers. *Thank You, Lord. You brought her back. Now show me how to keep her safe.*

Chapter Nineteen

Though she had a raging headache, Beth could only touch Hart's thick hair and marvel. Had she really heard words of love from his lips, or had she been dreaming?

"Miss Wallin." Doc bent over her, craggy face concerned. "You've had an accident, and we need to assess the extent of your injuries. Can you answer a few questions for me?"

Beth started to nod, then winced as her head protested. "I'll do my best."

Doc proceeded to ask about various aches and pains, requesting that she move this part of her body or another. Hart had straightened and stood with eyes narrowed, apparently daring Doc to treat her well or suffer the consequences.

Finally, Doc stepped back. "It seems the worst of your injuries is a concussion. I'm sure you'll have some discomfort from bumps and bruises over the next few days as well." He looked to Hart. "She'll need someone to watch her through the night. I suggest bed rest for the next few days. I'll send some laudanum with you."

They were treating her like a child. Beth tried to

sit up, and the room spun around her. Hart caught her shoulders.

"Easy," he murmured. He glanced at Doc. "Can I take her home?"

"If by home you mean Wallin Landing, I'd advise against it," Doc replied, lowering her spirits. "You know the road between here and there. Best not to jostle her any more than necessary."

"I'll speak to the Howards," Hart promised.

"I am capable of talking for myself," Beth informed them both.

Her irritation only grew when Doc smiled at Hart over her head. "I'll leave you to make the arrangements. Tell her brothers I'll send the bill shortly."

Beth opened her mouth to offer a stinging rebuke. She had her own money. She was her own person. She didn't need her brothers interceding for her.

But Hart scooped her up in his arms, and suddenly all she could see was him. The sweep of dark brows, the firm chin, the swirl of silver, gray and black that made up his irises.

"I'll take care of her," he told Doc, who slipped the bottle of laudanum into his pocket.

Beth didn't argue until they were out of the office. "I can't ask this of Allegra and Clay, Hart."

"They'll want to help," he countered, carrying her down the block. One look from him and everyone else scattered, the ladies with looks of compassion or surprise, the men with looks that bordered on envy.

"You can't carry me all the way to the Howards'," she protested.

"Are you impugning my strength or your weight?"

"Well, I never! Hart McCormick, you..." She sputtered to a stop at the look in his eyes. He was trying to distract her, but she could see that the accident had taken a toll on him. His face was lined, his mouth tight. Had he truly been so concerned about her?

"Don't worry," she told him. "You heard Doc. A few days' rest, and I'll be fine."

His only answer was a *humph*, but it might have been because they had reached the hitching post in front of Kelloggs', where Arno was tied. She recognized Billy from Lowe's standing beside the black gelding.

"I found the horses, Deputy McCormick," he said. "They were fine, just confused. I took them to the livery stable."

"Oh, thank you," Beth said before Hart could answer. "I don't know why I didn't think about Lance and Percy. The poor dears! And the wagon! We can't leave it standing in the middle of Second."

"I'll see to it," Hart said. He nodded to Billy. "Give me a hand, will you?"

Billy's eyes widened. So did Beth's, at the thought of Hart handing her to the youth. Instead, he set her up in the saddle. With Billy supporting her, Hart swung up beside her, bracketing her between his body and Arno's neck.

"Much obliged," Hart told the porter, his arms coming around her as he took the reins. "I'll speak to your manager, explain how you were a credit to the hotel with your quick thinking."

Billy grinned. "Thanks, Deputy." He touched his forelock. "Miss Wallin. I'm glad to see you weren't badly hurt. You gave us all a scare."

"Thank you for your concern, Mr. Prentice," Beth

said. Then she had to focus on keeping her seat as Hart turned Arno and started down the street at a gentle walk.

His body felt warm against hers. His arms cradled her close. She rested her head against his chest. He smelled like leather and mint. She fancied she could hear the beat of his heart. It seemed to match the throbbing in her head.

"Beth!"

She snapped open her eyes. They had turned onto Spring and started up the hill. He stared down at her, face white.

Perhaps she should be trying to distract *him*.

"I was just coming to find you when all this happened," she told him, rocking in the saddle as the horse headed up the hill. "When I left Kelloggs' I saw the man who threatened me."

His face tightened. "Where?"

"Across the street. He darted into an alley. I decided against following him."

"Smart."

She shouldn't be so pleased by his praise. "I knew you needed to talk to him. But as soon as I flicked the reins, the horses ran off."

"Taking you with them." His voice was grim.

"Now, Hart, don't blame Lance and Percy. They just did what they've been trained to do. They couldn't know that they were no longer hitched to the wagon." She frowned. "And why weren't they hitched to the wagon? We came all the way from Wallin Landing just fine. When were they let free, and still in harness?"

"That's what I intend to find out."

She met his gaze. "You think someone deliberately tampered with the wagon? Why?"

"Maybe the gang thinks you know more than you should. Maybe they think you're a danger to them."

Beth made a face. "Not that much of a danger. We never caught them, did we?"

His arms tightened around her as Arno reached the top of the hill. "There is no *we*, Beth. You will have nothing further to do with the investigation. With any investigation," he hurried to add when she opened her mouth to protest. "Leave the law to me and Sheriff Wyckoff."

"Go home, tend the stove and sweep the floor," she retorted. "Necessary tasks, of course, but I won't apologize if I think I was meant for more."

"And I won't apologize for keeping you safe. As soon as Doc approves, you're heading back to Wallin Landing. And you will stay there until I say otherwise."

The ice she felt crossed into her voice. "I am a grown woman. I am not related to you by blood or marriage. You have no call to order me about."

"I'm the Deputy Sheriff of King County. You'll do as I say."

"We'll see about that." She tossed her head, then gasped as the pain seized her.

He reined in Arno in front of the Howards', face tightening once more. "Beth, what is it? Are you hurt?"

"Terribly," she said. "Horribly. Utterly devastated that you have so little faith in me. Now, get me inside and get out of my sight, before I say something unladylike."

She rested the next few days as Doc requested. Her heart wouldn't have let her do otherwise. How dare Hart treat her like a child? She'd had quite enough of that from her brothers. She could certainly see the sense in laying low for a time, until she was healed. But to run off to Wallin Landing, as if she was afraid to stand on her own two feet? Bah! She had a dozen people she needed to address about moving forward with various activities like women's suffrage and the theatrical troupe, she must settle things with the Literary Society even if they ended up rejecting her, and she had to learn the truth about Evangeline Jamison and stop Scout from making a disastrous marriage.

Unfortunately, she had to heal first. Allegra and Gillian stayed with her the first day to make sure she was all right. Hart stopped by that evening and the next morning, but he didn't come back to her room to see her.

"Clay says the wagon's hitch broke free," Allegra reported instead. "Apparently, Deputy McCormick found that suspicious."

He would. He seemed to see darkness at every turn. But, given the circumstances, Beth couldn't deny that the accident might not be so accidental after all. It seemed she really was in danger. Perhaps Hart was right. The best place for her was at home until this business with the gang was settled.

"Though I feel as if I'm running away," she complained to Allegra as her friend helped her pack her things.

"A strategic retreat, as Catherine would say," Allegra replied with a smile. "You are very welcome to return at any time."

Beth kept that thought in mind on the way back to Wallin Landing. Drew himself came to get her, lifting her to the wagon's bench with so much concern on his face that she had to pat his powerful shoulder.

"It's all right, Drew," she assured him. "I'll be fine."

She had to repeat the statement to the rest of her brothers, their wives and several of her nieces and nephews before they consented to leave her alone in her cabin. In consideration of her injuries, Simon had moved the bed from the loft to the main floor, squeezing it between the hearth and the table.

Levi was the last to leave. They had been conspirators as well as competitors growing up. She still found it hard to look at those blond curls and clever grin and see a minister.

"You're sure you'll be all right?" he asked, tugging the quilt higher on the bed.

"Fine," Beth assured him as she sat on the edge. "I wish you all would accept that."

"Might as well ask the sun to stop shining," he said. "You're too important to us, Beth. We worry. Deputy McCormick was very persuasive when Drew talked to him in Seattle before fetching you."

She might have known her oldest brother would consult Hart first. "He told you to coddle me, didn't he?" Fury tightened her fists. "Stubborn, annoying…"

"Easy." Levi put a hand on her shoulder as if to keep her settled. "He's just doing his job."

"Not from my perspective. I don't need that kind of protection."

His smile humored her.

Beth sat up taller. "Who's the best shot at Wallin Landing?"

"John, but you're a close second."

"Who knows every inch of this town, helped plan it, keeps it going?"

"You and Simon."

"Who very likely could spot danger coming a mile away?"

Levi shook his head. "Sorry, Beth, but not you. You tend to look at the bright side of things. You don't expect evil, so you don't notice it as it creeps closer."

Beth sighed. "And I suppose you do."

He shrugged. "I have seen a bit more of the world than you have."

He must be thinking of the gold fields. He'd had a hard time there. Beth frowned up at him. "So, tell me this, oh wise one—how am I any safer surrounded by wilderness instead of in Seattle with a constable, a marshal and a sheriff and his deputy near at hand?"

Levi opened his mouth and promptly shut it again.

"See? It's Hart McCormick. He's determined to keep me swaddled like a newborn babe. I won't have it. Can't he see I'm capable of taking care of myself? I helped him look for a house, improved his wardrobe, introduced him to society and found him a cause to support. He won't let me help him investigate this gang. He won't listen to a word I say!"

Levi moved closer to the hearth, set another log in the grate. "Maybe he doesn't like feeling he needs help any more than you do."

Beth started. "I... I never thought of it that way. But it's not the same thing. He did need help."

"And you don't?"

She smoothed down her flannel nightgown. "I suppose anyone does, sometimes. I certainly haven't managed to do much on my claim, for instance."

Levi stirred the fire. "And is that what you want, to stay out here and farm?"

A shudder went through her before she could stop it,

and she hoped her brother hadn't noticed. "I'm not sure. Frankly, I enjoyed my time in town more than I thought I would. There's so much going on, so much to get involved with. I feel as if I could make a difference in the town, even in the territory. But you all need me here."

Levi turned to her with a smile. "We missed you, but we managed. Feel free to go where you want, Beth. Where God leads you."

He left her then, but his words lingered as she climbed into bed. Lying there, gazing at the dying fire, it was easy to paint a picture of the perfect life for her. A small house in town, work with a purpose, helping fight for worthy causes, concerts and plays in the evenings, church surrounded by friends. She'd never been one to lack for ideas. But where was God leading her? It seemed a long time since she'd asked. She closed her eyes.

Dear Lord, You've blessed me with so much—family, friends, resources. Looking back, it seems I just went on my way, with no thought beyond my current goal. If there's a path You want me to follow, would You make it clear?

The sounds of the room faded as sleep approached. Her last thought was of Hart. She'd been certain that door was closed. He could have little respect for her to order her about like this. How could he be the path God wanted her to take?

Hart wasn't sure of his reception when he rode out to Wallin Landing later in the week to check on Beth. For one thing, he didn't relish confessing he'd taken her advice in another area of courting and purchased a house. What if she took that as encouragement and went back to trying to find him a bride? For another, he didn't bring good news. No one else claimed to have seen the man Beth had spotted, even though Hart and the sheriff had shown the drawings to every man and woman in the city, it seemed. No one had seen who'd tampered with Beth's wagon either. So, her enemy was still at large. She would have to stay at Wallin Landing for her own good.

He had thought of no good way to break it to her, but it turned out he never had the opportunity to try. He had no sooner reached the main clearing when the schoolroom door burst opened, and Frisco, Sutter and three of the older children spilled out, their teacher right behind them.

"Hurry, run!" Rina ordered, clapping her hands.

He reined in as the children scattered in all directions. "Something wrong, ma'am?"

"There most certainly is," she said, head coming up in the regal way she had. "We've been expecting you, Deputy. Please go to the main cabin. We'll be along shortly."

"We?" he asked, but she'd already whisked back into the school and shut the door.

Bemused, he dismounted and let Arno into the pasture. Then he went to the main cabin.

It had changed little over the years since Beth and her brothers had lived in it together. The logs had weathered to a silver-gray, but flowers still grew in the boxes under the windows. Likely Beth tended them. Inside, the same collection of wooden benches and chairs, including a bentwood rocker, gathered around the stone hearth. Ma Wallin's quilts and pillows lay scattered here and there, as if her presence still blessed the home she'd made for her family.

He was considering whether to take a seat when Levi arrived, followed by James, then John and Simon. Last came Drew, shutting the door soundly behind him.

Hart widened his stance as the big logger approached him. His golden brows were heavy, his dark blue eyes narrowed.

"What's happened?" Hart asked, fearing the worst.

"A great tragedy," James assured him. "Or a tremendous opportunity, depending on your point of view."

A tragedy? Had something happened to Beth? Had she been more injured than Doc had thought? Had the gang come to avenge itself on her?

Simon pointed a long finger at Hart. "We have evidence you're in love with our sister."

What? Despite himself, Hart took a step back. "It's not like that."

Drew crossed his arms over his broad chest. "No? Then explain your behavior."

Hart felt as if his throat was tightening. "Behavior?"

James ticked it off on his fingers. "Heads close together at the Pastry Emporium. Hours arm in arm to select a home, choose a new wardrobe. Rescued from certain death not once but twice. And that's just Lance and Percy."

"She's helping me," Hart insisted.

"Helping you do what?" Levi asked.

If he said courting, they'd probably all jump him. Normally he could hold his own in a fight, but he wasn't sure about tussling with Beth's brothers. They were all big men, and they were clearly concerned.

"Listen," said John, always the peacemaker. "We

don't hold it against you, Hart. Beth's logic can be hard to resist."

"Logic?" Simon asked with a frown.

John waved him into silence. "But if you care about her as you seem to do, we expect there to be some sort of proposal coming."

James sidled up to him, put one hand on his shoulder. "On bended knee. In the moonlight. Spouting Everard's poetry."

"It doesn't matter how or where," Drew said with a look to James. "But we need to know your intentions are honorable."

Now they all had their arms crossed.

Just then the door opened, and their wives began filing in. Beth's sisters-in-law looked equally determined to give him a dressing-down, heads and color high. No way around it now. Hart readied himself for a fight.

"We would like a few words with Deputy McCormick," Catherine, the acknowledged leader, said.

"Quickly," Rina added. "I have to get back to the children."

He thought he heard whooping and hollering from the clearing.

Nora put her hand on Simon's arm. "Frisco and Sutter are minding the little ones."

Simon's brows shot up.

"Please, John," Dottie said.

Callie went so far as to open the door wider. "Out you go, now. We'll get back to you directly."

Drew inclined his head. "We've said our piece. We'll expect an answer shortly, Deputy." He strolled out the door, his brothers behind him.

Hart backed up as the women converged on him. He

wasn't sure whether to draw his Smith and Wesson or cover his head with his arms.

"It is clear to us that you care deeply about Beth," Catherine said.

Hart drew in a breath. "Your husbands already let me know where things stand, ma'am."

"We were certain they would," Rina told him. The others nodded.

"That's why we're here," Catherine said. "So there can be no misunderstanding."

He nodded as well. He wasn't sure what else to do with them all gazing at him so determinedly.

"We just want to know how we can help," Dottie said.

"She is such a dear," Nora put in with a sigh.

"So, what'll it be, Deputy?" Callie asked. "How can we get you and Beth hitched?"

Chapter Twenty

Beth drove in to Seattle to fetch the mail on Friday afternoon. She felt fully restored by then, at least physically, though she was aware of a distinct lowering of her spirits when it came to Hart. He hadn't so much as darkened her door the last few days, as if having handed her to her family he bore no more responsibility for her.

Perhaps he didn't. It wasn't as if he was in love with her. The kiss had clearly been a mistake, and one he regretted. A shame she couldn't find it in her heart to do the same.

Her family certainly showed their support. Levi escorted her to the main clearing, where the horses and wagon waited. She had to admit to a tremor when she climbed up onto the bench, but James insisted on accompanying her in to town, and Simon and Drew assured her that the wagon was repaired. John had figured out a way to put a padlock on the hitch, so no one could tamper with it again.

"And you and I have the only keys," he promised her.

They were all so encouraging she began to hope she might convince them of the plan she'd decided upon while she was recuperating. She'd prayed about it, thought about it and prayed some more. Yet her excitement only grew.

It was daring. She'd be the first Wallin to live in town, the second to pursue a business of her own. And there was no guarantee she would succeed. But she was determined to try.

She dropped James off at the Occidental, where they planned to spend the night, and promised to meet him for dinner at five.

"And don't buy out Kelloggs' in the meantime," he cautioned with a smile.

She didn't intend to. She wasn't going to shop at all, but she wasn't ready to explain to any of her brothers until she knew the plan was viable.

Mr. Weinclef came out of Kelloggs' to greet her when she pulled in. "It's good to see you up and about, Miss Wallin. What can I get you today? We have some lovely new cambric."

Just the thing for summer! She could rework her blue dress, perhaps add some lace…

Beth squared her shoulders. "No, thank you, Mr. Weinclef. I'm here on business. I'd like to speak to Mr. Kellogg and his brother, if I may."

The brothers who owned the store were delighted to meet with her, but they expressed skepticism about her idea.

"A professional matchmaking service, out of Kelloggs'?" the older brother mused, stroking his clean-shaven chin. "I'm not sure how that benefits the store."

"It's not like your sister-in-law's sewing service, making use of our merchandise," his younger brother agreed, blue eyes narrowing.

"No, it's much better," Beth told them. "Gentlemen frequently need new clothes, accessories and toiletries before going courting. They spruce up their accommodations, requiring cleaning supplies, material for drapes, housewares. Once they wed, their loving wives will feel nothing but confidence in the store that brought them together. Where else would they shop forevermore?"

The brothers exchanged glances.

"Why not?" the elder asked. "We can give it a trial, say six months."

"A year," Beth said. "Some courtships take longer than others. You should begin to see the full benefits by next Easter."

"A year then." He stuck out his hand.

"Actually," Beth said, reaching into her reticule, "I thought you might prefer a written agreement, so I prepared one. Sign here, gentlemen."

Beth couldn't stop smiling as she exited the store a short time later. The first part of her plan had gone better than she'd hoped. She had a respectable location to conduct her business, with no need to rent a shop of her own. Now on to step two, finding a place to live. She had a little money put by for the first two months' rent. She knew just the place.

There, unfortunately, she was doomed to disappointment, for Mr. David Denny sadly reported that the charming house she'd seen with Hart had been purchased. He promised to let her know if anything else that met her needs became available. She would simply have to find another way for now.

"Open the doors, Lord," she murmured as she returned to Second Avenue.

She had two more errands before she met James for dinner, and they were both likely to be difficult. She went to the Pastry Emporium and asked Aiden to bring Scout to her. She would have preferred to meet her friend in private, but she couldn't take a chance now with her reputation, not when she was about to embark on a new business.

"I'm so glad you weren't seriously hurt," Ciara told her while they waited. "You can be sure I'll check our harness and tack before driving from now on."

"The worst thing was how everyone treated me," Beth confided, "as if my capabilities had been knocked from my head in the fall."

"Ridiculous," Ciara said with a sniff. "You're the most capable woman I know."

Having been raised by Maddie Haggerty, her friend offered high praise indeed. "Thank you," Beth said. "After I talk to Scout, may I beg a moment of your and Maddie's time? I'd like to propose a business venture."

Ciara's eyes lit. "Oh? What? Do you want to bake too?"

"Not exactly," Beth said. "I'm starting a matchmaking service, and I'd like to bring clients here to meet their prospective spouses, besides having the Emporium bake for the weddings."

Ciara was as excited as Beth could have hoped. She listened as Beth provided more details. Beth had just finished when Aiden returned with Scout.

Ciara gave her hand a squeeze. "We'll talk more later, but I think it's a marvelous idea, and I'm certain Maddie will be happy to have the Emporium serve as a meeting place and baker to the bride." She went back through the curtain to the kitchen.

"What's happened?" Scout asked as he sat at one of the little tables with Beth. With a thumbs-up to Beth, Aiden went to take Ciara's place behind the counter.

"Nothing of concern," Beth assured him, clasping her hands on the tabletop. "I just wanted to apologize."

Scout's eyes widened. "To me? For what?"

"For not allowing you to pursue courting the way you wanted. I was argumentative and far too determined."

Scout grinned. "Same bossy Beth."

Beth raised her chin. "I prefer to think of it as taking care of my family."

His grin slipped. "Family. Now, that's an honor."

"Well deserved," she told him. "But I pressed my advantage, and it's clear I made you uncomfortable. For that I am sorry."

"Apology accepted," Scout said. "And I hope you'll wish me happy. I'm to be married."

Her smile froze. "Mrs. Jamison?"

He nodded. "She's everything I ever wanted, Beth. She listens to me, thinks of my needs before her own, has dreams big enough for the both of us. She wants to travel, to England, to France, and she makes me want to go with her. She's so beautiful."

If Beth had seen all that in the seamstress, she might have thought better of this. "I'm very glad she makes you happy, Scout. But are you sure?"

He shrugged, dropping his gaze, fingers rubbing at the top of the table. All at once he was the shy, lost boy she'd known.

"As sure as anyone can be, I suppose," he murmured. "And it's too late now in any event. I proposed, she accepted. A gentleman does not cry off. Your father's books taught me that."

For the first time, she wasn't so sure about her father's legacy. "If there is any doubt in your mind, Scout, about her feelings or your own, you must postpone the wedding. Marriage is for a lifetime."

He raised his gaze to meet hers. "I think I could be very happy with Evangeline for a lifetime. My doubts come from a different direction. Can she be happy with me?"

Beth reached out and took his hands. "Oh, Scout, any woman would be proud to have a husband like you. I hope Mrs. Jamison knows how blessed she is."

He demurred, and they spoke of other things for a time. After she had sent him on his way, she sat for a moment, thinking.

Lord, I'm trying not to run ahead of Your plans. I'm trying to listen for Your voice. I'm trying to be a good friend. But something tells me this marriage is wrong. Is that You leading, or my own prejudices getting in the way?

Before when she'd asked for guidance she'd felt a peace. This time, urgency poked at her shoulder blades. She had to be sure. Scout had to be sure. She rose and moved to the counter. Her face must have betrayed her thoughts, for Aiden frowned.

"What's happened?"

Beth drew in a breath. "Something I need to attend to. I'll just let Ciara know." She slipped behind the counter and poked her head through the curtain into the kitchen.

Ciara hurried to meet her.

"We'll have to talk another time," Beth told her. "I must find Deputy McCormick. It's a matter of life or marriage."

* * *

Hart had already spotted Lance and Percy outside the Pastry Emporium. He'd ridden by twice before he sighted Beth leaving. Something inside him tightened as she went to retrieve the reins. Why did that blue dress make her look soft, vulnerable? Even the feathered hat on her curls looked insubstantial. She was still the prettiest lady in Seattle.

He couldn't believe her family had encouraged him to marry her. Her brothers seemed determined to hear of a proposal. Her sisters-in-law were equally determined to help Hart craft one. All had had numerous suggestions as to what he should do to bring Beth to the altar.

As if she was the one who had to be convinced.

Then again, maybe she did. He'd already refused her. Who could blame her if she didn't want to try again?

He was talking himself into approaching her when she turned and saw him. Her smile brightened the day. Arno veered in her direction.

"You too?" Hart murmured.

"I was just coming to find you," Beth said, putting out a hand to stroke Arno's nose. "I need your help."

Hart stiffened in the saddle. "What's happened?"

"I don't much like that question," Beth said, dropping her hand and setting Arno to bobbing his head in protest. "Everyone keeps asking it as if something must be wrong because I want to speak to them."

Hart forced himself to relax. "Sorry. How can I help you, Miss Wallin?"

She glanced in both directions, then frowned at him. "Have I offended you, Hart?"

"No."

"Then why the formality? No one is near enough to question the use of my first name."

Even if using her last name made him more comfortable. "What do you need?"

"It's Scout," she said. "He's going to marry Mrs. Jamison."

And she wasn't pleased about it. "I thought we agreed it was his choice."

She sighed. "We did. And he's so happy. But Hart, would it be possible to check with San Francisco again, just in case?"

"They never answered the first time," he pointed out. "But I can try."

She sagged. "Oh, thank you. I knew I didn't have to investigate the matter myself. I trust you."

For some reason, his chest swelled.

She untied the reins from the hitching post. "I should be going. I have a lot to do."

"Like always," he said with a smile.

She returned his smile. "Even more than usual. I'll tell you all about it when I come back to town on Monday. Perhaps we can meet here."

He cocked his head. "Is that an invitation?"

She grinned. "Absolutely. And don't you dare accept anyone else's."

He touched his hat. "Wouldn't dream of it."

She clucked to the horses and set off. Hart watched her as she drove around the corner. Somehow he thought the sight of her would never grow old. But did it follow he should offer marriage? Just because he loved her didn't mean she returned his love. Deep in thought, he turned Arno and headed for the telegraph office.

"Wondered when you would turn up," the operator said. He dug under the desk and retrieved a telegram.

"How long have you had this?" Hart demanded, staring down at the block lettering.

"Since the day after you sent the original. I asked Bobby Donovan to tell you. He's been helping me run telegrams around town."

"I guess he never caught up with me." At least, not to deliver the message. One look at the short note from the San Francisco law officer, and he thought he knew why Bobby had balked if he had suspected the contents.

Jamison likely Jasson. Third husband murdered? Wanted for questioning. Detain and contact us.

Normally, such a request would have sent Hart after the person, who would be sitting in the county jail by nightfall. But this wasn't a common thief or brawling logger. This was a lady, a business owner, respected, engaged to be married to a friend. Scout wasn't likely to take kindly to the fact that his sweetheart was wanted for questioning. Until Hart had more proof, he wasn't about to lock her up. Besides, at the moment, he was more interested in knowing why Bobby hadn't told him about the telegram. Was he only protecting his sister? Or did his refusal stem from something more?

He thanked the telegraph operator, mounted Arno and rode up to the North School.

The new teacher, Miss Jenkins, beamed at the sight of him. Beth's campaign to make him attractive to the local ladies had obviously worked on this one, for she smoothed down her hair and fluttered her lashes as he asked her some questions.

"Robert Donovan?" She cocked her head. "Why, no, Deputy. We have no student by that name. But if you'd meet me at the Pastry Emporium later, I'm sure we could discuss it further."

"No time, ma'am," he told her, turning Arno. "But thank you for the kindness."

He thought he heard her sigh as he rode away.

So, Bobby hadn't started school after Easter as his sister had said. It was possible she'd decided to hire him a tutor instead, someone who could keep him current on his lessons while he worked. But why work at all? Were the pair so low on funds?

He did a sweep of the town, but caught no sign of the boy, his sister or Beth. He'd only looked for the last to be certain she wasn't investigating after all. Despite her declaration of faith in him, he found it hard to believe she'd simply step aside. Still, the fact that she had relinquished her search in favor of him only made him more determined to get to the bottom of things.

He hitched Arno down the street from the seamstress's shop and approached the door. It was locked, the window shade down, but he thought he saw a flicker of shadow behind it. Someone was inside.

He pounded on the door. "Open up. It's Deputy McCormick."

A moment later, the door cracked open, showing a slim slice of Mrs. Jamison. The crimson dress with its high neck and long sleeves might have graced the finest ladies in any town. A gold watch glimmered on a chain around her neck.

"Deputy, you startled me," she said, sounding a bit breathless. "I'm afraid now isn't a good time for you to come in. I'm doing inventory, and there are unmentionables everywhere."

He hadn't known she stocked ladies' underthings,

but he certainly didn't want to question her standing next to them. "This will only take a moment, ma'am. It's about Bobby."

"Bobby?" She frowned, then a concerned look slid into place on her lovely face. "Oh, Deputy McCormick, please tell me he hasn't been on the docks again."

"Not the docks," he said. "Not in school either."

She gasped. "Oh, you must find him. Give me a moment, and I'll come with you."

The door closed. Shadows passed the shade again, but before he could try the door, she was back, coat draped about her. She locked the door behind her.

"Now, then," she said with a brave smile, "let's find that naughty brother of mine." She took his arm and led him away. Hart glanced back in time to see a hand push the shade into place.

Who else was in there with her? Scout, helping his sweetheart with her work? Why not admit it? Bobby? Why claim he was elsewhere? He would have given a great deal to see what was happening inside that shop, but he didn't have a warrant. He'd have to play it her way.

"When was the last time you saw him?" Hart asked as they moved down the street.

"This morning, when I thought he was on the way to school. It's the company he keeps, Deputy. That awful O'Rourke boy and his sister."

Hart fought to maintain a civil tone. "They were both working at the Pastry Emporium this afternoon. Where would your brother have gone?"

She waved a hand. "Who knows how these children think?"

He was more interested in what she thought. "You must have some idea. He is your brother, after all."

"And a burden since the day he was born." She must have realized how hard she sounded, for she turned to him with a coy smile. "Forgive me, Deputy. It's so difficult raising a boy alone. And I'm so new to Seattle that I wouldn't know where to suggest we look for him." She put a hand on his arm and leaned closer, her frame brushing his. "I rely on you to guide me."

For someone engaged, she was rather forward. And for someone determined to find her brother, she wasn't much help. But perhaps that was the idea. Perhaps she didn't want him to find Bobby. She wanted him away from the shop.

Hart took her elbow. "Then allow me to do the guiding. I have a hunch we'll find Bobby right where you least expect him, hiding in your shop."

"What?" She dragged her feet as he drew her back toward the door. "No, Deputy. You're mistaken. I'd know if Bobby was hiding so close."

"Let's find out." He strode up to the door and looked expectantly at her.

She raised her chin and her voice at the same time, as if making sure anyone near heard her. "This is silly, Deputy. I'd much rather walk up to the school and ask where Bobby has gone. I'm sure it's all a misunderstanding."

He held out his hand. "Key."

She patted her coat pocket. "Now, where did I... I'm sure it's here somewhere."

"Key," Hart demanded.

She jumped, then yanked it out of her pocket and

dropped it into his hand. "Fine. See for yourself. Bobby isn't anywhere near here."

But someone was. He heard the motion just as he opened the door. He had a brief glimpse of broadcloth, a flash of metal, and something collided with his skull.

Chapter Twenty-One

She was nearly done. Beth drove the wagon up the hill to the Wyckoff residence and tied Lance and Percy before going to knock on the lacquered front door. Ursula seemed glad to see her, but when Beth broached the subject, the sheriff's wife leaned away from her on the sofa.

"Deputy McCormick is a private man, firm in his convictions," Beth told her. "Having worked with him these last few weeks, I think we do him a disservice by insisting that he wed."

Mrs. Wyckoff arranged her dun-colored skirts. "A challenging case, to be sure. Perhaps a full member of our Literary Society will be up to the task."

It seemed she wasn't to be accepted after all. What was more important was doing right by Hart. Beth squared her shoulders. "I assure you they will not. Short of tricking him to the altar, which I'm certain you agree is a shabby practice unworthy of the Literary Society or any lady of character, Hart McCormick cannot be brought up to scratch against his will."

Mrs. Wyckoff stilled, eyes narrowing. "But might he someday be willing?"

"I believe that to be the case," Beth said, refusing to blush. "And I promise you will be among the first to hear of that happy event."

Mrs. Wyckoff nodded. "Excellent. Perhaps you could give us an update at each meeting, among the other areas you'll have to report on for the society, of course."

Beth stared at her. "You're inviting me to join?"

Mrs. Wyckoff touched her hand as if to reassure her. "My dear, anyone who can serve so ably cannot be denied."

Beth had left smiling. She could hardly believe it— she was a member of the prestigious Literary Society. Pa and Ma would have been so proud. And that also meant the pressure was off, both her and Hart, at least for the moment. If he wanted to court, it was all up to him.

"And how is the good deputy today?" James greeted her when she met him in the Occidental dining room a short while later.

She allowed him to hold the chair for her while she sat. "Fine. Did you convince Mr. Black and Mr. Powell to let you carry their ready-mades at the store?"

James made a face as he sat. "Yes, and I cannot decide whether I'm pleased or disappointed. There's something about a tailor-made coat."

Her most flamboyant brother, in outlook and dress, James was forever offering Nora commissions for new outfits and coats. Even now, he was dressed in a spruce-colored frock coat and gold-shot waistcoat.

"Most of the men out our way will be happy for what they can get," she told him. "And if they want something fancier, there's always Nora."

"Or this Mrs. Jamison I keep hearing about."

Beth snapped the napkin open and draped it over her gown. "Inferior stuff, I assure you. What are you having for dinner?"

James was frowning toward the doorway of the establishment. "Now, what do you suppose brought Sheriff Wyckoff here tonight?"

She had an inkling. Beth grit her teeth. "Oh! I would not have expected Mrs. Wyckoff to exert her influence in this way, not after agreeing to my face. What, should I beg Drew to intercede for me when things don't go as I want?"

James eyed her, but the sheriff came unerringly toward their table. A tall, powerfully built man with a long narrow face half covered by a thick brown beard, he always smelled of tobacco. Now he nodded to them both as he planted himself beside the cloth-draped table.

"I won't do it," she told him. "And nothing you say will change my mind."

He took off his hat respectfully. "I'm sorry to hear that, ma'am. I was hoping you could tell me what's become of my deputy."

Beth reared back in her chair. "Your deputy? You mean Hart's missing?"

"Perhaps the sheriff's only misplaced him," James offered. "Did you look behind the sofa?"

Beth paid him no mind. Neither did the sheriff. "So, you haven't talked to McCormick recently?" he asked.

"This afternoon, around three, I suppose. Has no one seen him since?"

"No one I can find. He didn't sign out in the office at the end of his shift. Billy Prentice found Arno tied on Commercial, with no sign of McCormick."

Beth hopped to her feet, napkin sliding to the polished wood floor. "Something's happened! Those villains he's been chasing must have seized him to stop his interference."

Several of the other diners glanced their way. One of the waiters hurried in their direction. Sheriff Wyckoff looked more closely at her. "Which villains do you mean?"

Beth waved a hand. "The gang that's been robbing newcomers, the fellow who accosted me and very likely damaged our wagon. Deputy McCormick has been trying to bring them to justice."

"And we'd all like to help him," James put in with a firm tone she'd seldom heard him use.

Sheriff Wyckoff inclined his head. "I'm aware of the investigation, but I haven't heard he was close to making an arrest. I'll check further." He stepped back from the table. "Thank you for your help, Miss Wallin, Mr. Wallin." Turning, he started for the door.

James rose and eyed Beth. "He'll find McCormick. The good deputy is likely patrolling farther out of the city today."

"No," Beth said, watching the sheriff out the door. "He's always in town for the weekend. And he wouldn't have left without telling someone. Something's wrong." She turned to James. "We have to help him."

"Well, certainly," James agreed. "What do you have in mind?"

In truth, it was hard to order her thoughts. All she knew was that Hart was in danger, and she couldn't sit idly by waiting for word to come.

"What can I get you for dinner, folks?" the waiter asked, pad and pencil in hand.

"Not a thing," James told him. "My sister has work to do, and I mean to help her do it."

Beth shot him a grateful glance as they left the hotel. James strolled along beside her, as if nothing could be possibly wrong, yet she felt the tension in him. It nearly matched her own.

"When I talked with Hart this afternoon," she told her brother, turning toward the harbor, "he was going to send a telegram. I suggest we start there. Failing that, we could canvas the merchants. Or we could talk to Billy Prentice. He may have more to tell us about the circumstances of finding Arno like that. Oh, and Allegra might have something to say."

James quirked a brow. "You seem to have given this significant thought. Did you expect Deputy McCormick to disappear?"

"Certainly not!" Just the idea chilled her. "He can generally take care of himself."

"Which is why you've been trying to find him a bride."

Beth scowled at him as they turned onto Commercial. "I never told you that."

"No," he agreed, shoving his hands in his pants pockets. "But either he was courting you or you were matchmaking. There's no other explanation for it."

He was too clever by half. "That's all over now. If Hart McCormick wants to go courting, he can do it himself. I just want to make sure he's in a position to court."

She kept that in mind as they headed for the telegraph office. He had to be fine. If nothing more happened between them, he would always be a friend. He tempered her mad starts, helped her think through options. She couldn't lose him. Even the gang wouldn't dare harm a lawman. Would they?

She gave the telegraph operator, Mr. Dixon, her best smile. "Did Deputy McCormick come by here this afternoon to send a telegram?"

Dixon shook his head where he sat dutifully behind his desk, his brass equipment in front of him. "Deputy McCormick hasn't sent a telegraph for weeks."

What? Beth sagged. "I was so sure he came this way."

"Oh, he was here," Dixon said with maddening calm. "But he picked up a telegram. He didn't send one."

It took every ounce of control to keep her voice pleasant. "Oh? What time was that?"

The operator scratched his temple, making his cap slip on his brown hair. "Sometime before five. That's when I take my dinner break."

"Did you see where he went?" Beth pressed.

He shook his head. "I don't watch people. The line keeps me too busy."

As if to prove it, the telegraph started clacking, and he bent to take the message.

James drew Beth back toward the door. "Not the most helpful of fellows."

"Not at all." Beth tapped her foot, waiting, until the telegraph operator had finished, signed off and checked the message before looking up again. But instead of addressing her, he glanced around her as if expecting to see someone else.

"That boy! Where has he gone to now? Doesn't he know telegrams must be delivered?"

James stepped into his line of vision. "You were going to tell us about Deputy McCormick."

"Deputy McCormick?" He frowned as he straightened. "I already told you. He picked up a telegram and left."

"Who sent the telegram?" Beth asked. "What did it say?"

The operator drew himself up. "The telegraph office has a sacred duty. No one is to know the nature of the telegram except the one to whom it was sent."

"And apparently the delivery boy," James put in.

"No, sir," Dixon insisted. "Deputy McCormick was adamant. I send someone to tell him when a telegram comes. He fetches it. No one reads it but him. And me, of course."

Beth took a step forward, fists balling. "Deputy McCormick has disappeared, and it very likely has something to do with that telegram. You must tell me what it said. It could be important!"

Dixon took two fingers and pressed his lips together.

Oh! Beth squared her shoulders, but James stepped in front of her. "A shame about your delivery boy. Who was it?"

Dixon dropped his hand. "Bobby Donovan. Recently hired. And he won't be employed here long if he doesn't show up shortly."

Beth blinked, shoulders coming down. "Bobby Donovan?"

The telegraph operator nodded. "Seemed a dependable type, and he sure wanted the job. I haven't had any complaints until now. He assured me he'd found the deputy, but Mr. McCormick never came for the message. He seemed surprised to hear it had arrived. Apparently, the boy can't even do that errand right."

"I have a feeling he was doing exactly what he was

told," Beth said. "Thank you, Mr. Dixon. You've helped tremendously."

He puffed out his chest. "All in a day's work." The telegraph began working again, and he hurried to take the message.

James followed Beth out the door. "I learned nothing useful from that, but it's obvious you did."

Beth nodded, setting off down the street. "I certainly did. I asked Hart to look into Mrs. Jamison, the seamstress Scout intends to marry."

"Of what do you suspect her?" James asked, lengthening his stride to keep up. "Wearing a dress a year out of season?"

"Murdering three husbands for their money," Beth replied.

James whistled. "Scout can certainly pick them."

"Don't blame Scout," Beth scolded as they approached the lady's shop. "She's taken in the Denny ladies and most everyone in Seattle. Hart telegraphed the law in San Francisco, where she supposedly came from. I think that telegram told him something about Mrs. Jamison, he went to confront her and she captured him."

"And you base all that on a confused conversation with a telegraph operator who wouldn't even divulge the nature of the telegram?"

Beth paused to eye the shop door. "Yes. Besides, Bobby Donovan, the boy who forgot to tell Hart about the telegram and who can't be found now, is Mrs. Jamison's brother."

James's brows shot up. "Then let's find Sheriff Wyckoff, tell him what we suspect."

"No time," Beth assured him. "Who knows what foul things she has planned for Hart?"

James caught her arm. For once, no humor twinkled in his dark blue eyes. "Beth, if the woman hasn't scrupled to kill three husbands and kidnap a lawman, what makes you think she will listen to you?"

Beth pulled out of his grip. "Because I speak her language. Now, come on. We haven't much time."

Hart sat against the wall in the back of Evangeline Jamison's shop. At least that's where he thought he was. All he could see was a curtained doorway, some packing crates and a large trunk. He was a little concerned what might end up in the trunk.

His hands were tied behind his back with something that felt suspiciously like satin ribbon. His ankles were bound with yards of lace. If he was rescued in this state, he'd be laughed out of Seattle.

But he had to own that the ties were effective. Neither the lace nor the ribbon gave in the slightest no matter how he strained against them.

He'd been unconscious for a while, but near as he could figure it was after dinnertime. Would Wyckoff notice Hart hadn't signed out? Would he come looking? Who was Hart kidding? No one would think to look for him at the back of a shop specializing in ladies' clothing.

The curtain twitched, and Hart froze. But instead of Mrs. Jamison or his assailant, Bobby Donovan slipped into the room and came to crouch beside him. The boy's face was haggard, his clothing damp with sweat. He almost looked as if he'd been the one tied up and left behind.

"I'm sorry, Deputy," he whispered. "You've been nothing but a friend. I didn't want it to come to this."

So he knew at least some of what his sister was up to. Hart still wasn't sure.

"Then help me," Hart murmured back, wondering how many others waited on the other side of the curtain. "There has to be a pair of scissors in this place. Cut me loose."

Bobby's eyes dipped down at the corners. "I can't. She'd skin me alive if the others didn't beat me flat first."

"How many are we talking about?" Hart asked, watching him.

"Two. Tough characters. They do what Evie tells them to do, most of the time. Everyone does what Evie tells them to do, or there's trouble. Ask the men she's married."

He was beginning to see the picture. Two tough characters, Bobby had said. It couldn't be a coincidence. Evangeline Jamison must be the leader of the gang who'd been preying on the newcomers, and Bobby, it seemed, was an unwilling accomplice.

"I can protect you," Hart promised. "Just let me free."

Bobby glanced back over his shoulder, then rose and went to one of the packing cases. Returning, he slipped a crowbar behind Hart, between his bonds. "I can't, but maybe you can." Straightening, he slipped out of the room.

It took several tries for Hart to position the bar just right, but then he had the satisfaction of hearing a ribbon snap. A bit more pressure, and the rest gave as well. Shaking off the ties, he brought his hands forward to work on his ankles.

Voices rose on the other side of the curtain, angry, demanding. Was Bobby even now paying for his kindness? Yanking on the lace, Hart freed his legs and stood, keeping the crowbar at the ready.

"I have no idea what you're talking about." That was the seamstress at her most haughty. "I think you better leave."

She wasn't speaking to one of her henchmen, then. He crept closer to the curtain, listening.

"I'm going nowhere until you tell me what happened to Deputy McCormick."

The breath stopped in his lungs. Beth? No! He wanted to slam through the doorway, carry her to safety. But he couldn't risk that Mrs. Jamison would reach her first.

"I have no interest in your deputy," Mrs. Jamison informed her. "I'm to be married."

"Not if I have anything to say about the matter. You murdered your husbands. I won't see you do the same to Scout."

"How dare you!"

Would she strike Beth? Kill her for knowing the truth? He couldn't wait. He shoved through the curtain into the room, crowbar held high.

Mrs. Jamison was a few feet from Beth, the two women glaring at each other. The only other person in the room was James Wallin. He had his back to the door, as if to make sure no one got in or out. He sighted Hart first, and his eyes widened.

That was enough to tip off Mrs. Jamison. She leaped on Beth, pulled her close and turned with her as if to keep an eye on both Hart and James. A lethal-looking hatpin hovered near Beth's neck.

"That's far enough, Deputy," Mrs. Jamison said. "Drop the bar."

Pain shot through him, as if the pin had pricked every extremity. He bent and released the crowbar.

"Let her go," he told the seamstress.

Mrs. Jamison tsked. "I think not. Dear Miss Wallin has interfered quite enough." One hand on Beth's shoulder, she gave her a shake. Beth grimaced.

"Now, back you go into the rear room, Deputy. Mr. Wallin is going to tie you up again. I'll take Miss Wallin with me for safekeeping. Mr. Wallin will tell their family that you and their sister eloped."

"And why would I do anything so foolish?" James demanded, moving away from the door. "Don't answer that, Beth."

Beth rolled her eyes.

"Because if you don't," Mrs. Jamison said, "I'll use your sister as a pincushion."

James pulled up short with a look to Hart.

"She's right," Beth said calmly. "A hatpin, used strategically, can be quite a weapon. I could easily bleed to death before you brought help."

Hart felt sick.

"Clever girl," Mrs. Jamison purred with a smile. "Now, back away, Deputy."

He couldn't make his feet move. His gaze met Beth's.

"I won't let this happen again. I can't."

"I wouldn't ask it of you," she said. "And I'm not nearly so noble as your Annabelle."

Before he knew what she was about, she twirled to the left, taking herself down and under Mrs. Jamison's arm, which she grasped and wrenched up behind the woman. The hatpin flashed as it tumbled to the floor.

"Levi always fell for that one," Beth said with a shake of her head. "Deputy, I believe you have an arrest to make."

Chapter Twenty-Two

Beth was rather pleased with how the whole situation had turned out. Hart was free and apparently uninjured. She had escaped with only a scratch on her neck that would require her to wear an unfashionable ruff for a while, but sacrifices must be made. She thought she might hear a *job well done* from Hart as she handed Mrs. Jamison to him and retrieved the hatpin.

Instead, he pinioned the seamstress's arms to her sides and leaned around her to gaze at Beth, eyes hard. "There are two more of them who have been hiding out here. We need to find them and Bobby Donovan." He turned to her brother. "Normally the sheriff would do this, but there's no time. James Wallin, I hereby deputize you to serve the citizens of King County and uphold the laws of Washington Territory and these United States."

James blinked. "I'm honored, Deputy, but..."

Mrs. Jamison wiggled in Hart's grip. "This is ridiculous. I demand an attorney."

Hart ignored her. "James, take Mrs. Jamison to the office and send word to Sheriff Wyckoff to lock her up on charges of kidnapping and assault. Tell him there may be other charges as well after we contact the sheriff in San Francisco."

"A lady has a right to protect her property, her person," Mrs. Jamison protested as James took charge of her.

"Not at the expense of other people's lives and property," Beth told her.

The woman was still sputtering and dragging her feet as James muscled her out of the shop.

The moment he was through the door, Hart surged forward and wrapped Beth in his arms. Startled, she couldn't move as his mouth descended on hers. Then she found it hard to even think. She'd never imagined a kiss could feel so urgent. She leaned in, gave as she was given, delight bubbling up inside her.

He pulled away all too soon. "Stay here. I'll come for you when it's safe."

"Don't be ridiculous," Beth said, tucking a strand of hair behind her ear and trying to gather her composure while her blood still sang. "I have no intention of waiting here while you face all the danger."

"Beth."

Oh, how she loved that growl. "Think, Hart. Wherever these men are, you said this was their hideout. They're just as likely to return here as anywhere else in Seattle. I'd rather not meet them alone, even with a hatpin for defense."

He took her arm and pulled her from the shop.

"If you would listen," she said as he all but dragged her down the block, "I'm sure Aiden and Ciara would be happy to help us search. Clay and Allegra too, for that matter. And as soon as Sheriff Wyckoff locks up Mrs. Jamison, he and James will be available."

Some of the fire went out of him. "At least you didn't come alone this time."

"I'm not daft, you know. I do realize the danger."

"Do you?" He stopped and glared at her. "Mrs. Jamison is wanted for questioning about the death of her husband in San Francisco. She may well have murdered him and two others."

"That's what I've been trying to tell you! I'm quite glad to have my suspicions confirmed. Well, not glad, precisely, but vindicated. Who are her accomplices?"

He started walking again, as if he had to do something to relieve his tension. "Unless I miss my guess, they're the gang I've been trying to catch."

Now Beth stopped. "Really? Mrs. Jamison was behind the robberies and beatings as well?"

His breath was coming fast. "Now do you see why I'm worried about you? If anything had happened to you, Beth…"

She put a hand on his arm. "It didn't. I'm fine. And even if I wasn't, my brothers would never blame you. They know how I am."

"I wasn't worried about how your brothers would react," he said, eyes haunted. "I was worried about you. When I think of you hurt, my body tightens into a knot, and I'm no good for anything."

Before the words could sink in, he grabbed her arm and pulled her forward again. "We don't have time to talk now. Come on."

He kept going at such a pace that conversation and even breaths became difficult. Yet she couldn't forget his words. He had been frightened for her, to the point of pain. He'd kissed her as if his very life depended on it. If she'd read of such a situation in a book, she'd have said the hero felt deep love for the lady in question.

Had she won his heart at last?

Hart felt as if his body was encased in steel. No time to talk, no luxury to feel. He had to catch the rest of the Jamison gang. Beth's and Bobby's lives could be in danger otherwise.

And yet he could not forget how she had bested the seamstress. She had been fearless, clever and determined. She hadn't just reacted. She'd planned, chosen her movements with precision. Perhaps, like her family, he would always want to protect her, but he had to own she could take care of herself.

"I never saw her accomplices," Hart told her now as they approached the sheriff's office. "But they must still be in the area. Bobby helped me escape. He was scared of being caught."

She beamed at him. "I'm so glad to hear Bobby didn't go along willingly. I imagine his sister bullied him into helping. So, what's our plan?"

He started to protest that she could have no part in this, then forced himself to stop. After all she'd done, she had every right to see this through. "I'll work with the sheriff to deputize more men. We'll search the town, then spread out around the area."

"No one's admitted to seeing them before," she pointed out. "But perhaps having additional people searching will help. At least we can cover more ground than just you and the sheriff. A shame we don't have more information."

Hart eyed her. "Would you talk to Mrs. Jamison?

I have a feeling she'll tell you the truth sooner than she'd tell me. What you learn could well turn the tide in our favor."

She rolled her eyes. "She'll no doubt have a wealth of information, and I'm sure I can extract it from her, but don't think I'm unaware of what you're doing."

He made his eyes as wide as possible. "Me?"

The sound of her laughter eased his tight muscles. "You want me out of the way. I'll go, but only because it might do some good and give you some peace." Stopping him short of the office door, she stood on tiptoe and pressed a kiss to his cheek. Then she hurried inside.

It was nearly midnight before they caught the pair. In the meantime, Beth collected quite a story from Mrs. Jamison, who was no doubt attempting to build a case that would prove her an unwilling dupe.

"You have no idea of the pressure I was under," Hart heard her lament to Beth as he loaded a shotgun. "A widow alone, with a child to consider. Of course I co-operated with anything they demanded. I was afraid to refuse."

Hart very much doubted that.

At least Beth was able to get her to confirm that the two men who had robbed and beaten the newcomers were still in Seattle waiting until she had won more money from Scout to make their escape. She seemed to think they had gone hunting.

"Though she's rather vague about how much money she expected and when," Beth told him before he and the sheriff headed out. "I'm not sure poor Scout was supposed to survive his wedding night."

Her look to the jail cell hinted of her anger, but she

schooled her face and returned to her questioning. For a moment, he almost pitied Mrs. Jamison.

While some deputized townsmen scoured the city, James, Sheriff Wyckoff and Hart waited at the shop. He was only glad that silence was necessary. He wasn't willing to answer the questions he saw in James's eyes. Beth's brother had to have noticed the way Hart had reacted to the danger facing Beth, heard the tremor in his voice. If the Wallin brothers had wondered how Hart truly felt about their sister, there could be no doubt now.

Hart certainly had no doubt. His only question was how he could go about proving his love to Beth.

He heard the snick of the lock a moment before the rear door of the shop opened. Finally, his quarry! They were as Schneider had described, as tough a pair of customers as Bobby had intimated. They shambled into the shop, gazes wary. One shut the door behind them.

Sheriff Wyckoff rose from behind a crate and leveled his rifle. "Stop right there. Lay down your weapons and put up your hands. You're under arrest."

Hart thought they'd run for it or shoot it out, but they exchanged glances, and the taller made a dive for the sheriff. The next few minutes was nothing but flying fists and grappling men. In the end, Hart and the others triumphed with no more to show than some bruised knuckles.

"Well done, Deputy," James said, clapping Hart on the shoulder as the sheriff locked up the men. "You survived a vicious gang and my sister. Few men can make that claim."

Beth shook her head, then stifled a yawn. "Mrs. Jamison still maintains she loves Scout and wants to marry him. I don't believe her."

James took a step back. "What? My sister, the match-maker, the romantic?"

She cast Hart a quick glance. "I will probably always be a romantic, James, but I'm not so naive to believe every story told me. Mrs. Jamison had the opportunity when she was with Scout to confess, to ask for help. She could even have told Hart the truth, assisted him in catching her confederates. She did nothing but aid their schemes, each step of the way. And don't get me started on what she claims happened to her husbands. Three accidents? Unlikely."

She turned to Sheriff Wyckoff. "What news of Bobby Donovan? As far as I can tell, he's another victim in all this, forced to do as his sister said."

"No sign of him," the sheriff reported, pocketing the key to the cells. "We'll keep looking tomorrow."

Beth nodded. There was so much Hart wanted to say to her, but the crowded office wasn't the place or time. She'd once braved censure to tell him how she felt. If he was going to convince her of his feelings, he needed something grander, more eloquent than a simple acknowledgment. For now, he merely tipped his hat as James led her out to return to the hotel.

Though morning was only a few hours away, it seemed a long time coming. His mind kept turning over plans, thinking through options. Beth deserved the best, something spectacular, something that would appeal to her heart. James had called her a romantic. Hart had never considered himself such. He'd need help, and he'd have to swallow his pride to ask, but the chance that she'd agree was worth any trouble.

He rose early, walked down to the Occidental. He wanted to thank James again for his help, but he knew the effort was more about seeing Beth. She'd found a way past his defenses, reached the heart he'd kept guarded for so long. He was ready to admit defeat and win the prize. But he had a few things to take care of first.

"Any news about Bobby?" she asked after he'd greeted her and her brother outside the hotel. James had Lance and Percy already in harness, ready to return to Wallin Landing.

"Not yet," Hart told her. "He may be afraid to come out of hiding. He knows he's been an accessory to a crime at the least. When I think back, I can see a few times he tried to get my attention. He was just too frightened of his sister to do more."

"The jury should take that into account," Beth said.

"In the meantime, the sheriff will be busy lining up witnesses to the gang's crimes. Now that the victims understand the law didn't condone the violence, they'll be more likely to come forward."

"There's just one last person to notify, then," Beth murmured, slumping. "Will you come with me, Hart, when I tell Scout?"

They found him at home in the big house he'd purchased. Their voices echoed in the entry as he showed them in. Before Beth could tell him about Mrs. Jamison, he held up a hand.

"It's all right, Beth. I know. Bobby came to see me last night. It seems you were right. Evangeline never cared for me, only my money."

The words fell from his lips like deadwood. He looked nearly spent. Hart wasn't sure what to say, but Beth threw her arms around Scout and hugged him close.

"She doesn't deserve you," she told him. "The woman you thought you knew was a fiction. We'll find you someone better, someone real." She drew back with a watery smile. "I've decided to make matchmaking my vocation, and you'll be my first client, no charge."

Scout chuckled. "Might be hard to run a business if you don't charge your clients."

Beth waved a hand. "We'll work all that out later. In the meantime, do you know where Bobby went?"

Scout jerked his head toward the stairs. "He's staying with me. I thought he'd be safer. I was going to come down to the sheriff's office this morning and let you know, Deputy."

"You're a good man, Rankin," Hart said.

Scout seemed to stand a little taller. "You too, Deputy. Go easy on him. He's been through a lot."

"I'll talk to the sheriff. For now, let him know not to leave town but that we're on his side."

And then Beth had hugged him. He willed himself not to react the way he wanted in front of Scout. He didn't have the right, not yet. But soon.

Please, Lord!

She bustled along at her usual pace as Hart escorted her back to the hotel.

"You see what I mean about a lady being just as capable as a gentleman?" she asked with a sidelong look his way.

"You got the advantage over her," Hart admitted.

There was a decided wiggle in her walk, as if she was well pleased with herself. "Thank you, but that wasn't what I meant. All this time, we've been looking for men, when the person in charge was a woman."

She almost sounded admiring. "I won't argue that

Mrs. Jamison was as coldhearted a villain as one could ask. I hope you don't plan to take her example."

Beth snorted. "Certainly not. Oh, I understand the allure of fine clothes, pretty things. It seems she wanted the best. To dress well, eat well, move in the finest circles, travel. I think she must have been raised in a rough environment, which is probably where she met her henchmen. Her first husband wasn't as rich as she'd been led to believe, so she used her wiles to plot some crimes for her men. That went so well she continued the pattern with her second and third husbands. I imagine there's quite a sum built up in her name at the bank in San Francisco."

"Though not enough, it seems, to satisfy her," Hart said as they neared the bottom of the hill. "When the sheriff in San Francisco started asking questions, she knew it was best to leave town."

"In case he discovered her other activities," Beth agreed. "She came to Seattle, set up shop in more ways than one."

Hart helped her up onto the boardwalk as they reached the center of town. "And then she sighted Scout."

"And his money." Beth sighed. "I suppose that's when the gang disappeared for a while. She didn't want to take the chance they might be caught and reveal her when she was so close to achieving her goal. She kept them closed up in her shop and convinced Scout to pay for the supplies." Beth shook her head. "Very clever. Wicked, but clever."

Hart thought it time to change the subject. "What's this about you opening a matchmaking business?"

"Shh!" she cautioned as they approached the hotel

and her waiting brother. "I haven't told my family yet. I'll explain it to you next week, when I come back to town to stay. I've taken a room with Mrs. Elliott, at the ladies' boardinghouse."

She was willing to leave Wallin Landing to live in town? That might improve his chances. But he'd need to move fast. She might be starting a matchmaking service, but he had no doubt that a good many men in Seattle would be only too happy to make a match, with her.

Chapter Twenty-Three

Beth stood on the boardwalk outside Kelloggs', fingering the note from her latest client. Only two weeks as a professional matchmaker and already she had three gentlemen to help, besides Scout. Two she had introduced to prospective brides around the area, and the courtships seemed to be progressing. Scout and the mail-order bride she'd identified were corresponding, and light seemed to be returning to his eyes. All expressed complete confidence in her ability to see the tasks through. She shared their confidence.

But she couldn't help remembering the one time she'd given up.

She was certain she'd see more of Hart now that she lived in Seattle, but after she'd met him at the Pastry Emporium and told him all about her plans they kept missing each other. She was busy helping organize the women's suffrage march, memorizing her lines for the upcoming theatrical. But he knew how to find her. Perhaps he didn't believe her promise to never again turn her matchmaking skills on him.

Scout had told her Hart had convinced the sheriff to

let Bobby remain in Scout's custody. The boy had confessed to helping his sister out of fear. She'd kept him close, threatened harm to anyone he'd tried to befriend. His ability to identify his sister's accomplices and detail their crimes would go a long way toward proving his willingness to lead a law-abiding life from here on. Mrs. Jamison and her confederates were awaiting trial when the judge sat in May. So, Hart's investigation of that case was over. Beth hadn't heard of any other major crimes that might be keeping him busy. He clearly didn't want to spend time with her.

She might as well admit it. Though she still loved him and probably always would, he might never return her feelings. She had to accept that, and get on with her life.

Her family had seemed surprised but supportive of her decision to give up her claim for a vocation. Simon intended to see whether the territory would allow them to purchase Beth's land instead of her earning it. She had promised to put what she could toward the cost. It was a small price to pay for the freedom to do what she felt called to do.

She glanced down at the note, delivered only this morning. It was a bit mysterious—with no signature or anything that might suggest its writer. She was requested for tea *al fresco*. Likely that meant the note came from a gentleman attempting to ensure that propriety would be satisfied. She recognized the location. It was the house she'd hoped Hart would purchase, the one she'd tried to rent. At least this client had good taste. She adjusted her pink sleeves and headed for her appointment.

The owner, it seemed, had seen to her every comfort. A

table draped in white sat on the wide front porch, flanked by a pair of fanciful wrought-iron chairs that reminded her of the ones at the Pastry Emporium. The table gleamed with white bone china and silver. Good taste and money as well. Who was this paragon?

The door of the house opened, and Beth put on her best smile to meet the fellow. Instead, Maddie Haggerty, swathed in a frilly white apron, came out to set a plate of lemon drops and a pot of tea on the table.

"And a very fine afternoon to you, Miss Wallin," she said, twinkle evident in her eyes. "Your host will be with you shortly."

"Since when do you play French maid?" Beth teased, climbing to the porch.

Maddie winked at her. "Since you're involved, me darling girl. Have a seat, and try to be kind."

Kind? When had she been unkind? Did her mysterious client have some visible flaw? Was he lame, perhaps? Disfigured in some terrible accident? Or merely so shy he could not express himself well?

"Who is it, Maddie?" she whispered, attempting to peer inside the house.

Maddie put a finger to her lips. "Never will you be hearing it from me." She disappeared into the house again before Beth could beg, leaving her no choice but to sit on one of the elegant chairs.

The breeze caught her hair, pulling a strand loose. She tucked it back. It couldn't be Scout—he already had a perfectly fine house just down the hill. It wouldn't be Clay—he was happily married to Allegra. Most of the men with any money were married already. Most of the unmarried men in town hadn't purchased or built houses yet.

A noise caught her attention, the sound of a horse approaching. Was this her host? She raised her head, craned her neck to catch sight of him.

Arno trotted around the corner of the house, black sides gleaming, and her breath left her. Hart sat tall in the saddle, one hand on the reins, the other brandishing a sword. His black duster had been replaced with a white shirt from a previous age, the front and cuffs trimmed in lace. He reined in in front of her, then clicked to the gelding. Arno extended one leg and bent over it, as if offering her a bow.

Beth clasped her hands together to keep them from trembling as the horse rose, and Hart swung down from the saddle. Her legs pushed her to her feet and up against the railing.

He went down on one knee and planted the sword before him like a cross. "Lady Beth, I have ridden far in my life. But never have I beheld a fairer flower."

Beth swallowed. "Hart, this is all very nice, but…"

He held up a hand. "Let me finish. I've been practicing for two weeks. This stuff isn't easy to say, you know."

Two weeks? Oh, the dear man. She clamped her mouth shut.

He raised his head as if determined to get through his speech. "I'll never be a poet with gilded words to please you or a king with a castle and knights to place at your command. But I promise to tell you every day how much I admire you and to treat you like a queen. I will love, honor and cherish you all the days of my life. Will you marry me?"

Beth's heart blocked her throat. She couldn't speak,

couldn't breathe. She launched herself off the porch and into his arms.

He rose to catch her and held her close. Murmuring her name, he pressed a kiss against her hair. Then he leaned back to eye her. "I take it that was a yes?"

"Yes," Beth told him, happiness flowing into every part of her. "Yes, yes, yes. I so appreciate you going to all this trouble, but I find it's better if you just show someone how you feel."

He chuckled. "I wish you'd told me that sooner. It would have been a whole lot easier." He bent his head and kissed her, and it was a long while before either spoke again.

When he finally released her, it was to take her hand and lead her back onto the porch.

"So, you convinced Maddie to cater," Beth surmised, feeling flushed even on the cool spring day.

"And Michael to make me that sword," he confessed. "Ursula Wyckoff loaned me the shirt. It belonged to her grandfather." He plucked at the frills, and Beth laughed at the look on his face.

"And who let you borrow the house?" she asked, clinging to his hand, a little afraid it all might evaporate if she let go.

He smiled. "No one. A person I admire advised me my wife might like it, so I purchased it."

Beth gasped. "Oh, Hart, truly?"

"Truly," he promised. Then he sobered. "It's a good house, Beth, just as you said. But it will only be a home if you share it with me."

"What a lovely proposal, Mr. McCormick," Beth said, tears welling. "Have I told you how very much I admire you?"

"Yes, and to my sorrow I sent you away. Never again. I love you, Beth, and I want to spend the rest of my life showing you how much."

"I love you too, Hart. So much." Once more she had to hold him. She had a feeling that would happen a lot. Like the characters in her father's books, like each of her brothers and their wives, like Allegra and Clay and Maddie and Michael, she had every hope that she and Hart would live happily ever after.

And they did.

* * * * *

Don't miss these other
FRONTIER BACHELORS *stories*
from Regina Scott:

THE BRIDE SHIP
WOULD-BE WILDERNESS WIFE
FRONTIER ENGAGEMENT
INSTANT FRONTIER FAMILY
A CONVENIENT CHRISTMAS WEDDING
MAIL-ORDER MARRIAGE PROMISE
HIS FRONTIER CHRISTMAS FAMILY

Find more great reads at www.LoveInspired.com

Dear Reader,

Thank you for choosing Beth and Hart's story. I hope you enjoyed watching the youngest, and most determined, Wallin meet her match. If you missed any of the other stories in the Frontier Bachelors series, look for *The Bride Ship* (Allegra and Clay), *Would-Be Wilderness Wife* (Catherine and Drew), *Frontier Engagement* (James and Rina), *Instant Frontier Family* (Maddie and Michael), *A Convenient Christmas Wedding* (Simon and Nora), *Mail-Order Marriage Promise* (John and Dottie) and *His Frontier Christmas Family* (Levi and Callie). It has been my pleasure to bring their stories to you.

You can find more information on my books and sign up for a free email alert when the next book is out at my website at www.reginascott.com.

Blessings!
Regina Scott

We hope you enjoyed this story from
Love Inspired® Historical.

Love Inspired® Historical is coming to
an end but be sure to discover more
inspirational stories to warm your heart
from **Love Inspired®** and
Love Inspired® Suspense!

Love Inspired stories show that
faith, forgiveness and hope have the power
to lift spirits and change lives—always.

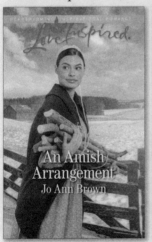
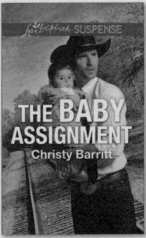

Look for six new romances every month
from **Love Inspired®** and
Love Inspired® Suspense!

Get 2 Free Books,

Plus 2 Free Gifts—
just for trying the **Reader Service!**

SPECIAL EXCERPT FROM

Love Inspired HISTORICAL

When rancher Seth Halloway inherits a trio of
orphaned boys, he has nowhere to turn—except to lovely
schoolteacher Marigold Brewster. Together, they'll learn
to open their hearts to new family...and new love.

Read on for a sneak preview of
THE RANCHER INHERITS A FAMILY
by *Cheryl St.John*, the touching beginning of the
series RETURN TO COWBOY CREEK.

"Mr. Halloway." The soft voice near his side added to his
disorientation. "Are you in pain?"

Ivory-skinned and hazel-eyed, with a halo of red-gold
hair, the woman from the train came into view. She had
only a scrape on her chin as a result of the ordeal. "You
fared well," he managed.

"I'm perfectly fine, thank you."

"And the children?"

"They have a few bumps and bruises from the crash,
but they're safe."

He closed his eyes with grim satisfaction.

"I'm Marigold Brewster. Thank you for rescuing me."

"I'm glad you and your boys are all right."

"Well, that's the thing..."

His head throbbed and the light hurt. "What's the
thing?"

"They're not my boys."

"They're not?"

"I never saw them before I boarded the train headed for Kansas."

"Well, then—"

"They're yours."

With his uninjured hand, he touched his forehead gingerly. Had that blow to his head rattled his senses? No, he hadn't lost his memory. He remembered what he'd been doing before heading off to the wreckage. "I assure you I'd know if I had children."

"Well, as soon as you read this letter, along with a copy of a will, you'll know. It seems a friend of yours by the name of Tessa Radner wanted you to take her children upon her death."

Tessa Radner? "She's dead?"

"This letter says she is. I'm sorry. Did you know her?"

Remembering her well, he nodded. They'd been neighbors and classmates in Big Bend, Missouri. He'd joined the infantry alongside her husband, Jessie, who had been killed in Northern Virginia's final battle. Seth winced at the magnitude of senseless loss.

Seth's chest ached with sorrow and sympathy for his childhood friend. But sending her beloved babies to *him*? She must have been desperate to believe he was her best choice. What was he going to do with them?

Don't miss
THE RANCHER INHERITS A FAMILY
by Cheryl St.John, available April 2018 wherever
Love Inspired® Historical books and ebooks are sold.

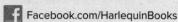
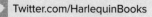
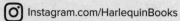